Because there was a moon George decided to walk back to the Mill along the shore. It was quicker and he was already very cold. Old age, he supposed, creeping up on him ...

He walked briskly, hoping the movement would bring some feeling back into his feet, keeping his eyes on the ground just ahead of him so he would not trip on loose shingle or a boulder. He stopped for a moment to get his bearings and catch his breath, to make sure that he was taking the shortest route to the Mill. At the high water mark he saw a pile of rubbish, a pale shape caught in the moonlight. He thought it might be another swan and he went to investigate. But as he approached he saw that it was too big to be a swan. It was Aidan Moore, drowned, and washed up by the tide. . . .

Also by Ann Cleeves
Published by Fawcett Books:

The George Palmer-Jones Series
ANOTHER MAN'S POISON
A BIRD IN THE HAND
COME DEATH AND HIGH WATER
MURDER IN PARADISE
A PREY TO MURDER
SEA FEVER

The Stephen Ramsay Series
MURDER IN MY BACKYARD
A LESSON IN DYING
A DAY IN THE DEATH OF DOROTHEA CASSIDY

THE MILL ON THE SHORE

Ann Cleeves

FAWCETT GOLD MEDAL • NEW YORK

A Fawcett Gold Medal Book
Published by Ballantine Books
Copyright © 1994 by Ann Cleeves

All rights reserved under International and Pan-American Copyright Conventions. Published in the United States of America by
Ballantine Books, a division of Random House, Inc., New York,
and simultaneously in Canada by Random House of Canada Limited, Toronto.

Library of Congress Catalog Card Number: 94-94204

ISBN 0-449-14918-8

Manufactured in the United States of America

First Edition: September 1994

10 9 8 7 6 5 4 3 2 1

1

There was no funeral, because there was no body. The disposal of James Morrissey's remains had turned into a farce, as Ruth had suspected it might. James's attitude to the established church had been sneering, even blasphemous, and Meg had taken it into her head that a humanist should lead the ceremony. But outside London, it seemed, humanist funerals were unknown, certainly out here in the sticks. Then they had discovered that James had arranged for his remains to be donated for medical research and after the post mortem they had been shipped discreetly to the nearest university in a van. To be giggled over, Ruth supposed, by medical students.

Ruth had thought that would settle the matter, but Meg wanted a show, a formal gathering, and had decided on a memorial service in the church nearest the Mill. So they had turned to the parish priest after all and although he did his best he seemed overawed by the event. He had never seen the church so full. In his address he said he had not realized James Morrissey was such a celebrity. He spoke with disappointment, as if at an opportunity missed, giving the impression that he wished he had cultivated James's friendship before it was too late.

Ruth wore black to the service because she always wore black, not as an expression of grief. She was

1

surprised to find she felt so little sadness. She was irritated by the trivial inconveniences caused by James's death—the disruption to her studies, the endless phone calls of condolence—but that hardly counted as grief. Perhaps, she thought, as the vicar stumbled nervously through his speech, she was so detached because of the special circumstances of the family. If James had been her natural father, she might feel differently. As it was, throughout the service she looked around her with curiosity, admiring the women's stylish hats, seeing how many people she recognized, unmoved by emotion.

The contingent from the Mill sat together, near the front, with Meg and the children in one pew and the rest behind them. They were unfamiliar in their funeral clothes, and Ruth, sitting next to the aisle, twisting her head slightly to look at them, saw them as if for the first time. We live on top of each other, she thought, but we're not close at all. I know nothing about them, about Rosie and Jane, the Cairnses, even Aidan. The idea was a shock, a revelation, and she put it down to the unaccustomed surroundings. Perhaps she should come to church more often. As she turned back to face the altar, the vicar ran out of platitudes and sat down gratefully. There was a rustle of coats as they stood to sing the Twenty-third Psalm and then it was all over.

They stood outside in the narrow lane waiting for someone to take a lead, self-consciously aware of the cameras from the local television station. It was January, cold and dull with spikes of hail in the easterly wind. The church was on a small hill with a view over flat fields to the sea, very exposed, apparently miles from anywhere. The village was a mile farther inland, sheltered by a belt of Scots pine. A sudden gust lifted one of the hats that Ruth had admired—a flat wide-brimmed straw—from its owner's head and sent it spinning like a Frisbee down the lane. They all watched, glad of the distraction, until it was caught in the hawthorn hedge and retrieved by a young man who presented a natural history quiz on Radio 4. The younger children, who had behaved immaculately throughout the service, began to laugh.

Ruth hesitated just inside the church gate and watched the scene from a distance, still intrigued by the idea that they were all strangers. She was eighteen, naive, and the obvious psychological insight seemed now the most important thing to have come from James's death. She looked around her for examples and saw Cathy Cairns. She had always thought Mrs. Cairns a well-groomed and sophisticated woman but saw now that she had something of the air of a water rat, with big front teeth, a faint moustache, and fair tufts of hair escaping from her hat. No wonder James ditched her, Ruth thought, though she had always liked Cathy before, felt very close to her, and turned back to the church to wait for her mother, who was, even now after four children, still beautiful.

Meg, her mother, was the last person out of the church. She stood for a moment to compose herself and then took charge, shepherding the guests to their cars, flattering the vicar with her thanks. Meg was magnificent, Ruth thought, but then she had known that all along. Meg was always magnificent.

As she walked towards the car, Ruth allowed herself to look at Aidan Moore. She watched with disappointment as he climbed into the Cairnses' Land Rover without seeming to see her. She had planned to invite him to accompany her in Meg's car, imagined them squeezed together in the back along with the children. It occurred to her that she might be in love with him and that was a revelation, too.

They drove the three miles to Markham Mill in a convoy, which caused quite a stir in the hamlet of Markham Law. So many smart cars, all in a row. So many women in hats. The residents had heard about the memorial service from Florrie Duffy, who cleaned at the Mill when her health allowed, and they were looking out. More like a wedding, one said, than a funeral. What a shame they'd had such a cold and rainy day!

When they arrived at the Mill, the drive was already full and they had to park in the lane outside. This minor disruption to the usual practice seemed to upset Meg, and Ruth saw that her mother's composure was precarious and she was more distressed than she was letting on.

"It's too bad," she said. "Too inconsiderate." And there were tears of frustration in her eyes. She slammed the car doors loudly, hardly giving the children time to scramble out. Ruth found the show of ill temper disturbing. It was unlike her mother to lose control in such an obvious way.

In the late-afternoon gloom the Mill still looked half derelict, a rickety wooden structure far too big for its position there at the mouth of the bay. Ruth had always thought that the Mill was too romantic a name for it. The Mill conjured up wind sails, waterwheels. This building had been put up in the thirties for the preparation of animal feeds and the family business had struggled on until 1960 when it finally went bankrupt. Then the Mill had stood empty for more than thirty years. There had been many schemes for its restoration. It had such potential for development, right on the shore, surrounded by unspoilt countryside. There were plans for a holiday complex, a hotel. But these involved the demolition of the Mill or a dramatic change to its structure and for some reason it had become a listed building. And Markham Bay was a wildlife sanctuary, internationally recognized. Prospective developers were put off by the possibility of objections by conservation groups. So the Mill had remained empty until Ruth's mother, Meg Morrissey, had arrived to take it on, with her grand vision of a different sort of field centre, a college of the countryside. She had seemed to sweep them all along, even James, with her

4

enthusiasm. They had uprooted from London, left friends behind, to make the project a reality. Now it was the family's home and workplace and to Ruth it was unthinkable that they would live anywhere else.

Meg stood at the wide door to the big room, part lecture theatre, part common room, where all the indoor teaching took place. She seemed to have calmed her crossness at the lack of parking space and was greeting her guests affectionately, by name, as if their presence gave her enormous pleasure and consolation. Although many of the mourners must have been only distant acquaintances, there was a lot of hugging and kissing. Ruth found such physical contact disconcerting and slipped past her mother while she was engaged in a particularly extravagant embrace. Then she stood in a corner and watched what was going on. This was her favourite room in the Mill and she resented its invasion by people she hardly knew. It was an impressive space on the second floor, stretching the width of the building. Once perhaps it had been a sort of storeroom. Three walls were wood panelled. The fourth, which faced the sea, was formed almost entirely of glass. The last of the daylight was reflected from the water and the view of the shore and the wide, darkening sky was uninterrupted.

"Too distracting," James had said when he first saw it. "You'll not get anyone to concentrate with a view like that. Especially not in Aidan's classes. An artist needs a blank wall and an imagination."

But in his last months he had spent a lot of his time there, sitting in a straight-backed chair with his binoculars on a table beside him, hunched over a notebook, writing frantically. Ruth suddenly missed him with a sharp and physical pain.

The room began to fill with people and they were all talking about James. All around her she heard scraps of conversation, recycled anecdotes, and the stories turned

5

her stepfather into someone she hardly recognized. He became a mythical character: Jimmy Morrissey, the great naturalist, television presenter, writer. The person who first brought conservation to the people, who awakened the green conscience of the nation.

"Do you remember filming in Burma?" said a fat, grey-haired man with bulldog jowls and a mouth full of vol-au-vent. "I really thought the bloody elephant would get him that time."

Jimmy Morrissey, adventurer and hero.

"Never thought he'd marry again," said the companion, poorly shaven, leering. "Not after Cathy. Thought he'd make the most of his freedom after that little disaster. Could have knocked me down with a feather when he got hitched to Meg. That was some bloody party, mind you. I had a hangover for a fortnight after that. I was booked to do the sound for Attenborough in the Galapagos and nearly missed the sodding plane."

Jimmy Morrissey, the great lover.

What was wrong with Mother? Ruth thought defensively. She looked back to the door where Meg still stood and began to worry about her again. There was no specific cause for concern. Meg was performing her role to perfection. But the welcome to the last of the guests now seemed slightly too loud, tinged with hysteria and desperation.

What else would I expect? Ruth thought. A week ago her husband committed suicide. Isn't she entitled at a time like this to be hysterical? But the shaky public image was so unlike her mother that Ruth became tense and anxious. She looked around for Aidan, thinking that he might reassure her, but he was not there. As the afternoon wore on and the light faded over the mudflats and the brent geese flew low over the water to roost, she waited breathlessly, expecting some new disaster.

Ruth was the oldest, Meg's child by a previous marriage. She'd always been a worrier. Caitlin was her full sister; the younger two were James's. All the children had been in the church. Meg had said they could stay at home, but they had chosen to go, afraid, Ruth supposed, of missing something.

Caitlin's laughter floated to her over the crowd. Ruth stared in her direction, hoping to make her see that mirth was hardly appropriate, but she was surrounded by people and did not notice. Ruth had thought that Caitlin would miss James most. They had been very close, wrapped up in each other. He had spoiled her more than his own children, taken a delight in her beauty, demanding her company even when Meg said she should be studying. But now she seemed to treat his death as a joke. Perhaps the actress in her was enjoying the melodrama of it and grief would come later. Caitlin was sixteen, very arty and posy. She played the flute and painted, wore strange home-dyed long skirts and large floppy hats. Ruth worried occasionally about the gaps in Caitlin's education. She did well enough there, showing off in front of the students, chatting up the single men, but how would she survive in a world away from Markham Mill? For three years she had known nothing else. Meg seemed unbothered and assumed that Caitlin would find a niche somewhere, in the theatre perhaps or television. Ruth suspected that it was not that easy. Even in television, wasn't there a requirement these days for A levels, a degree? But Caitlin was beautiful, with wide flute-player's lips and an oval Bardot face, and perhaps that would see her through just as well.

She caught Ruth's eye across the crowd and came over to her, with a glass of wine in one hand and a plate in the other.

"What a load of bores!" she said in a stage whisper. "When do you think they'll all go home?"

"You seem to be enjoying yourself well enough," Ruth said.

7

"Oh well!" Caitlin said. "You have to put on a show, don't you?"

"I don't know," Ruth said. Perhaps that's where I go wrong, she thought. I'm no good at pretending. "I shouldn't suppose they'll stay long," she said. "Most of them have a long way to go."

But the gathering had turned into a party. There was a sudden outburst of giggling and people shouted to be heard above the noise. Ruth turned away from it and stared out at the shore, her nose pressed against the glass like a child's. It was nearly dark and the buoy that marked the shingle spit at the far end of the bay was already lit. Ruth could make out, silhouetted against the water, the row of staithes that had once formed a pier. Boats carrying grain had tied up there and unloaded their cargoes for the Mill, but now they were broken and rotten, perches for cormorants and gulls. The glass was cold and she realized that there were tears on her cheeks.

"Ruth!" It was an insistent whisper and she recognized the voice not as Caitlin's but as Timothy's. She took a tissue from her sleeve and wiped her eyes before turning to face him. Of all the children Tim was her favourite and she didn't want to upset him. He was an earnest ten-year-old, solitary, uncertain. She often thought that like Caitlin he would be better off at school, but from the beginning Meg had been convinced that formal education destroyed creativity in a child and she saw schools as prisons. Her first husband had been a master at a minor public school and she said that had put her off for life. They had all been educated at home. When Ruth had broached the subject of school discreetly with Tim he had been unenthusiastic.

"I don't know," he had said. "I'd have to be indoors all day, wouldn't I? There's my project on the shore. When would I find time to finish that?"

"You might make friends," Ruth had said. "There'd be more to do. Football. That sort of thing."

But it seemed football was not much of an attraction when compared with a study of the Markham Mill rock pools, so he continued to be taught by Meg at home.

Today he looked scrubbed and uncomfortable in a white shirt and tie. Ruth had got him ready for the service herself and she was sorry she had been so hard on him. A clean sweater would have done. She put her arm around his shoulder, but he pulled away, embarrassed by the gesture, not wanting to be shown up in front of all these friends of his father's.

"What is it?" she said, smiling, whispering, too. "Fed up?"

He nodded. "Do you think Mum would mind if Em and I went to the flat to watch telly?"

Emily was eight, considered the baby, indulged by them all.

"Why don't you ask her?" Ruth said. She never liked to make decisions for her mother.

"I don't know," he said. "I don't like to bother her really. . . ."

They both looked at Meg, who had moved away from the door and was walking slowly among the crowd. Ruth could understand his diffidence. Their mother seemed tense and preoccupied. As they watched, she took a glass of wine from Rosie, the housekeeper, and drank it very quickly. The action surprised them both. Usually she drank very little, preferring mineral water to wine at dinner, getting angry when Caitlin persuaded the students to buy her beer at the bar or take her to the Dead Dog in Markham Law.

"Why aren't the Cairnses here?" Tim asked suddenly as if it had just occurred to him.

"I don't know," Ruth said. "They were asked." She was surprised by the question and wondered what lay behind it. "Look," she went on, "I'm sure Mum wouldn't mind you watching television. I'll tell her where you are." It had come to her again that Meg's control was fragile, that it could give way at any moment, and she wanted the children out of the way before her mother broke down.

"There's a survival programme on," Tim said. "I don't suppose Em will want to watch that. . . . She'll make me put on some ghastly game show. Or *Neighbours*."

"I tell you what," Ruth said hurriedly, "if there's any problem you can watch the television in my room. Then you can choose whichever programme you like. But take Emily with you now. I expect she's had enough, too."

"She's had four meringues already," he said gloomily. "You know what she's like with Rosie's meringues. She'll probably be sick."

But he went without a fuss to fetch his sister, who was standing by the buffet, staring covetously at the last piece of coffee gateau. With relief Ruth watched them go quietly from the room.

She took a deep breath to calm her nerves, then went over to her mother and shyly took her hand.

"Are you all right?" she said. "You don't have to go through all this, you know. We can tell them to go home."

They're only showing off, she thought. Claiming they're important because they knew the great Jimmy Morrissey. And they didn't really know him at all. Not like we did.

"No," Meg said. "We can't send them away. Not yet. I've got something to say."

She was a small woman, dark and fine-featured, compelling. Ruth towered over her and always felt clumsy in comparison. After years of living in England Meg's voice could still become Welsh when she was emotional. "Moulded by chapel and the valleys," James

10

would say of her, half teasing. "And very principled indeed. When it suits."

He thought Mother was stupid, Ruth realized in surprise. And she saw that in one way her mother was indeed stupid. Her reactions were always passionate and instinctive. She was incapable of cool thought, of seeing anyone else's point of view. For the first time she wondered how James could have liked her mother. It was an uncomfortable thought and she returned to the conversation.

"What do you want to say?" she demanded, confused, but her mother ignored the question and looked around her.

"Where are Tim and Emily?" she asked.

"Watching television in the flat." She knew Meg disapproved strongly of the television. "They did ask. Is that OK?"

Why does my mother always make me feel so nervous? she wondered. Why can't I trust my own judgement for once? She's made us all too dependent on her.

"Yes," Meg said, absent-mindedly, almost to herself. "Of course. It's as well they're not here. I'd be reluctant to speak in front of them. But it has to be said . . ."

"What has to be said?" Ruth cried. She thought her mother was going mad.

But Meg seemed not to hear and walked to the front of the room, where she clapped her hands like a teacher calling for attention. The noise in the room subsided and they jostled forward so they could see her.

"My friends . . ." she said. Ruth stood with her back to the window. Meg's slight figure was hidden by the crowd, but her words were quite audible.

"My friends . . ." Meg went on. "I want to talk to you about my husband, to make one thing clear. . . ."

Ruth wished she had the courage to interrupt. Don't listen to her! she wanted to shout to all the people in the room. My mother's distressed. She doesn't know what she's doing. She can't think it through. But she wasn't sufficiently brave and the guests listened sympathetically, admiring Meg's calm, thinking that she would make a short loving speech to Jimmy's memory and that then they could go back to the booze.

"The verdict of the inquest was that James took his own life when the balance of his mind was disturbed. It was a reasonable decision considering his medical history. We all know that since his accident he'd suffered periods of depression. But it wasn't a true verdict. I know that James didn't kill himself. He wouldn't have done it. As the days have passed since his death I've become more convinced—" Her voice broke off. "I just can't let it go!" she said desperately. "There has to be an investigation. I have to know if there was a dreadful accident or some malicious intent." She stopped again. Perhaps she expected some reaction or encouragement but there was only awkwardness, a cough, an uneasy murmur from the back that Meg had been under considerable strain for years and it was hardly surprising if she broke down now.

Meg looked around her and suddenly seemed her old self. She smiled.

"It's been a terrible day," she said. "I'm sure you'll understand that I want to be on my own now."

And she left the room without saying anything more. There was a stunned silence and the crowd broke up. Ruth stood at the front door and watched them run through the wind to their cars. She had expected some comment about Meg's state of mind, but no one spoke to her. There were only sympathetic and embarrassed glances as they dashed away.

When she returned to the common room, Caitlin was draining dregs of wine from the empty bottles.

"What was all that about?" she demanded. She was flushed and unsteady. "What the hell was she trying to say?"

"I rather think," Ruth said quietly, annoyed by

Caitlin's flippancy, wanting to shock, "I rather think she was trying to say that James had been murdered."

Caitlin went very pale, dropped heavily into a chair, and began to laugh out loud.

2

*C*athy *Cairns* was pleased when Aidan Moore asked for a lift to the church with them. She thought her husband, Phil, would want to talk about James. She had avoided the subject since his death and was still not quite sure what to say. In Aidan's presence, surely, even Phil would restrain himself to polite and superficial expressions of sorrow.

They arrived at the church early and waited outside for the family to arrive, shivering in the cold. Phil, who usually seemed impervious to extremes of temperature, bounced around like a puppy, slapping himself to keep warm. He was a plump, jolly man with a thick black beard and boundless nervous energy. He could never stand still. At last Meg's car drew up, and it was like a royal procession when she and the children paraded into the church, the flashlights snapping as the local press took pictures.

Cathy, as usual, felt the shock of recognition as Emily climbed out of the car, then the old bitterness and anger. The girl looked so like Hannah at the same age that she wanted to go up to her and take her into her arms. She turned away with tears in her eyes. Phil, who had never noticed her reaction to Emily, patted her shoulder and said: "Nay, lass, don't cry. He had a good life," which made her smile despite herself because

14

"good" was never an adjective to describe Jimmy Morrissey in any context.

Cathy had been married to James Morrissey briefly in the early seventies. During the courtship she had been overwhelmed by him, infatuated beyond reason, but after the wedding she had seen quite soon that it would not work out. The main problem was that he was never there. He was at the height of his fame, and besides the routine trips abroad to film for the BBC, he was invited to lecture, to advise, to promote internationally the interests of conservation. He had been public property and had never really belonged to her. It would never have occurred to him to turn down these invitations. He needed the admiration and the excitement, the sense that life was full, that he was always rushed off his feet. So Cathy had been left on her own, abandoned, she felt, out of preference for elephants and rhinos. Even when Hannah was born James had turned up late, still dressed in some ridiculous safari suit, and had entranced the midwives and doctors so they clustered around him asking for autographs while she and the baby were left alone, forgotten.

She saw now that she had not made sufficient fuss. Meg had not let him get away with anything like that.

How had she managed it? Cathy wondered, looking at the little woman in the pew in front of her. How had Meg managed to tame him? Perhaps James had been prepared to make the sacrifice because he loved Meg more, but that seemed unlikely. None of his loves had been *that* important. Perhaps she had just been better at maintaining the façade of family life. The accident, of course, had been the best thing that had ever happened to her. After that James had been dependent on her and it seemed she could do what she liked with him.

The organ played a phrase of the first hymn and they stood up to sing. Cathy was reminded of Hannah's funeral and how James had been late even for that. Then there was a scuffle at the back of the church; Rosie and

15

Jane the two young housekeepers from the Mill, flew in, scarves and coats flapping. Cathy smiled, pleased that someone was late for him, too.

Phil was worried about Cathy. He thought she was grieving for James more than she was prepared to let on and it would do her good to talk about it. She should know by now that he wasn't jealous, not of Jimmy Morrissey. He was grateful because it was Jimmy, in a way, who had brought them together.

Phil had been brought up locally in Salter's Cottage, the whitewashed single-storey house where he still lived, facing the Mill across the bay. His dad had worked in the Mill when it was operating and in his spare time he'd been a bit of a fisherman, going out in a small boat for crab and lobster. Phil had thought he would work in the Mill, too, but it had closed the year he left school and he was taken on as an apprentice at Mardon Wools, the textile factory up the river. He had never considered leaving the district, moving away like his school friends. His passion was the wildlife on the shore. He was something of a botanist, too, but the birds were most important to him. Since he was a child he had kept regular wildfowl and wader counts and every spring he had ringed the arctic tern chicks that were born on the shingle. He had been the county's British Trust for Ornithology rep for years.

He threw himself into work with the same enthusiasm as he did his birdwatching, staying on late even when there was no overtime to be had, going to college in the evenings. He had worked his way up to become manager and could do the job now, he thought, standing on his head.

Cathy had joined Mardon Wools some years after her divorce from James. The company had wanted to change its image. It had a reputation for quality, but the clothes it produced were staid, boring. The loyal customers were slowly dying off and it needed to attract a

16

younger clientele. After her separation from James, Cathy had established her own company, designing sweaters, selling the patterns and the wool for customers to knit in their own homes. She had been head-hunted by Mardon, offered a good salary, substantial perks if she became their chief designer. She had been flattered by the approach and accepted. She had never liked the idea of Hannah being a teenager in London.

Phil had fallen for Cathy as soon as he saw her. He had a romantic nature sustained since adolescence through lack of experience. Women had always seemed unable to take him seriously. The glamour of her name and the fact that she had intimately known Jimmy Morrissey, his great hero, added to her appeal. He still could not believe his luck that she had agreed to marry him. He loved her with a boyish devotion and would have done anything for her.

Cathy had been attracted to Phil Cairns because he was everything James was not: reliable, self-effacing, considerate. She had been reluctant to take the step of a second marriage and he had wooed her in a diffident, old-fashioned way with presents and flowers. Sex, which had been the impetus for all of Jimmy's relationships with women, had hardly come into it.

Now he supposed they were still happy, living in Salter's Cottage. She had been glad of him at the time of crisis after Hannah's death. He had never let her down. She had left Mardon Wools when Hannah died. She couldn't face seeing them all every day and thought anyway that self-employment suited her better. Phil was still there, making the best of it, looking forward to early retirement when he could spend all his time on the shore.

He had taken a day's leave to be at the memorial service and though he was too good-natured to resent it, it came to him now as he stood through the dreary hymns that his time would have been better spent counting the brent geese on the mudflats. Jimmy would have thought so, too.

Aidan Moore had been a tutor at Markham Mill every winter since the field centre opened three years before. He spent January and February there as artist in residence and taught one long course and three weekends. Aidan was famous. There was always a waiting list for his courses and some students booked one year for the next. Meg could charge double the usual fees.

Aidan had first come to the attention of James Morrissey when he was a boy and James was editor of *Green Scenes*, a campaigning natural history magazine taken by everyone working in conservation. The magazine had run an annual competition for amateur artists. Aidan, ten years younger than any of the other competitors, had won with a pen-and-ink drawing of goldfinches on a thistle head. The picture had appeared on the front cover of *Green Scenes* and the original now hung in the Morrisseys' flat in the Mill. James had gone on to commission other work for the magazine and to support the teenager through art school by employing him during the holidays as a junior reporter and general dogsbody. As soon as he left college Aidan had managed to make a living out of wildlife art and he had become a very highly respected illustrator.

Now in his late twenties he still had the look of a student, with sandy hair and small oval spectacles. He was a shy, inarticulate man. Teaching was a trial to him and he came to the field centre only as a favour to James. This year he had tried to cancel the arrangement, had made the excuse that he was too busy, but James had insisted.

"Come on, old boy, you can't let me down. Don't leave me to face all the bloody punters without a friend in the camp."

So as he had always done, whenever James asked anything of him, Aidan had agreed, only to find that he

18

was as miserable as he was every year. He was frightened of offending and found it impossible to criticize the students' work, even the appalling daubs turned out by some of the regulars. He made stammered suggestions then escaped out into the saltmarsh with his sketch book until it was dark. He could only relax in the evenings after a few beers. Then James would invite him into the flat to spend some time with the family and there he seemed to lose all his inhibitions, laughing and telling jokes to Emily and Tim, drawing cartoons for them of all the visitors.

He went to the memorial service because it was expected of him and to please Meg, but he thought it was a pointless exhibition. James would have mocked the occasion and it seemed to Aidan appropriately ironic that he would not be present even in his physical form. He supposed the service provided some comfort to Meg, who seemed frightened now of being alone. On the morning after James's death he had said to her:

"I expect you'd like us all to go now so you can spend some time on your own with the children. I'll see to it, if you like, talk to the students. They're a good crowd. But perhaps we should offer a refund?"

It would be less embarrassing, he thought, to send the students packing if he could offer them a financial incentive. He was shocked that James's death had left him with a sense of relief. At least there need be no more teaching. Meg, however, had been surprised by the suggestion, as if it had never occurred to her that the students should leave.

"I suppose that would be best," she said at last. "If you don't think it would appear rude. But you stay on, Aidan. The children are wonderful, of course, but I don't want them to feel responsible for me. Do stay, Aidan, and see me through it."

Of course he had agreed, though the sentimentality of her plea had embarrassed him. Her bereavement gave her a special status. She could ask anything of anyone.

And now he thought it was a mistake to have sent the students away. The Mill seemed so dead, the dormitories echoing, everywhere lifeless and cold. He saw that he would have to stay on as long as Meg needed him.

Aidan had never learnt to drive. When his parents gave him lessons for his twenty-first birthday present, he had been sick with fear and had a nightmare about the car he was driving going out of control and killing a child. The nightmare had recurred regularly after the accident when Hannah died and James was injured and still haunted him when he was anxious. Lately even being a passenger was an ordeal and he was glad when Phil Cairns offered him a lift to the church. Phil was practical, optimistic, and he inspired Aidan with confidence. And he drove a Land Rover, which was strong enough, Aidan thought, to survive most kinds of disasters.

They arrived at the church early. Cathy made a joke of it. That was Phil for you, she said. He got everywhere early. They stood outside, sheltering from the wind as best they could and waited for Meg and the children to come. In the lane a young man from the local BBC station was doing a piece to the camera, describing some of the famous mourners who were starting to gather. Then the family arrived, seemed to emerge from the car as a group, a single unit, and Aidan thought with dismay that it would be impossible for an outsider to break it up.

Aidan listened to the vicar's address with some surprise. There was so much to say about James Morrissey. He had been a writer of distinction, author of many field guides, most of which were still in print. For five years he had hosted BBC2's serious natural history programme and had found a means of describing complex conservation issues in a way the viewer could understand. He had gone on to found *Green Scenes* and had taken it from a small, photostated newsletter to a magazine with a circulation that other specialist journals en-

20

vied. Even after the accident, when he had resigned as editor of *Green Scenes*, there had been achievements. He and Meg had discovered Markham Mill, seen its potential, and developed a field centre that everyone agreed was a success. Despite astronomic fees and a recession, the most popular courses had a two-year waiting list and the academic research that had come out of the place had rocked established notions of estuarine ecology. Meg had sold the place to the punters, made them so welcome that they wanted to come back, but the science had been James's.

The vicar, however, mentioned none of that. He burbled at length about James as a family man and husband. It seemed to Aidan that Meg and the children were so close that James had been excluded from the family. His attitude to his children had been unpredictable—he had either lavished them with affection so they felt smothered or had been moody and bad-tempered. The relationship between Meg and James had been so strained and odd that Aidan felt unable to make a judgement about it, but it was hardly worthy, he thought, to be celebrated at a memorial service. He was pleased when at last the whole thing was over and he was out in the open air. The salt wind blowing from the sea revived him.

He would have liked to get back to the Mill immediately. He wanted to change out of the uncomfortable clothes, the black tie lent him for the occasion by Phil Cairns, and get out on to the shore. But Cathy had been accosted by old acquaintances, people she had known in London when she was married to James, and he had to wait.

Through the crowd he saw Grace Sharland, the community nurse who had come occasionally to visit James. She had taken off a small round hat and shaken out the hair that had been piled inside. It was the copper colour of the hair that had caught his attention. He had not noticed her in the church and he wondered why she was there. It was beyond the call of duty surely to attend the

21

memorial service of a patient. She stood alone, as awkwardly as he, and on impulse he began to push past the other mourners to speak to her. She turned and saw him approaching. For a moment she hesitated and he thought she would join him, but she turned away abruptly and hurried down the lane to where the cars were parked. He could not chase after her without appearing ridiculous.

Phil Cairns bounded excitedly beside him. "Look," he said. "Waxwings!" And Aidan was immediately distracted by the shape of the sturdy, thick-billed birds that clustered on the bare oak beside the church. He concentrated on the delicate shading, the splash of colour on their wings, the background of fine, intertwined branches. He would do a painting, he thought. It would be more of a memorial to James than that vicar's speech.

"We're not going back to the Mill," Phil said. "Cathy doesn't fancy it." He was disappointed, Aidan could see. He would have liked to mix with all the famous people. "She thinks it might be a bit awkward for Meg. I suppose you can understand why. But we'll drop you off, of course, on our way home."

At the Mill Aidan avoided the smart people crowded in the lobby and slipped away to his room. He had done his duty by attending the service but could not face the prospect of standing in the common room making small talk and drinking tepid wine. Besides, his feelings about James were too confused. He changed into jeans and stood at his window, looking down at the garden, waiting for a time when he could leave the building without being seen. At last all the cars seemed to have arrived and he padded down the stairs, his thick woollen socks making no sound on the bare wood. In the porch he stopped to pull on Wellingtons and then he went out.

There was no way directly from the Mill on to the marsh. At one time there had been wide doors so the grain could be unloaded directly from the boats for storage, but they let in the east wind and the high tides and the whole of the front of the building had been made weatherproof. Now the only entrance was at the back of the house, which faced the road. It opened on to a garden that had been specially planted to attract migrant birds with hardy bushes, stunted trees, and a pond. Phil Cairns must have been ringing that morning because mist nets were still strung between bamboo poles but furled and tied. Aidan walked around the building and on to the marsh.

James had recently commissioned Aidan to design the cover for his latest book, an autobiography. James had wanted a picture of the Mill. "My last resting place after all, I suppose," he had said, grinning bitterly. Aidan had thought the autobiography a bad idea. He suspected it would only cause mischief. But as usual he had been unable to refuse a request from James and despite himself he had become engrossed in the painting. He thought that the Mill should be seen in perspective on the design, as one feature of the bay, not dominating it. So he had begun to sketch it from the shingle spit, with the mud and the staithes in the foreground as part of the landscape. This late-afternoon winter light was perfect. The mud and the Mill and the woodland behind it all seemed different shades of the same colour. Aidan was not sure what would happen to James's autobiography now—but he had been obsessed all week by the idea of the picture and knew he would have to finish it whether he got paid for it or not.

His boots on the shingle startled the waders and sent them wheeling and calling into the air. He sat with his back to the marker buoy and looked across the bay to Markham Mill. The light in the common room had already been switched on and he imagined he heard voices and laughter coming over the water. Farther south at the opposite end of the inlet to the spit stood the Cairnses' cottage, its white-washed walls standing

23

out against the prevailing grey, a light from the uncurtained window reflected on the wet mud.

He stayed out on the saltmarsh until it was quite
dark. When he arrived back at the Mill he was surprised
to find that all the cars had gone and the common room
was empty.

For Rosie and Jane the gathering in the Mill after the
memorial service represented hard work. It wasn't much
fun preparing food for that crowd and there were only
the two of them to do all the serving. Florrie Duffy
would come in later to help with the clearing up, but, as
Rosie said, since her operation she'd been neither use
nor ornament.

Rosie had been up since dawn and Jane had had to
drag her out of the kitchen for the service, and then
they'd almost been late. Rosie wouldn't trust Jane with
the cooking. She might have been to a smart girls'
school and have A levels, but her pastry turned out like
lead.

Yet, she thought, as she stood in the huge room surrounded by famous people, pouring wine, refilling
plates, it had been worth the effort. She could be proud
of the spread she'd laid on. She wished she could tell
her dad about it. He'd been a great James Morrissey
fan. There'd always had to be silence in their house
when *Morrissey on Mammals* came on the telly. It was
one of her earliest childhood memories. But her dad
was dead and would never know how involved she had
become with his great hero. There was only Jane to
share her excitement and even she couldn't understand
how important it was to have everything perfect. It was
her own memorial to a dead man.

Grace Sharland made tea in her house in the small grey
town that straddled the River Marr. She was disappointed by her lack of control at the memorial service.
What had possessed her to run away? What, if it came

24

to that, had possessed her to go to the church in the first place? She drew the heavy curtains against the windy afternoon and lit the fire. It seemed to her friends that she gathered around her the clutter of a middle-aged spinster, though she was only in her mid-thirties, hardly old at all these days when menopausal film stars were having first babies. The room was already warm, lit by a standard lamp with a heavy fringe. There were paintings, a chintz sofa, bowls of dried flowers. James had asked once if it was all an elaborate joke. Surely this mock Edwardian nonsense didn't really reflect her taste. She wondered what she had replied and found she could no longer remember.

She carried the tea from the kitchen to the living room on a pretty enamelled tray and poured it not into a mug as her friends would have done, but into a white fluted cup made of china so fine that it was almost transparent.

After the turbulence of the previous months there was something pleasant about being here, alone, with no prospect of further excitement or disorder. She finished her tea, let in her cats, and felt a surprised relief that the business with James Morrissey was over.

3

George Palmer-Jones read James Morrissey's obituary in *The Times*. It listed his achievements, gave a glowing account of his contribution to natural history, yet it left George disappointed. George had known James Morrissey well over the years. They had been of the same generation, the first conservationists to care more about the behaviour and habitat of living creatures than dead specimens in a museum or collections of birds' eggs.

George folded the newspaper tidily and thought of the Jimmy Morrissey he had known: gaunt, hollow-eyed, with a smoker's cough and a wild, spontaneous laugh that racked his whole body. George had been one of the ornithological consultants for *Green Scenes* and had gone to the office in London occasionally for editorial meetings. The meetings were always occasions of drama, wreathed in cigarette smoke despite the muttered complaints of Morrisey's environmentally conscious colleagues. James would prowl around the room, drinking cup after cup of strong black coffee, firing ideas into the air, demanding an immediate and intelligent response. It was all very different from the calm reserve of Whitehall where George worked and he would leave the meeting excited, his head full of new ideas, thinking that perhaps he was in the wrong job.

He had been surprised when James retired from

26

Green Scenes. The resignation seemed to come out of the blue. There was the accident, of course, but James seemed to have recovered from that. He wasn't the sort to brood. George had learned of his decision to leave the last time they had met. Jimmy had turned up in the doorway of George's office looking sheepish.

"I thought you might be knocking off soon," he had said, "and might fancy a drink."

It was obviously more than a courtesy call. He had never been to the office before.

George had taken him into a dark, unfashionable pub, which was almost empty. The barmaid had recognized James from a repeat of his television series and brought drinks to the table, flushed from her contact with someone famous. James still limped and walked with a stick.

"I haven't got the heart for it since the accident," he had said. "And the doctor thinks I should slow down a bit." He had leaned across the table, willing George to believe him. In the past George had heard him dismiss the opinions of doctors with unrepeatable oaths and wondered what lay behind the move. Reserve and a misguided notion of good manners had prevented him from asking.

"Meg's seen this place," Jimmy went on, "at Markham Bay, near Cathy's cottage actually. It's an old mill. She thinks it would make a good field centre. Somewhere decent for the children to grow up. She's never liked them living in London."

And he had stared sadly into his beer.

"I'll miss the old *Green Scenes*," he said. "But there you are. Nothing I can do about it. Have to accept, I suppose, that I'm getting old."

He looked up at George plaintively. Perhaps he was hoping for contradiction but George could only murmur polite regret. When he went out, jauntily waving his stick at the barmaid, George was left with the impression that he could have said more if he had been pressed, that he could have been persuaded to pass on some confidence. He had been too scared of intruding. Molly would have handled it better.

The letter from Meg arrived two days after the memorial service. He and Molly were in the kitchen enjoying a leisurely breakfast. Since Christmas business had been quiet. Soon he would experience the panic that was the inevitable result of boredom, but these few weeks of long meals and empty afternoons had been relaxing, an indulgence. Outside it was cold and blustery, just light. George had seen the service advertised in the press but had decided not to go. It was a long trek to Markham Mill, especially in the winter, and he did not need to attend a service to remember James.

Meg's letter was formal and brief:

"Dear Mr. Palmer-Jones," it said. "I should like to hire you to investigate the circumstances surrounding the death of my husband James. I know that you were friends and your involvement with conservation makes you, of all private detectives, most suited for this commission. You will stay, of course, at the Mill and I will pay your normal daily fee plus expenses. I will be available to receive you on Friday, January 29th, and if I don't hear from you I shall expect you then. I enclose a map for your convenience." The letter was signed "Margaret Morrissey."

George disliked the term "private detective" but that, in effect, was what he had become. He had spent his career as a civil servant, working for the Home Office, liaising between the police and bureaucrats. He had expected to enjoy retirement. It would give him the opportunity to devote all his energies to birdwatching. He was an obsessive birder, a twitcher, and he hoped to extend his list of species seen, even to reach his target of two thousand for the world. But soon he found that he was becoming restless and dissatisfied. Birdwatching was a compulsive hobby, but it did not fill the gap of work. So in partnership with his wife, Molly, he had founded an enquiry agency. They had thought it would

28

be an outlet for both their skills—Molly had been a social worker for forty years. They seemed to work well enough together though Molly was becoming increasingly sensitive about her role in the business. It seemed to her sometimes, she said, that she was a glorified personal assistant, not a partner at all. Conscious of past complaints about heavy-handedness and a failure to consult, he handed the letter to her.

"What do you think?" he said. "Should we go?"

"She hasn't asked me," Molly said. "Only you."

"I'll phone her," he said. "Explain that we only work as a team."

She looked at him suspiciously, fearing mockery, but he seemed perfectly serious.

"Meg Morrissey," she said. "She became famous for being a sort of professional mother, didn't she? Belongs to the 'mother's place is in the home' school. Writes articles and appears on TV talking about it. Nice work if you can get it. Shame some of us had to go *out* to earn a living."

George listened patiently. The venom was directed as much at him as at Meg, though he had always approved of Molly's decision to work.

"That's right," he said. "She's educated all four children at home. I've met her several times. Actually, I found her charming."

Molly sniffed. She knew she was being deliberately provoked, teased because her reaction to the woman was so predictable.

"What does she mean, 'investigate the circumstances' of his death?" she demanded. "He committed suicide, didn't he? Didn't you say he took an overdose of those old-fashioned anti-depressants sensible GPs stopped prescribing years ago? Does she want us to find out what particular event triggered the decision to take his own life? That might not be easy. If he were particularly low it could have been something quite trivial. . . ."

29

"I don't know. . . ." George found it hard to imagine James giving in to that sort of despair. At their last meeting in the pub he had been subdued but quite rational. He picked up the letter and read it again. "Perhaps she doesn't believe he committed suicide at all."

"What do you mean?" Molly looked up at him sharply.

"I'm not sure." He knew his judgement was suspect. He had been enormously attracted by James and didn't want to believe him capable of cowardice. But he could understand Meg's unease. "If he was going to commit suicide I would have thought he would make an event of it. Taking an overdose doesn't seem his style at all. . . ."

There was a silence. Molly stood up and poured coffee from the filter machine.

"I think we should go," she said.

He said nothing. She would give her reasons in her own time. He was learning to treat her more carefully.

"Not because I don't believe he committed suicide," she said. "But because Meg's mixed up and can't accept what happened." She realized suddenly that she sounded patronizing, the bloody superior social worker, and added: "If she knows the facts she might find it easier."

And you, she thought. You might find it easier, too.

"So it's social work," he said. "Not detection."

"That's right," she said, grinning. "And I think that makes me senior partner on this case."

They arrived at the Mill at dusk. The wind of the previous week had dropped and everywhere was icy and still. There was frost under the hedges where the sun had not reached it and when they got out of the car their breath came in white clouds. From the top floor suddenly came the clear notes of a flute, first a series of scales then an Irish folk tune. They stood for a moment, entranced, until the music stopped, then they heard the beating of wings overhead as a skein of geese flew in to roost.

There was a wild garden, then a large wooden porch where all the outdoor coats and boots were kept. The door to that was open. While they were still hesitating, unsure how to attract the attention of the occupants, a boy walked around the side of the building through the garden and joined them. He was wearing a long brown duffel coat that reached the top of his Wellingtons and in one hand he carried a large bucket and a trowel. He stopped on the drive and considered them seriously.

"Are you visitors?" he said. "There isn't a course this weekend. It's been cancelled."

"We're visitors," George said, "but we're not here on a course. We've come to see Mrs. Morrissey. She's expecting us."

"You'd better come in then." He showed no curiosity but opened the door to the porch and sat on a square of coconut matting to pull off his wellingtons. When he took down the hood of his duffel coat they saw that he had large, jug-handle ears and a shock of brown hair.

"What's in the bucket?" George asked to make conversation.

"Lugworms."

"Going fishing?"

"Of course not." The boy was disapproving. "It's part of my study of the shore. I'm doing a real survey. It's all marked out in quadrats. I've taken a sample to see how big they are, but I'll put them back."

"Very impressive," George said.

Precocious brat, Molly thought. That's what home education does for you.

"Mum'll be in the flat," the boy said. "I'll show you." He covered the bucket with a plastic lid and led them into the Mill. They stood in a large hall the height of the building, lit by a slanting skylight in the roof. On each of the three floors a balcony overlooked the space. From the balconies, presumably, would lead bedrooms, dormitories, laboratories. A huge oil painting of barnacle geese hung on the ground floor opposite them.

"That's an Aidan Moore," the boy said. Perhaps he was used to giving conducted tours. "He's staying here, too." He pushed through some swing doors to a staircase. "Come on," he said. "The flat's on the top."

As he climbed the stairs behind the boy, George hoped that Meg and Molly would get on, would at least find something in common apart from the suspicion that, he had discovered, was mutual. When he had phoned Meg to arrange the visit and had said that Molly would be with him she had been less than welcoming.

"This is a serious commission," she had said sharply. "Not a family outing."

"Of course," he had said, "but we work together. I couldn't contemplate taking on the investigation without Molly's assistance."

There had been a silence and he had almost expected her to say that it was all a mistake or she would find someone else to contemplate the investigation. But she had said grudgingly: "Very well then. I agree to your terms. I really feel I have very little choice." But, she had implied, don't expect me to like it.

The image they had of Meg Morrissey when Tim pushed open the door of the family living room was calculated to confirm all Molly's prejudices. She sat in a low chair by the fire with a wicker sewing basket beside her and a pile of mending on her knee. Molly had never darned a sock in her life. The room was warmly lit by the fire, the last of the daylight reflected from the water through the large uncurtained window and a single spot that shone over Meg's shoulder on to her work. As they came in she stood up, set the jeans she was patching on the arm of the chair, and slipped a thimble from her finger. She wore a calf-length cord skirt and a hand-knitted, blackberry-coloured sweater. Very cosy and domestic, Molly thought. The perfect picture of a wonder mother. She probably bakes her own bread, too.

32

Then she remembered that the woman had only recently lost her husband and wondered that she could be so bitchy.

"George!" Meg said. "It is nice to see you. It's been such a long time. And Mrs. Palmer-Jones. I'm very pleased to meet you after all these years."

Her words were cordial. She looked tired, but she was putting on a good show. George thought optimistically that the women might get on after all. The boy stood fidgeting just inside the door, bored by the adult politeness. Meg turned to him.

"Why don't you join Emily in the school room, Tim," she said. Her words were calm and reasonable. This was a mother who would never lose her temper. "I'll send Caitlin down, too, when she's done her practice. I'd like that history project finished before supper. I'll come down in half an hour and see how you're getting on."

"I was hoping to start on the lugworm samples," he said sulkily.

"There'll be plenty of time for that tomorrow," Meg said, and Molly was struck by her confidence. She was quite certain that the boy would obey her, without argument. Molly's relations with her own children had never been that simple. Tim shrugged and left the room.

"Now," Meg said brightly. "What can I get you? I expect you'd like some tea. Even now that the students have gone we usually eat in the refectory downstairs. It's easier for Rosie and Jane, who do the cooking. But I made sure that I had a little kitchen of my own in the flat. Tea I can manage."

She stopped abruptly, aware perhaps that she was talking too much, and disappeared from the room without waiting for them to answer.

George stood by the window. The bay was already lit by pale moonlight. "What a place!" he said, almost to himself. "I've heard of it, of course, from people

33

who've stayed at the field centre as students, but I hadn't expected anything on such a scale."

"Quite an enterprise to take on in retirement," Molly said. "Especially after a serious accident."

"Oh," he said. "I think Meg was behind the organization."

"I bet she was," Molly said under her breath, forgetting for a moment that she had decided to be compassionate.

Meg came in then, carrying a tray that she set on a small table close to the hearth. Molly saw fine china, a plate of home-made biscuits.

"We were just admiring the view," George said. "It's quite splendid!"

"Isn't it wonderful?" Meg said automatically, then sensing that more was expected of her, "It's a great comfort at a time like this."

She paused as if she expected an expression of sympathy. There was a moment of silence as the fire spat and sparks flew up the chimney.

"Perhaps you could explain why you asked us to come," George said gently. "It wasn't quite clear from your letter . . ."

"It's simple," Meg said. "James didn't commit suicide. He wouldn't have done. Not now. I'm hiring you to find out how he died. . . ."

"There must have been a post mortem report," Molly said.

"He was poisoned by the anti-depressants he'd been prescribed," Meg said sharply. George was suddenly aware again of the hostility between the women. "A post mortem can't tell us how he came to take them."

"I can't see," Molly said, "that he could have taken them by accident. Unless perhaps he'd been drinking. Had he been drinking?"

"He'd taken some alcohol," Meg said dismissively, "but not enough to cloud his judgement."

"So what are you saying?" Molly demanded. "That your husband was murdered?"

Meg turned in her chair to face her. "Yes," she said. "I think that is what I'm saying."

"Perhaps," George said, interrupting, not wanting any overt confrontation between the women, "you could explain why you believe that. You must have a reason." He paused, then added apologetically: "It wouldn't be easy, you know, to force-feed an unwilling adult enough pills to kill him."

"Of course I have a reason." She sat back in the chair and looked into the fire.

"You must tell us," George said at last, "if you have any suspicions."

But she seemed unwilling to answer directly.

"James wasn't depressed all the time," she said. "Not even after the accident. He could go for months without needing any medication at all, then, without any apparent reason, he'd hit a low time. It was guilt, I suppose, about Hannah."

"Hannah?" George prompted. He knew about Hannah, but he wanted to hear it from Meg.

"She was his daughter," Meg said. "From his first marriage to Cathy. She was killed in the road accident that caused his spinal injury."

"How did the accident happen?" Molly asked. Meg looked at her with disapproval as if the question was impolite but answered.

"Cathy was already married to Phil and living in Salter's Cottage. Hannah lived there, too, but came occasionally for holidays to her father. She enjoyed coming to stay with us. It was exciting, I suppose. James was still editor of *Green Scenes* then, something of a celebrity. On the night of the accident he had collected her and was driving her back to London. The crash happened before they even reached the motorway. No other cars were involved."

"Did you ever find out what caused the accident?"

She shook her head. "The police could find nothing wrong with the car, but it was such a mess that they couldn't be sure that there wasn't some freak mechanical failure. James couldn't remember anything about it. He was unconscious after the crash and lost his memory of everything that happened after leaving Salter's Cottage. He blamed himself, of course. He'd been tired, thought even that he might have fallen asleep at the wheel."

"And after the accident he changed," George said. It was not a question. He remembered his last encounter with Jimmy Morrissey in the pub in Whitehall, the sense that something important had been left unsaid. Had he wanted to talk about his daughter? Was it a need for confession that had prompted him to invite George for the drink?

"Yes," Meg said. "He changed."

"And the decision to leave *Green Scenes*?" George said. "Was that the result of the accident? There was nothing else?" He remembered again the meeting in the pub, Jimmy's reluctance to leave the venture behind him.

"It was too much for him," Meg said sharply. "He couldn't stand the stress. Not on top of everything else."

"I'd always thought Jimmy thrived on stress," George said mildly.

"Not after the accident," she said. "You said yourself: he changed."

There was a silence.

"You said that he had periods of depression." Molly spoke carefully. "Had he been depressed recently?"

"No," Meg said. "Not for months. The tablets came from an old prescription. He hadn't felt the need to complete the course of treatment. Since the autumn he's almost been his old self."

"Can you account for the change of mood?"

"It was the Mill," she said. "I knew that the move would be good for him in the end."

But George was not convinced. They had been at Markham Mill for two years and the Jimmy he knew would have been bored by spending that long in one place, even a place as beautiful and full of birds as this.

"There wasn't any new project," he said, "something to excite him?"

She hesitated.

"There was his autobiography," she said. "That was his latest enthusiasm." She spoke with a bitterness that surprised George. An autobiography seemed a tame enough project. It would at least keep him at home, which, he suspected, was all Meg had wanted. He said nothing and allowed her to continue.

"I wasn't sure it was a good idea," she said at last. "To relive all those experiences of the past when he was so much more active. I thought it would only make him more depressed. But Grace encouraged him. I suppose she was right. He seemed very keen."

"Grace?"

"Grace Sharland, a community nurse attached to our GP's practice. She visited occasionally. She seemed to amuse James."

"How far had he got with the book?" George asked.

"It was nearly finished. He'd written it all out in long-hand. He'd never taken to computers. He wouldn't let any of us see it. It would be a surprise to us all, he said. A revelation. I believe a number of publishers had expressed interest in it."

"You won't have any objection to our looking at it?" George said. "It might help in our enquiry. . . ."

He phrased the request carefully. He was reluctant to encourage Meg in the belief that James had been murdered.

"No," she said, "I wouldn't have any objection. But I'm afraid you won't be able to see it. James's notebooks have all disappeared."

She spoke flatly, without any sense of making a dramatic revelation.

"And that's why you believe James was murdered?" asked George. "Because of the theft?" He thought she must realize the implication of the notebooks' disappearance. Why else had she called them in?

"I don't know," she said. "I don't know what to think any more. But you must find the autobiography. That's obvious, isn't it?"

Then she put her head in her hands as if the strain of the previous few days had been too much for her. "I'm sorry," she said, I can't think straight. It's all been a nightmare."

George looked at her with sympathy. "Of course," he said. "Of course."

But Molly, sitting at some distance from the woman, was not convinced by the grief. She thought, cynically, that Meg had simply decided she did not want to answer any more of George's questions.

4

"*He* doesn't *look* like a detective," Tim said. "He's old."

"What's his wife like?" Emily looked up from a collage of a Viking boat. She was sticking milk-bottle tops along its side to make shields.

"She's old, too. And scruffy. Very short hair and specs. Caitlin said that the detectives were coming today so it must be them."

"Schoolroom" sounded quaint and Victorian, which was what Meg intended, but this was filled with equipment many schools would have been proud of. There were two computer terminals and screens, an overhead projector, and a flip chart. Each child had his or her own space marked out with the sort of screen you find in a high-tech open-plan office. Emily's had a box of Legos and a construction kit, a shelf of Roald Dahls, a tray of felt pens and paints, mounds of coloured paper. Vikings figured largely—Meg tried to follow the National Curriculum, though not too closely, and the subject was a Year Four topic. There was a model helmet made of papier-mâché and a street plan of Viking York.

Tim's space had a children's series of natural history field guides, a lizard in an aquarium, and a tank full of stick insects. There was a faintly reptilian smell. One shelf held a collection of bird skulls—mostly mute swan and oystercatcher.

Caitlin's project concerned a play she had written, a fantasy tale of knights and ladies. There were shoe boxes made into three-dimensional stage sets, a huge easel with the costume designs, scraps of fabric. Everything was piled into a chaotic heap. Meg nagged her routinely for being untidy.

Ruth had surprised her mother by deciding to go in for A levels. Her corner was designed to resemble an undergraduate's study. There were shelves of textbooks, a file of previous exam papers that she was slowly working through, and a tape recorder so she could practise her French.

Tim and Emily were sitting at a large table in the middle of the room. Tim was supposed to be working on the Vikings, too, but his attention was not on the book in front of him.

"Ruth!" He raised his voice so it penetrated her corner. "Do you think they're detectives?"

Ruth sighed, put a bookmark between the pages of *La Peste*, and went to join them. She thought Meg was making a dreadful mistake. The outburst after the memorial service had been embarrassing but understandable. To pursue the matter by hiring private detectives was so bizarre that she wondered about her mother's sanity. She must have known that the children's interest would be aroused. How did she think she could explain the couple's presence?

"They're sort of detectives," Ruth said at last. "Mum wants to find out how your father died so she's asked these people to come and look into it. That's all."

"But the police came before," Tim said. "That morning we found him. The fat one must have been a detective because he wasn't wearing a uniform." The logic seemed to him unanswerable. He considered. "He didn't *do* very much though," he said at last. "He sat in the kitchen with Rosie and Jane all morning drinking tea and eating flapjacks. He talked to Mum in the flat, but he didn't see anyone else. Not as far as I know."

And he would know, Ruth thought. Tim knew everything that went on at the Mill.

"Mr. Palmer-Jones isn't that sort of detective," she
said. "He's not a policeman. He'll have time to ask
questions and find out what actually happened."

"But we know what happened," Tim objected. "Dad
killed himself some time that evening when we thought
he was in the study working on his book." His face was
pinched and Ruth thought that uncertainty and muddle
would make it harder for him to accept James's death.
What was Meg thinking of?

Emily had finished her picture. She set the paper
aside and began to peel strips of dried glue from her
fingers.

"I don't think he killed himself," she said calmly. "I
think Mum's right."

She stood up and went to wash her hands in the deep
sink under the window. Before Ruth could ask what she
meant, the bell rang for dinner and the children ran off.

They ate in the field centre dining room, which could
hold eighty people at six large tables. Now only one
was laid. It was covered by a white linen cloth and set
with heavy cutlery and glasses. Most of the lights in the
room had been switched off. The table where they sat
was in one corner, lit by a single bulb on a long flex
covered by a wicker shade and by candles. The shad-
owy space beyond them seemed vast. The room was
rather cold and their voices seemed to echo.

Molly wondered at the formality of the occasion.
With such a small number wouldn't it have been easier
to eat in the kitchen? At least there it might have been
warm. But Meg seemed concerned to maintain the ritual
of the Markham communal meal. She had changed from
her sweater and skirt into a soft grey wool frock and
there were pearls around her neck. Molly, who had felt
liberated from the need to consider clothes with the
coming to fashion of the track suit and who was still in

the navy joggers and sweatshirt she had worn for travelling, felt decidedly underdressed.

"We always try to eat together in the evening," Meg was saying as the children came in. "Family and students together when the courses are running. I like to think it typifies the atmosphere of the place. Now let me introduce you to my wonderful brood."

And they were, Molly saw at once, all too wonderful for words. It was as if each child had been moulded with a different personality only to reflect Meg's creativity and range of interests. There was Ruth of the good sense and the brains, artistic Caitlin, the boy who was being groomed to be a biologist. And the youngest girl? Molly wondered. What does Meg intend for her? Then it came to her in a flash that Emily would be the carer, the homemaker. She would be expected to look after her mother in her old age. The work of art that was Meg's family was complete.

"Ruth's preparing for A levels," Meg was saying, completing the introductions. "We're very proud of her. She's hoping to go to York to read French. I'm not convinced of the value of A levels, of course—so much rote learning still—but the way the university entrance system's organized at the moment I suppose exams are essential." She beamed at them all.

Where had Jimmy fit into all this? Molly wondered. What need had these children had of a father? She felt suddenly as she had done when her own children were teenagers. Each Christmas a school friend had sent a circular letter extolling the virtues of her model family, their achievements during the year, the exams they had passed, the musical instruments they played. Molly had read these letters with a mixture of envy, guilt, and shame. Where had she gone wrong? Her children had dabbled in drugs, got drunk and thrown up on the carpet, threatened to drop out of college. They had turned out all right in the end, of course, were now almost frighteningly decent and respectable, but then she had read the woman's smug letters with fury, as if their complacency were an accusation of her own incompetence. Meg aroused the same emotion.

With relief Molly turned her attention from the children to a latecomer, who hovered awkwardly at the edge of the pool of light.

"Aidan," Meg said, "come and join us. This is Aidan Moore, our most famous tutor and great friend. You'll know his work. Aidan, perhaps you'll have met George Palmer-Jones. He's here to help sort out what happened to James."

And me, Molly thought. I'm here, too. But having shown off her children, Meg ignored her throughout the rest of the meal.

The food was served by two cheerful young women who sat together later at the end of the table to eat. They were competent and energetic, the sort of girls, George thought, you'd expect to find running riding stables. Very healthy and fit with strong, red hands.

"You'll have to talk to Rosie and Jane," Meg said. "They run this place between them. Jimmy and I always said that we'd never manage it without them."

The young women smiled politely. They were not taken in, George thought, by the flattery but were too good-humoured to resent Meg's patronizing manner. They ladled home-made soup into bowls that they carried deftly around the table on trays. The bread, Meg said proudly, had been baked by them this morning.

As the excellent dinner progressed, George found it increasingly difficult to imagine James in this setting. The Jimmy Morrissey he had known had never been able to sit still for the length of a meal. He would jump to his feet between courses and move restlessly around the room, even if he were in a restaurant. In a private home he would pick up objects of interest: a book from a shelf, a photograph, then discard them immediately. He had considered food as a fuel, eating ravenously whatever was to hand if he was hungry. It would not

43

have mattered a jot to him if the bread had been baked that morning or bought from a supermarket the week before.

George listened with detachment to the conversation going on around him. Meg led it all. Without her prompting they would probably have eaten in silence. The talk was of local people, the children's school work, and domestic problems related to the field centre. They really would have to buy new sheets and towels before the summer, she said, as if it were a matter of extreme importance. And if Florrie wasn't more reliable this year they'd have to consider someone else from the village for the cleaning. She was obviously determined to make a go of the Mill on her own.

James would have been bored to distraction by the subjects under discussion and George wondered if at last he had found a convincing motive for suicide. Perhaps it had been triggered by nothing more sinister than the tedium of his life there, the endless family dinners. Then he thought that James had had other means of escape. He had never cared much for convention. What had there been to stop him just walking out and leaving Meg to carry on the show alone? Or had his bouts of depression made him too dependent on her to run away?

"And James?" George asked, interrupting Meg in full flow. "Did he always eat with you?"

"Of course," she said, but at the same time Caitlin across the table broke in with, "Not if he could help it!"

It was the first spontaneous statement of the evening and they all stared at her.

"Well, it's true," she said defensively. "He hated this kind of thing."

"Sometimes he didn't feel up to it," Meg conceded. "Since his accident he sometimes felt uncomfortable in a crowd. Then Rosie or Jane took him something on a tray to the flat."

There was an awkward silence.

"Is it all right if I go out tonight?" Caitlin said, taking advantage of her mother's lack of composure.

"Where do you want to go?"

"Rosie and Jane are going to the Dead Dog. They said I could go, too."

There was another silence.

"You may go," Meg said at last, "if Ruth will be there, too."

"Oh, Mum, she's not my minder!"

"And no alcohol."

Caitlin appeared to sulk, but she had got her way and she left the table happily.

After dinner Meg took George and Molly to her flat for coffee. The younger children had been sent to bed. Heavy brocade curtains had been drawn across the large window, and the room was warm.

"Now," Meg said bravely. "George, I expect you'd like to ask me some questions."

"Thank you," George said. "I'm sure Molly and I *both* have questions to ask."

The dear, Molly thought. He's learning!

"Of course," Meg said. "Of course."

"Did James eat with you on the evening of his death?" George asked. It was a development of the conversation begun in the dining room.

"No," Meg said reluctantly. "He decided not to come in to dinner that night. He said he was engrossed in his autobiography. He could see the end of it, he said, and wanted to crack on until it was done."

"So somebody brought him a meal on a tray?"

"Yes," she said. "I believe Rosie took dinner to him in his study."

"Where is that?"

"It's on the ground floor," Meg said. "As far away from the guests and the family as he could manage." She smiled but could not hide her resentment.

"What time was dinner?"

"At seven o'clock," she said. "We always eat at seven so the children can join us."

"You and the children ate with the guests as usual?"

She nodded.

"Did you come back to the flat for coffee?"

"Yes," she said. "Aidan was here, too. He needed a break occasionally from the students."

"But James didn't join you?"

"No. I went in to see him after dinner. He seemed preoccupied, excited. He'd hardly touched his meal, and when I asked him about it, it was clear he'd forgotten it was there. I asked him to have coffee with us. The study's close to the front door and rather draughty. I thought he might like to come and get warm by the fire. It was a freezing night. There'd been snow."

"But he didn't come?"

She shook her head. "He said: 'It's nearly finished, Meg, and I'm not going to stop until it's done even if it takes me all night.' So I asked Jane to take him coffee to the study."

"Did he drink it?" Molly asked. "Did you find the cup the next day? Was it empty?"

Meg seemed surprised and confused by the question. "I'm not sure," she said. "One of the girls in the kitchen might know."

"Do they do the cleaning as well as the cooking?"

"They supervise," Meg said. "A couple of women come in from Markham Law for a few hours to do the bulk of the cleaning, but I leave the organization to Rosie and Jane."

How very convenient! Molly thought. It must be much easier to be a wonder mother without having to worry about the cooking and the cleaning.

"What time was that?" George asked gently. "What time did you ask Jane to take the coffee in to James?"

Meg shrugged. "I'm not sure. Eight-thirty. Nine o'clock. I'd read to Emily and Tim and put them to bed."

"Did you see your husband again that evening?" George asked.

She shook her head. "I didn't want to disturb him," she said. "He seemed so involved." She paused, then added hurriedly: "Before I went to bed I walked down to his study. I knew he was there because his light was on, but in the end I decided not to go in. He was always accusing me of fussing. I thought he'd be angry if I interrupted. So I came back to the flat and went to bed."

"What time was that?"

"Ten-thirty," she said. "I read for a while, hoping that he might join me, then I must have fallen asleep."

"Did James have any other visitors that night?"

"I wouldn't know," she said. "He didn't mention anyone when I asked about the coffee. Someone might have come to the study later, but I don't think he would have encouraged the disruption."

"What about Aidan? Did he spend all evening with you?"

"Yes. He left at about ten."

There was a silence. George tried to picture the events of that night. The atmosphere of the Mill must have been very different when it was full of students. Presumably some of them, like Rosie and Jane, must have been tempted to visit the village pub.

"Was the front door of the Mill left open?" he asked. "Or did the students have their own keys?"

"It's locked at midnight," Meg said. "Usually by Rosie, who doesn't mind staying up late. If a student wanted to be in after that we'd give them a key."

"But before midnight anyone could have got in?"

"Oh yes," she said. "Anyone in the world." She got up from her chair by the fire and filled their cups with coffee.

"Had James seen anyone earlier in the day?" George asked. If this was suicide, he thought, something must have triggered it, something must have made that day different from all the rest.

She paused. "Grace Sharland, the nurse, came at about three," she said at last, and added lightly: "James always seemed to find time to talk to her."

"That was the woman who encouraged him to write the autobiography?"

"Yes. Our GP arranged for her to visit when we first moved here. After his accident James suffered from spells of depression and anxiety and the doctor thought it might help. For some reason James seemed to take to her and she came every month even when he wasn't feeling particularly low."

"Was this one of her regular visits?"

"No." Her voice was even, but he sensed her irritation. "I was surprised to see her."

"Did you ask why she had called?"

"No," Meg said frostily. "She made it clear from the start that her interviews with James were confidential. I suppose he must have phoned her. He did that occasionally. I think he liked the attention."

"You didn't ask James why he'd sent for her?"

"No," she said. "It never came up."

George did not believe her. From her attitude it was clear that Ms. Sharland had been a subject of contention, an unwelcome intrusion. He thought there would have been arguments. Meg would have wanted to know what the visit was about.

"Where did he see the nurse?" George asked. "Here or in the study?"

"In his study. He spent most of the day there." She stopped suddenly as if remembering. "He did come out at lunch-time to go for a walk along the shore," she said. "Towards Salter's Cottage. He probably called to see Phil. It was a Saturday so he would have been there."

"Were your husband and Mr. Cairns friends?" Molly asked. "They didn't find the situation awkward?" Although they had shared a wife, she almost added, but there was no need. The question was understood.

"Of course not," Meg's voice was sharp. "Why should it be? We're civilized adults."

"Didn't you feel any reluctance about moving here so close to James's first wife?"

"None at all. Phil and Cathy are happily married. We'd all become rather good friends, actually. We first saw the Mill when we came to visit them for a week-end."

Like Meg's perfect family, it was too good to be true, Molly thought. In her career as a social worker she had never known separation or divorce without bitterness.

"Whose idea was it to take on the Mill?" she asked.

"It was a joint decision," Meg said firmly. "We both fell in love with the place as soon as we saw it."

"But James must have seen it before then," Molly said, "when he came to collect Hannah for access visits."

"Of course he had seen it before." Meg allowed her voice to become impatient. "But that was before his accident. His attitude to everything changed then. He realized that he couldn't cope with the stress of running *Green Scenes*. Starting our own field centre in the Mill seemed a practical alternative."

"Did he realize or did you realize?" Molly asked.

"What do you mean?"

"People who are under stress find it hard to step away from it, to admit that they can't cope. I wondered if you had to persuade James to consider resignation."

Meg hesitated, unsure whether criticism was implied in the statement, defensive.

"I told him I was worried about him," she said at last. "*Green Scenes* was going through a turbulent time. The board was very demanding. James was a fighter. It would never have occurred to him to change the magazine's policy without a battle. I showed him that there was an alternative. Once he'd grasped that, he didn't need any persuasion."

They sat for a moment in silence. It was plausible,

49

George thought. Just. If James had lost all his confidence after Hannah's death he would have been susceptible to Meg's suggestions. He thought Molly was being too hard on Meg, that she should be more sympathetic.

"So James went to see the Cairnses at lunch-time and he saw the community psychiatric nurse in the afternoon," he said gently, intending to bring the interview to a conclusion. "And the rest of the time he was working alone in the study?"

"So far as I know," she said. "He may have gone down to the schoolroom to see if any of the children were there. He did that occasionally if he'd come to a break in his work. He liked to see them then."

"You don't mind our talking to the children?"

"I don't mind anything," she cried, "so long as it helps find out what happened."

"I'm sorry," George said, "to have to ask all these questions. I expect the police went over the same ground."

"No," she said. She sounded exhausted. "The police assumed from the beginning that James had killed himself. They sent a man called Porter whose attitude I found very offensive. Once he heard that James had been treated for depression he stopped asking questions. He just gave up. It's discrimination, isn't it? James should be treated in death like everyone else, not dismissed as a madman."

"Where did James keep his pills?" George asked, prompted by her talk of his illness. "Here in the flat or in the study?"

"Here," she said. "In the bathroom. There's a cupboard where we keep all our medicines. They'd have been in there."

"So he'd have had to fetch them specially?"

She nodded.

"He could have done that easily, I suppose, without your knowing. For example, while you were at dinner?"

She nodded again.

"Do you lock the flat when no-one's in it?" he asked.

"Of course not," she said. "What danger could there be here?" She stirred in her chair and seemed to be trying to find the energy to move. "I expect you'd like to see his study," she said. "I'll show you."

"No," George said. He felt sorry for her. "Tomorrow will do."

And he and Molly left her sitting by the dying fire with the pile of mending still at her feet.

5

The pub in Markham Law was called the Lord Nelson but was known to the locals as the Dead Dog because of a stuffed terrier in a glass case that stood on a shelf behind the bar. Ruth did not like going to the pub much. She had the feeling that most of the regulars resented their presence. It was like gate-crashing a private party, if you could call such a sombre gathering a party.

They always sat in the public bar. Rosie and Jane saw that as a sort of political statement. They said only yuppies went in the lounge, though Ruth thought that in Markham Law yuppies were pretty thin on the ground. In her experience the lounge bar was inhabited by pleasant middle-aged couples out for a drive from Mardon or students from the Mill who had escaped for the evening. She suspected they would be better company than the public bar regulars, who were without exception unfriendly and miserable.

The room was long and narrow with a brown lino-leum floor and brown varnished tables. It was usually heated by a calor gas heater in one corner and the smell of its fumes always caught at Ruth's throat when she walked in. She would recoil from the smell and from the stares of the old men who spent all evening at the table next to the heater. They must have known who she was—she knew most of them by name—but whenever she entered they glowered as if she were a stranger. Once she had plucked up courage and shouted: "Hello, Ron!" to a retired farm worker who helped occasionally in the garden at the Mill, but he had ignored her. Since then she had crept into the pub and sat on the bench nearest to the door pretending to be invisible.

Not all the regulars of the Dead Dog were old. There was Florrie Duffy's son who worked in the tannery in Mardon and came with his biker friends because they had been banned from all the pubs in town. The atmosphere of the Dog seemed to affect them. They caused no trouble there but sat in a gloomy silence, their leather-clad elbows on the tables, steadily swallowing beer, as unwelcoming as the old men playing cards.

Rosie and Jane had breezed into the place as if they owned it right from the beginning. They drank pints in straight glasses and kept their own darts behind the bar. Young women had never behaved like that in the experience of the Dog regulars, especially well-spoken young women like Jane. They should have been in the lounge making a glass of lager and lime last all night. But since their first appearance the attitude of the drinkers had softened. They admitted that "those girls from the Mill" were all right. They recruited them into the pub darts team and let them play cribbage if they were short-handed. But their suspicion towards Meg's daughters remained.

Tonight Ruth felt her usual reluctance as she entered the bar. She would have refused to go despite her mother if Aidan had not asked to join the party. If anything it would be worse tonight because they would be curious about James's death. They might even have heard of the Palmer-Joneses' arrival at the Mill—Florrie saw it as the main responsibility of her post as cleaner to pass on information about the Morrisseys to her friends. The regulars of the Dog weren't known for their sensitivity and Ruth imagined probing questions about her stepfather's suicide and a discussion about her mother's sanity.

Caitlin, she saw, would make an exhibition of herself as she always did when she was released from her mother's supervision. She was in Morticia mode, wearing a long, closely fitting black dress that almost reached the floor. She had already made her way to the table where the bikers sat and draped herself around the neck of Florrie's son, Malcolm.

"Go on, Malcolm," she said. "Buy me a drink."

He stared in front of him, hardly seeming to notice she was there.

"Can't," he said at last. "You're under age."

"Cedric won't mind, will you, Cedric?" she said, and pranced towards the bar. "You don't know how old I am, do you, Cedric? You could always say I look eighteen."

Cedric was the only son of the owners of the Dog, an overweight and pimply man with a nervous disposition. In the village he was considered rather odd. Partly it was his name that had made him a figure of fun since he started infants' school, partly it was his sheltered upbringing. He had gone away once to college to study horticulture and landscape design, but there had been some crisis or breakdown in the first month and his doting parents had brought him home. They had vowed never to subject him to such stress again. He worked for them in the pub but only doing the light work. There would be no lifting of barrels for Cedric.

Caitlin teased him dreadfully because he was an easy target. She pointed out that his hands were shaking when he pulled the pints and commented on his acne. Yet she held a fearful fascination for him. He knew she would torment him, but he looked forward to her occasional visits to the Dog with a mixture of fear and erotic excitement.

"I don't know," he said now in answer to her question. Then bravely: "I don't suppose anyone need know. What do you want?"

"An orange juice," said Rosie firmly. "You know what your mother's like, Cat. If she thinks you've been drinking she won't let you out with us again. And I'm not prepared to get into bother by lying on your behalf."

"Oh well," Caitlin said, giving in gracefully. "An orange juice then, Cedric. And a bag of crisps. I know how to live dangerously."

She smiled at him sexily and waited for him to blush.

The five of them sat at the table by the door. Ruth wondered why Aidan had come—he looked tense and ill at ease. Her only experience of romantic love came from nineteenth-century novels and she hoped for some dramatic declaration of affection from him. She had no idea how to go about the business of showing him that she was interested in him.

"Well," Rosie said, breaking in on her thoughts, "what do you think of Sherlock and Watson? I must admit that they're not quite what I expected. They hardly inspire confidence, do they?"

"You shouldn't underestimate George," Aidan said. "He might have retired, but he's no fool. There was a case in Norfolk a few years ago when a young birder died . . . The police didn't have a clue, but he sorted out what happened."

"So he really is a great detective?" Rosie said. "Well, I'll take your word for it, but I'm not convinced."

In the awkward silence that followed the bikers got up as a group and clattered out. There was a clanking of chains and a pounding of steel-capped boots, then the roar of their motorbikes as they sped away to find fun elsewhere.

"I think Mum's off her head," Caitlin said. "She's done some pretty weird things in her time but this beats them all." She turned to Ruth for support. "Well?" she demanded. "Don't you think the idea that James was murdered is preposterous? He could be a moody bastard, but you can't imagine that anyone would want to *kill* him."

"No," Ruth said. "Of course not." But she wondered immediately if that were true. There had certainly been times when she had wished him out of her life.

"Why don't we change the subject?" It was tactful Jane, who hated a fuss. Caitlin took no notice.

"But I *want* to discuss it," she said. "It's so bloody frustrating being kept in the dark. Mother won't tell us anything. She says there's nothing to tell until Mr. Palmer-Jones has made his report. If that's true, why did she ask him here in the first place? What made her suspicious?"

Rosie and Jane looked at each other. Ruth caught the look and envied their friendship. She had never been that close to anyone of her own age. Meg's philosophy of educating her children at home had made that sort of easy relationship impossible. There had been Hannah, of course. Ruth had always thought of Hannah as a kindred spirit, but they hadn't seen each other that often, only during the school holidays. And she was almost a relative, so it hardly seemed to count. Rosie and Jane had quite different backgrounds: Rosie had a mother she described as "barking mad" and had been in and out of children's homes during her teens; Jane came from a wealthy family and a posh school. Yet now they were so close that they communicated without speaking. Ruth looked across the table at Aidan and wondered if they would ever be that intimate, but he seemed preoccupied and took no notice of her.

"Well?" Caitlin demanded again. "Is anyone going to tell me what it's all about?"

"The autobiography has disappeared," Rosie said. "Meg didn't tell you that?"

Caitlin shook her head.

"She thinks it's a peculiar coincidence," Rosie went on. "You can understand her point of view."

"Who'd want to read James's boring autobiography?"

Caitlin said extravagantly. "It was all trips down the Amazon and how I saved the rain forest for mankind."

"How do you know?" Aidan Moore asked. "Did you get to read it?"

His voice was light, but Ruth was struck by the notion that the question was desperately important to him. Caitlin could not have noticed his anxiety or she would have strung the story out. She just shrugged.

"I didn't read all of it," she said. "I couldn't have coped. Did you see how long it was? But he showed me bits he was specially proud of. Or he read them out loud to me."

"What else was there?" Aidan asked carefully. "Besides the piece on the rain forest?"

"Oh, God, I don't know," she said. "There was a chapter on the setting up of *Green Scenes* called something pompous like 'The Moral Dilemma—Private Interest or Public Good.' He gave me that the day before he died, but it was so tedious that I put it back in the study without reading it. I hoped he wouldn't ask me questions on it and catch me out. He would have been livid. But in the end he didn't have the chance, did he?"

Ruth, who had been watching Aidan's reactions carefully, saw that he was still troubled.

"How do you know that the book's disappeared?" she asked.

"Your mother asked Jane if she'd seen it," Rosie said. "We helped her to look for it in the study and the flat, but we couldn't find it."

"Why did Mother want it, anyway?" Caitlin demanded. "She's never been interested in James's work."

The question went unanswered.

"Meg didn't tell me about the autobiography," Aidan said. "I've been working on the jacket. You'd have thought she'd have let me know."

Of course, Ruth thought. That's why he was so interest in James's book. He's been working on the jacket design ever since he arrived. "What will happen to your drawing now?" she asked.

"I'll finish it anyway," he said. "It'll make a reasonable painting. I could give it to Meg as a present. Besides, the book might turn up. James was never very organized."

"I don't think it's at the Mill," Rosie said. "Meg made us look everywhere. She wanted to be sure it had gone, you see, before she brought in Mr. Palmer-Jones."

"Yes," he said. "I see." He felt absent-mindedly in his pocket for his wallet and went to the bar to buy another round of drinks. When he returned with a tray, they were still talking about the autobiography.

"But I don't understand," Caitlin was saying, "what the book going missing has to do with James dying. Why did Mum think she had to rush out and hire private detectives? It's completely bizarre." She looked around the group for a response. "Or am I just being dense?"

Jane answered gently. "Perhaps he was prepared to dish the dirt in his book. He must have come across information during his career that would have been embarrassing. . . ."

"Like politicians, you mean? Or film stars?" Caitlin was intrigued by the notion.

"Yes," Jane said. "Something like that."

"And he was killed to stop him revealing all?" She was incredulous.

"I think that might be the way Meg's mind is working."

"Well," Caitlin said. "I wish I'd taken more notice of the bloody book now."

"It seems very unlikely to me," Aidan said diffidently. "Any embarrassment caused by the book would have been to large corporations or government departments, bodies whose inefficiency or greed had a cost in conservation terms. For example, he might have been interested in following up a lead on the company that owned the *Braer*, the tanker that went aground on Shetland. But he'd hardly have given out embarrassing information about individuals."

Ruth, who had experience of her stepfather's capacity for mischief, wasn't so sure. What did he say about us? she wondered. Or Mother? She certainly wasn't sorry that the notebooks had gone missing.

"Meg didn't want to believe James had killed himself," Jane said. "The disappearance of the autobiography just confirmed her view. It didn't have a lot to do with logic."

Rosie nodded in agreement. "The inquest verdict was suicide," she said. "If Mr. Palmer-Jones is as perceptive as Aidan says, he'll soon realize that it was right. The problem will be to convince Meg of that."

They stayed in the pub until closing time and then drove back to the Mill, crammed inside Jane's Mini.

"You should let me drive," Caitlin said. "I'm the only one who's not been drinking."

"You must be joking," Rosie said. "Jane could find her way from the Dog to the Mill blindfolded. Come to that, the car could probably drive itself."

Ruth, in the back of the car, found herself sitting next to Aidan. As the car hurtled around the sharp bends in the road she was thrown against him. She could smell the wool of his jersey. She wished she had the courage to reach out and take his hand but even the drinks in the Dead Dog had not made her sufficiently brave for that.

Molly would have liked to go to the pub after they had finished with Meg Morrissey. She was already finding the atmosphere of the Mill oppressive and would have liked to get away for a couple of hours, a beer, some normal conversation. But when she suggested it to George he shook his head disapprovingly.

"Meg already thinks we're treating this like a holiday camp," he said.

59

"It's not Colditz," she retorted. "She'll let us out occasionally."

"Not tonight," he said. "Really. I think we have things to discuss. Where we won't be overheard."

She shrugged and followed George to their room. The bedrooms at Markham had nothing in common with Colditz. They would not have been out of place in a smart hotel and were nothing like the field centre rooms where George had stayed in the past, and where rows of beds and moth-eaten blankets had reminded him of the deprivations of National Service. There *were* dormitories at Markham Mill, discreetly hidden away at the end of corridors, where for a discount school and college groups could stay, but the emphasis here was on style and comfort. There was a wide double-glazed window with a view over the bay, Scandinavian furniture, an oatmeal-coloured carpet, and a folk-weave bedspread. On a low pine table there was a tray with kettle, earthenware mugs decorated with hand-painted oystercatchers, sachets of instant coffee, teabags on strings, and plastic pots of vile UHT milk. Molly made tea—without milk—and they sat by the window and watched the flashing marker buoy on the end of Salter's Spit.

"Even if this place was nearly derelict and cheap to buy, it must have cost a fortune to do it up," Molly said. "Where do you think they got the money?"

George seemed mesmerized by the flashing light and Molly had to wait for an answer. "James sold his controlling interest in *Green Scenes* when he retired," he said. "One of the conglomerate publishers that prints everything from the *Methodist Times* to *Angling Today* took it on. They'd been interested in buying him out for some time and would have paid well for it. Then there was a big house in Putney where the family was living before they moved. James inherited that from his parents and they sold just before the property market crashed. That must have given them sufficient working capital to get started. And now the Mill is curiously

60

successful despite the recession. It fills a gap in the market. There are lots of people who want the atmosphere but not the discomfort of a traditional field centre and who are prepared to pay."

"Yes," Molly said. "I suppose so." But Markham Mill seemed to her less a successful business than a monstrous white elephant, created simply to provide Meg with the lifestyle she had wanted for her children. The place might have space, stimulating company, security—everything Meg wanted for her family—but what had it provided for Jimmy Morrissey and why had he gone along with her plans?

"I wish I'd seen him more recently," George said suddenly, his train of thought following hers. "I wish I'd come here when he was still alive. . . ."

"Do you really think he came here of his own free will?" she asked.

He shrugged. "I've never known Jimmy to do anything for any other reason," he said. "He was the most selfish man I've ever met. Charming, of course, but quite selfish. I can't believe that he'd respond to the sort of emotional blackmail Meg may have tried about the move being best for the children. Not unless the accident changed him dramatically."

"Ah yes," Molly said sceptically. "The accident. I don't believe anyone changes that much. Do you?"

"I don't know," George said. "The last time I met him he was certainly different, less sure of himself."

"But not so insecure, surely, that he would volunteer to move here to become a glorified hotelier, just because Meg wanted him to?"

"What are you saying then?" George demanded. "That he had his own reasons for choosing to retire here? Or that he was put under so much pressure that he couldn't refuse?"

"The latter," Molly said quickly. "He must have seen that it would be like a prison for him. Even if he were depressed he wouldn't have chosen that. So we'll need

61

to find out what Meg used to put pressure on him, why he couldn't stand up to her or just run away."

"I can't believe that Meg forced Jimmy into a situation when she knew he would be unhappy," George said. "She loved him. She must genuinely have thought he'd find it easier to get well here."

"Do you really believe that?" Molly demanded.

He thought romantically of the gentle woman sitting by the fire.

"Yes," he said. "Of course."

"Then you're more of a fool than I took you for," she said.

6

They woke to another clear, freezing day. There was ice on the mudflats and a thick frost on the grass. The tension of the previous night remained between George and Molly though neither mentioned the disagreement. They treated each other politely, with detachment, and went to the dining room without discussing James Morrissey's death.

Aidan Moore sat alone at the large table, eating muesli in a preoccupied, mechanical way. When he saw them come in he stood awkwardly.

"We didn't have a chance to talk last night," George said. "It's a pleasure to meet you again even under these circumstances. Perhaps you don't remember but we met a few times at Cley. Nancy introduced us." Nancy had run a small café patronized by birders.

"Yes," Aidan said. "I remember." He returned to his breakfast. George helped himself to porridge from a heated dish.

"We never bumped into each other at *Green Scenes*," George went on, "though Jimmy always showed me your latest contribution, and I've admired all your illustrations. The plates for the *Estuaries* book are my favourites. You must have taken some inspiration from the bay here. I hadn't realized before, of course. It's a wonderful place for a field centre."

"Yes," Aidan said. "It is."

"You'd normally be teaching a course now?" George persisted. He was surprised by the monosyllabic answers. He would have expected more co-operation. Aidan owed his career to Jimmy Morrissey.

"Normally, yes. When Jimmy died we sent all the students home but Meg asked me to stay. Perhaps now you're here she won't mind if I go ..." His voice trailed off.

"It couldn't have been easy," George said, "teaching amateurs. Quite a different skill from painting itself."

"It was dreadful!" Aidan replied spontaneously at last. "They expected me to talk, to explain, to criticize. As if that mattered. But they wouldn't just stand still and *look*." He shook his head. "I'm sorry," he said. "I wasn't very patient."

"Why did you agree to come," George asked cheerfully, "if it was such a trial? It can't have been because you needed the money. Not now."

"It wasn't for the money," Aidan said. "It was because Jimmy asked me. You know what he was like. I couldn't refuse him anything."

"And I suppose while you were here you did get a chance to do your own work, too?"

Aidan nodded. "It was only that which kept me sane."

"What are you working on now?"

He hesitated. "The jacket for a book of Jimmy's," he said. "It doesn't seem likely now that it'll be published, but I'd like to finish it."

"He commissioned you to design the jacket for his autobiography?"

"Yes, he wrote to me about it in the autumn."

"You know the book's disappeared?"

Aidan nodded.

"Did he talk to you about the book at all?"

Aidan looked up sharply. "No, not specifically. Why should he?"

"If you were designing the jacket he might talk about the contents, even let you see a draft of the text . . ."

"No," Aidan said vehemently. "There was no need for that. He wanted a picture of the Mill. That was clear from the beginning."

"Why did he choose the Mill?" George asked. "Because he'd been specially happy here?"

"I don't know," Aidan said abruptly. "He never said. He just gave me the commission. Now I'll try to get it finished so I can go away and leave Meg in peace."

"*Was* he happy here?" George asked.

There was a shocked silence. Aidan looked up and met his eyes. But before he could answer Meg and the children arrived at the table with a scraping of chairs and a babble of murmured greetings. Aidan excused himself and left.

Molly had been listening to the conversation with interest. There was, she thought, in Aidan's attitude to Jimmy Morrissey an ambiguity. There was admiration certainly, but a resentment, too, a sense of impotence perhaps because he did not have the courage to stand up to the older man. Frustration. Neither did it escape her notice that Ruth watched Aidan's departure with disappointment.

Meg nodded to them as she sat down but seemed not to feel the need for constant conversation as she had at dinner. The children were quiet and morose and Molly wondered if there had been a family row. With some guilt she realized that the thought gave her considerable pleasure. She passed her empty plate to Jane and turned to George thinking that this coldness between them was childish. She would not allow Meg to come between them. But George, with his breakfast finished, had turned his chair to face the window and was staring at the birds on the shore. As he watched, Aidan Moore appeared, silhouetted against the startling morning light, and made his way slowly down Salter's Spit. He focused the binoculars that he had brought to the table

65

with him on a flock of waders. Molly might as well not have been there.

If I asked him to choose, she thought, between me and the birds, I wonder which way he would go.

The thought had not occurred to her for thirty years, since the babies were young and demanding and she was working full-time. George had recognized she never had a minute to herself but had still found time to go birding every weekend even if it were only to a piece of local woodland or a nearby reservoir. She had not dared to ask him to make the choice then, had seen, except in her most desperate moments, that the demand would be unreasonable. She supposed it was too late now. Perhaps Meg Morrissey had found more courage. Perhaps she had expected James to commit himself to the family and choose between the ruling passion of his interest in natural history and his love for her.

George took the binoculars, a pair of East German Zeiss he had bought before the wall went down and the prices went up, from his eyes. But he kept the strap around his neck and she could tell that he wanted to be outside. He turned back to the room, unaware that she had been watching him.

"Ready?" he said. She nodded and followed him.

When they were out of the Morrisseys' hearing he said: "I thought I'd go to Salter's Cottage this morning. Phil will be out, but I could talk to Cathy."

It was an excuse to be out, walking along the shore, and they both knew it.

"Why not?" she said. She had decided to be forgiving. Meg had forced Jimmy to change and look what had happened to him. "What do you want me to do?"

He looked at her with surprise and answered carefully, afraid of being accused of bossiness.

"What do you suggest?" he said at last.

"I could speak to the two housekeepers. They should have a reasonably objective opinion of James's state of mind before he died and they'll know as much about what went on in the family as anyone. Then I thought I'd make an appointment to see Grace Sharland, the community nurse. We need to know exactly what the medical position was."

"Yes," he said. "Thanks." He was grateful because she was being so reasonable, but his mind was already on the shore outside, the possibility of shore lark or lapland bunting. He hurried away before she could change her mind.

Molly thought that there was a Victorian quality in the way Meg spoke of her domestic staff always as a couple. They had become "Rosie and Jane" as if, because they were servants of a sort, they were not allowed personalities of their own. Now she saw that they were quite different in almost every way, apart perhaps from their age.

She found them in the kitchen. The breakfast dishes had been loaded into a large industrial dishwasher that churned away in a corner and they were drinking coffee. They seemed to take her interruption for granted and were quite prepared to talk about themselves.

Rosie had long tawny hair that she tied back in a thick, untidy plait when she was working. She had a local accent and an air of perpetual aggression that made it clear that she would allow no one to push *her* around. The family had come from Mardon originally—her father had worked in a factory there. He'd been made redundant when she was still at school, then they'd all had to uproot to a soulless Midlands new town that she described as "the pits."

"It killed the old man," she said. "He hated the work and he'd left all his mates behind. They said it was a stroke, but he had nothing left to live for. Me mam's still there, but she never settled. She's suffered from depression since I can remember, but the move made it worse. And now there's no way out. She'd not get a council house back here after all this time."

Rosie, it seemed, had gone to catering college because she liked cooking but starting at the bottom in some posh hotel where they mucked the food around and charged you the earth wasn't for her. Nor sweating away in a bloody works canteen where you churned out pie and chips all day. You might just as well be on the factory floor as *that*. She'd wanted the job at Markham Mill as soon as she'd seen the advert. It was a chance to get back home, to the place where she'd been happy as a kid. She even dreamed of bringing her mam back some time and renting a cottage in the village for her—if ever she managed to save anything out of the pittance Meg Morrissey paid.

All this she told Molly as they sat in the large, rather gloomy kitchen, told it almost without prompting. Astounded that anyone could be interested enough to listen so intently. She'd had a tough time, Molly could tell, seeing through the jokey presentation.

"And did it live up to expectations?" she asked, hoping that it had.

"Aye," Rosie said cheerfully. "I suppose it did. We're our own bosses at least. No one breathing down our necks all the time. Long hours, of course, but you expect that in catering. It's not always as quiet as this. Sometimes in the summer there are three courses running at once and day visitors wanting lunch. And Mrs. Morrissey throwing dinner parties for her fancy guests. Then it's pretty hectic. But it could be worse."

Jane was quieter, slighter, more hesitant. She had a pretty face, dark, curly hair, and an air of nervousness that disappeared slowly as she continued. She felt safer in Rosie's shadow but could speak for herself if she had to. Her voice was southern BBC and she had impeccable manners. She'd started off at university, she said. Reading chemistry. It hadn't been difficult to get into her provincial university—the famous girls' day school she'd attended could get a donkey through A levels. But when she'd got there she'd seen it was beyond her. She hadn't realized that the students would be left so much

68

to themselves, that everyone would be so bright. She saw she'd never be able to keep up so she'd dropped out before the humiliation of failing the first-year exams. She was rather proud of that, actually. She'd never said boo to a goose before. Of course her parents had been frantic. They'd both got firsts from Cambridge and it had never occurred to them that she wouldn't get a degree. They hadn't considered any other option for her. Her mother had been a close friend of Meg's. They, too, had lived in Putney and they'd kept in touch after the Morrisseys moved. Jane had been sent to Markham Mill to give her time to sort herself out, to decide what she wanted to do with her life.

"But really, of course," she added candidly, "to get me out of the way. Much worse, in my parents' view, to fail academically than if I'd got myself pregnant. They couldn't stand the shame. What would they tell all their intellectual friends? I couldn't cook, of course—nothing so useful—but they didn't seem to think that would matter. And it doesn't really. Rosie does all the difficult bits, I'm just the dogsbody."

They looked at each other affectionately. Molly wondered briefly if there were more to the relationship than friendship but decided it was none of her business at this stage.

"Do you know why my husband and I are here?" she asked.

"Not officially," Rosie said. "No one tells us anything officially."

"But unofficially?"

"I heard the kids talking about it. Meg can't accept that James committed suicide."

"What about you?" Molly said. "You must have known him. Were you surprised at the way he died?"

The girls looked at each other again. In the end it was Rosie who spoke for them both.

"Aye," she said. "I suppose I am. If it had happened two years ago when I first started here it would have been different. He seemed more nervy then. Not ill as far as I could tell. Not mad, any road. But anxious. I suppose he'd lost all his confidence after the accident. You had the feeling he wouldn't go for a pee without asking Meg first. . . ."

She paused.

"But more recently he changed?" Molly said.

"Yeah. He was much more lively. More full of himself."

"Do you know what brought that about?"

"Not really. Time, I suppose. If he'd had some sort of breakdown." But the explanation did not seem to Molly quite convincing.

"And he was more confident?" she said.

"Much more confident. He went out more. He started driving again and organizing his own bird surveys up the coast. And he wouldn't let Meg boss him around anymore. He spent hours in the common room if it was quiet or in his study working on his book and she didn't like it. She wanted him mixing with the students, especially at meal times. I heard her say to him once: 'We can charge such high fees for Markham Mill because everyone wants to meet the famous Jimmy Morrissey. You can't hide away in here so they go away at the end of a fortnight without having caught a glimpse of you.' "

"What did he say to that?" Molly asked.

Rosie grinned. She was enjoying the opportunity to gossip. "He said: 'Sod off! If they want to know all about the famous Jimmy Morrissey they'll be able to read about it soon in my autobiography.' "

"So everyone knew about the autobiography?" Molly said.

The girls did not answer immediately. They had work to do. Jane took a scarred wooden chopping board and set it on the table in front of her. She began to peel and chop onions, carrots, and leeks.

"Soup for lunch," she said. "I told you I'm the dogsbody."

"So you both knew that James was writing an autobiography?" Molly persisted.

Rosie was weighing flour. She tipped it into a large stainless-steel bowl and stood for a moment with her hands poised over it. "Yes," she said. "Everyone knew that."

"Did he ever talk to you about it?"

"Once," she said. "But nothing serious. I asked him if he were going to put me in it. For a joke, like. 'Oh no, Rosie,' he said. 'You wouldn't want to be in it. Everyone who's in it has got something to hide.' And then he laughed, like a kid would if he were up to mischief."

"You never saw what he'd written?"

She shook her head. "I didn't go into the study much. If he didn't want to eat in the dining room he usually came in here to the kitchen to make himself a sandwich then took it back with him. Sometimes Meg would ask me to take in a tray to him, but he didn't really like to be disturbed."

"And you?" Molly turned to Jane, who was slicing carrots with great concentration. "Did you ever come into Mr. Morrissey's study?"

Jane set the knife on the table in front of her as if it were beyond her to do two things at once.

"I went in there lots of times to clean," she said. "When Florrie from the village was off with her hysterectomy I took over most of the cleaning in the Mill. But I never read any of the book. He was quite secretive about it, you know, and that wasn't like him. Whenever I went in with the Hoover he'd shut all his notebooks in the filing-cabinet drawer. I told him he needn't stop writing on my account. I wasn't as fussy about the dusting as Florrie and I wouldn't pry. 'Of course not Jane,' he said. 'But it's a journalist's habit to protect his sources.'"

"What do you think he meant by that?"

"I'm not sure. I thought he was showing off, reminding me that he'd once been the editor of a famous magazine." She paused. "I did see the manuscript once when I went in to clean. He'd left it on the desk. But it didn't mean much to me. It was open at a chart with a lot of figures."

"Did James lock the filing cabinet when he put the notebooks away?"

"I hope not!" Jane was indignant. "He knew I wouldn't snoop." She returned conscientiously to slicing leeks.

Molly turned back to Rosie. "On the day before James's body was found you did take a tray in to him, didn't you? He didn't come into the kitchen for a sandwich that day?"

"No," Rosie agreed. "Meg asked me to take something in to him. He'd gone for a walk along the shore instead of coming in for lunch, and when she went to remind him he'd not eaten all day he sent her away with a flea in her ear. So she asked me to take in a tray."

"How did he seem then?"

"Excited," she said. "Really pleased with himself."

"Did he say anything to you?"

"No," Rosie said. "He hardly noticed I was there. I could see damn fine that it was a waste of good food. He'd not stop to eat it." That, at least, Molly thought, tied in with what Meg had told them.

"Mrs. Morrissey asked you to take her husband a cup of coffee that night," Molly said. "Do you know if he drank it? Who cleaned the study the next day?"

"I did," Jane said. "Usually it would be Florrie's job, but she said she couldn't face it. The ambulance had come and taken James away. Nobody had told us he was dead, but we could tell there wasn't much hope. She tends to get a bit emotional, our Florrie, especially since her operation. So I went in, just to make sure it was tidy for Meg when she came back from the hospital."

"Had the coffee been drunk?"

"Yes," she said. "The mug was empty. And the glasses."

"What glasses?"

"There were two glasses, smelling of whisky. James didn't only keep his notebooks in the filing cabinet. He always had a supply of booze in there. Meg must have known, but she didn't approve. I washed the glasses up and took them to the flat where they belonged."

"So James must have had a visitor," Molly said, almost to herself, "after Meg had gone to bed."

"I suppose so." Jane seemed hardly interested.

"What about the autobiography?" Molly asked. "Were the notebooks still there?"

"They weren't on the desk," Jane said. "They might have been in the filing cabinet, but of course I wouldn't know about that."

She turned to Rosie with a little smile so that Molly wondered suddenly if the girls shared a secret, if this whole conversation was a performance that they had prepared beforehand.

"No," she said. "Of course you wouldn't know about that."

7

George walked along the shore to Salter's Cottage. He wanted to make the most of the morning, the brilliant light. He even stopped and set up his telescope to count a flock of scoter that were bobbing in the swell beyond the spit. Even now, when he should have been engrossed in the investigation, he was hoping for something rarer. As this time of year a surf scoter or king eider was a possibility. Why can I never quite be satisfied? he thought. All this should be enough for me, but I'm always wanting something more, some new bird or new excitement. Molly said he was like a spoilt kid or one of those raffish fictional gentlemen of the twenties and thirties who tried to forget the horrors of the first war by seeking adventure. But I've no excuse, he thought. Jimmy would have understood this restlessness. If anything, he was more easily bored than me.

He twisted the legs of his tripod so it collapsed to a manageable size and continued along the beach. There was access directly from the shore into the Salter's Cottage garden. Some steps had been cut out of the rock and there was a wooden gate in a white-washed stone wall. He saw Cathy Cairns before he reached the top of the slippery, seaweed-covered steps. She was throwing rubbish on to a bonfire, then she stood back to watch the smoke rise straight up in the still air. She was muffled in a heavy Berghaus jacket, her hood pulled over her head, and had not heard him approach.

"That's not very environmentally friendly," he said. He had meant it as a joke, but she looked up, startled, and backed away.

"George Palmer-Jones," he said. "We met a couple of times in London."

"Oh yes," she said. "Of course." It was impossible to tell if she really recognized him. He had been a guest at a dinner party she and Jimmy had given soon after their marriage, and they had had a long conversation then. He did not think he would have known her again. Then she had been striking, confident, talking about her designs and her plans for the future. Her hair had been cropped short, he remembered, almost punk. She had said that things were changing and the seventies would be a great time for her. Now she looked middle-aged and ordinary. He wondered if Jimmy had, in part, been responsible for the change.

She turned and threw another pile of garden waste on to the fire. He was still standing beyond the gate. "I know it's not really eco-sound," she said defensively. "And there's a shredder at the Mill that I usually borrow, but sometimes, with diseased wood, it's the only way . . ."

The garden was small and there were only a few misshapen trees in the shelter of the house, but George did not argue. He wanted to be invited in.

"Therapeutic, too," he said.

"Yes," she said. "I suppose it is." They watched as a scrap of charred paper flew out of the fire and above their heads.

"Had you heard that we were coming to stay at the Mill?"

"Yes," she said. "Meg explained to Phil . . ." She stooped and shovelled a pile of leaf mould on to the fire. It steamed gently. "That'll be safe now," she said. "I'm rather cold already. I think I'll call it a day."

75

She was about to turn away from him and walk into the house.

"I'd like to talk to you," he called.

"Phil's at work," she said. "I expect you'd like to talk to him, too, so perhaps it would be better if you came back later."

"I'd like to talk to *you*," he insisted. She hesitated and could not quite bring herself to be rude enough to send him away.

He wondered again at the change in her. "You'd better come in then," she said at last. "I was going to make some coffee." He would not have thought her capable of this shyness, this blushing awkwardness. Perhaps she had been altered by her daughter's death as deeply, if not as dramatically, as Jimmy.

She led him through a tidy garden cleared for the winter to the kitchen door. There was moment of farce when George, trying to take off his Wellington by standing on one leg, toppled over and put the stockinged foot into a puddle of ice-covered water, but although he laughed at the fool he had made of himself, she remained tense.

"You'd better come in," she said. "There'll be a dry sock of Phil's you can borrow."

He stepped into a square kitchen. Breakfast dishes remained piled on a draining board. A washing line was suspended from the ceiling over a range that must have been there since Phil's parents had lived in the place. She unhooked a rope from a hook in the wall and lowered the line until she could reach a hand-knitted sock. She handed it to George without a word.

"Where does Phil work?" George asked.

She filled an electric kettle and plugged it in. Even such a simple question seemed to disturb her and she did not answer immediately.

"Mardon Wools," she said. "It's a textile factory in Mardon, the town up the river. You've probably heard of it."

He had, of course, heard of it. The Mardon logo could often be seen on television on jerseys worn by sports people, the county set at play, and even the royal family. It represented quality and gracious country living.

Cathy spooned coffee into a pot. "Phil's production manager," she said. "He's been there since he left school."

She paused, as if she expected George to continue the conversation, but he seemed engrossed in pulling on his clean sock. The silence seemed to increase her discomfort and she added: "That's where we met. When I first separated from Jimmy I knew I'd have to get away from London. By that time, despite my career, I seemed to be known to everyone just as 'Jimmy Morrissey's wife.' I wanted to work somewhere where my work would be judged on merit. Mardon approached me because they wanted to develop a younger, more fashionable image. I suppose the connection with Jimmy helped—ironically they suggested that the first year's designs should be on an environmental theme—but I felt at least that I had space to breathe here. I introduced brighter colours, looser styles, and they sold very well. The company were pleased."

"But you don't work there now?"

"No," she said. "I run my own business from home. It's not very lucrative, but it gives me something to do."

"Didn't you enjoy working at Mardon?"

"Of course I enjoyed it," she said bitterly. "But after Hannah died I went to pieces. Nothing seemed important enough to get up for."

"I suppose that's how Jimmy felt," George said. It seemed a good time to introduce him into the conversation.

She looked at him sharply, then let go the coffee spoon she'd been twisting between her fingers so it clattered on to the table. "No," she said. "That's not how

77

Jimmy felt. He felt guilt, responsibility. And so he should. He caused her death. But he was never close to Hannah. Even while we were married he hardly saw her. He would be out of the house in the morning before she got up and he was seldom home in the evening before she went to bed. And then there were all the foreign trips when he was away for months. I sometimes thought that if he saw her in the street with a group of other children he wouldn't recognize her." She stared ahead of her. "Of course he was depressed," she said. "The idea that he might have been careless or incompetent, the cause of the crash, hurt his pride and shattered his confidence, but you can't grieve properly for someone you hardly know."

The outburst had surprised her as much as it had shocked George and she turned away from him, pale and shaking.

"So you blamed Jimmy for Hannah's death?" George asked gently.

"Of course I blamed him," she said. "He killed her. Who else would I blame? Myself, I suppose, for trusting her to someone so obviously reckless. And I've done enough of that, too."

"Meg told me that you and Jimmy stayed friends," George said. "How did you manage to get on with him if you felt so strongly?"

"We were friendly enough after the divorce," she said. "Jimmy didn't care much either way. My leaving him was just a minor inconvenience. And I thought it would be better for Hannah if we stayed on good terms. But after Hannah died I never wanted to see Jimmy again. I made that perfectly clear."

"But Meg told me that they came to visit you," George persisted. He needed to sort out exactly how things had been between the two couples. "You were married to Phil and living in Salter's Cottage. It must have been after the accident. Meg said that was when they first realized the Mill would make a field centre. She implied you were all close friends."

"Meg remembers things as she would like them to be," Cathy said. "They turned up once on their way south from a trip to Scotland. We had no warning and I could hardly turn them away. We gave them a meal, that was all, and Phil took Jimmy for a walk along the shore. It was spring, I remember, a beautiful day. Phil was like a big kid showing off the place. He thought Jimmy was doing him a great honour by going out with him. He would have asked them all to stay the night, but I wouldn't have it. Meg had all the children with her. I couldn't imagine how anyone could be so insensitive."

"So it came as a shock when you heard they'd decided to buy the Mill?"

"It was a nightmare. We'd heard rumours in the area that it had been sold for development, and we'd been concerned that there would be a horrible holiday camp or hotel. Then Meg phoned up, full of her plans, expecting us to be excited, too. Phil was relieved, but I would have preferred a night club and a row of concrete chalets. I was starting to be happy again, Phil was training me to be a ringer, I was making new friends. It wasn't the exciting roller-coaster of a life I'd had with Jimmy but it suited me." She paused, determined to make George understand. "I knew that if they came here to take over the Mill *everything* would be different. It wasn't only that I was still bitter about Hannah. It was more trivial than that. I thought, I suppose, that they'd take Phil away from me, too. That he'd change. He'd already been taken in by the myth of the glamorous Jimmy Morrissey. And then Meg is such a dominating character that I thought our relationships with friends here would be thrown out of balance. I was afraid I'd be reduced to competing with her in some way. I didn't want them here. I even hoped that they'd be refused planning permission." She smiled. "If I'd known how to go about it I'd have bribed the council."

"But the plans went ahead without any problems?"

She nodded. "I suppose they were relieved at last to find someone who was willing to take the place on. The fact that Jimmy had a good green image was an added bonus."

"What did Phil think about your opposition to their moving here?"

She gave a little laugh. "He had some strange notion that I was still in love with Jimmy. 'I can handle that,' he said. 'You mustn't think I'd be jealous. There's no reason why we shouldn't all get on together.' "

"And there wasn't any truth in that idea?"

"Of course not," she said. "If anyone was in love it was Phil. He was in love with the idea of being part of the Morrissey clan. He was like a star-struck teenager. There was no way I could make him see sense."

She hesitated, came to a decision to speak.

"I went to see Jimmy," she said, "just before they signed the contract on the place. I never told Phil. He thought I was going to London to meet some old friends. But I arranged to see Jimmy on his own and I tried to persuade him to change his mind. . . ."

"What happened?"

"He agreed to meet me and that was surprising enough. The old Jimmy would have been too busy. I should have known then that he had changed. We went for a walk in Battersea Park, along the river. It was probably the longest conversation we ever had without interruption, but I could see straight away that it would do no good."

"Why?"

"Not because he'd made up his mind to take on the Mill and was determined nothing would make him change it. I'd expected that. But because he refused to take any responsibility for the decision. He left all that sort of thing to Meg, he said. It didn't matter to him one way or the other, but Meg had made up her mind so he supposed that they'd go. I couldn't pin him down to anything, couldn't even provoke an argument. All my anger just washed over him. Meg would do what was best, he said, and that was that. I was astonished. I knew she wanted him to spend more time with the family, but I never thought he'd give up *Green Scenes*, all the telly appearances, without a fight."

"Don't you think it was the accident that changed him?" George asked.

"Partly," she said. "But there was more to it than that. Remorse was never his thing and whatever else you might think of Jimmy he could always put up with physical pain."

"But the depression?" George said. "That must have been real. He was treated for it."

"I think the depression was the result of the move, not the cause of it."

There was a silence.

"Did you ever approach Meg to try to persuade her not to move?" George asked at last.

"No," Cathy said. "I knew it would be no use."

"How did it work out with them living so close to you? Was it as bad as you'd expected?"

She shrugged. "I suppose not. Nothing ever is, is it? Nothing ever quite lives up to the fears you create in your imagination. Except losing Hannah and I'd never imagined for a moment that could happen. Meg doesn't bother with us much. When Jimmy was alive, occasionally we'd receive a royal summons to Sunday tea and sit in the flat eating crumpets and making polite conversation."

"You went then?" George was surprised.

"I was never keen, but Phil liked to go. He could never see what she was up to."

"What was she up to?"

"She was showing the world how civilized and reasonable she was. As you've said, she liked to pretend that we were all close friends. . . ." She paused. "And there was another reason for the invitations, too. She wanted to show off her family, her miraculous bloody children. We had to listen to their music, admire their art, hear about their school work. It made me sick because, of course, it wasn't them we were supposed to admire, it was Meg for having created such a tribe of geniuses." She smiled bitterly. "I suppose I'm just jealous. They're really quite nice kids despite their mother."

"It was hardly the most tactful way to carry on," George said. He was encouraged by Cathy's openness. The shyness seemed to have gone.

"Oh no," Cathy said. "Tact's never been one of Meg's virtues. She's too self-centred for that. Tact requires the appreciation that other people have feelings." She smiled at him. "I'm sorry," she said. "What must you think? I'm getting bitchy in my old age."

She leaned across the table to refill his coffee cup. He saw that her hand still shook slightly. She noticed, too. "I'm sorry," she said again. "I get so wound up because there's no one I can moan to. Phil thinks they're all wonderful."

"I've only spent a day there," George said slowly, "but I find it hard to imagine Jimmy at the Mill. . . . Tea and crumpets and polite conversation . . . Not really his thing."

She grinned and there was pure delight on her face. He saw the old Cathy of the London dinner party. "He hated it," she said. "I suppose it's not charitable, but it was a sort of revenge. . . ."

"Did he always hate it?" George said. "How did he stick it for so long?"

"Yes," she said. "I think he always hated it. In the beginning he was really apathetic. Nothing seemed to matter. More recently I had the feeling that he was prepared to do something about it. I never thought he'd

82

take his own life, of course, but I thought he was looking for some way out."

"When did his mood change?"

She shook her head. "I'm not sure," she said. "As I told you I didn't see him very often. The last ritual Sunday tea was just before Christmas and he was certainly more his old self by then. When we arrived Meg was trying to persuade him to do something domestic and he told her to fuck off. He disappeared off to his study and didn't emerge until we were about to leave, all charm and apologies because he'd been too busy to talk to us. You know, the old Jimmy."

"Could his new assertiveness have coincided with the decision to write his autobiography?"

"I don't know anything about that," she said shortly. "I wasn't even aware that he proposed to write one."

"Didn't he discuss it with you? Surely you would have featured in the book. It would have been courteous to mention it to you, especially if he intended to include an account of the accident. . . ."

"Courtesy never featured largely in his range of responses," she said. "You should know that, George."

He nodded but did not believe she had known nothing of Jimmy's book. There must have been talk of the autobiography at Salter's Cottage. Everyone at the Mill had been aware of it.

"Did you know the autobiography had been stolen?"

"No," she said. "How could I know that? I didn't know it existed."

She seemed to lose patience with the questions. She stood up and moved restlessly around the kitchen, collecting coffee cups to set on the draining board, wringing a cloth to wipe stains from the table.

"Look," she said, "is that all? Jimmy might have been a bastard, but I don't find this easy."

"He came here on the day he died," George said. "What did he want?"

"I don't know," she said. The earlier tension had returned and her voice was angry and shrill. "I wasn't here."

"Where were you?"

"I was in Mardon," she said. "For the January sales. If you like I can show you the coat that I bought. Not exactly the height of fashion, but I don't expect that any more."

George ignored the challenge.

"But he was here?" he said. "Did he talk to Phil?"

"Yes," she said. "I think so. I think Phil mentioned it."

"What was the conversation about?"

"How should I know?" She was beginning to lose control. "I wasn't here. I presume it was just a social call. Jimmy was always looking for an excuse to escape from the Mill. Why don't you ask Phil if you're so interested? He'll remember every word the great man said."

"Of course," George said. "I intend to do that."

He sat for a moment looking at her over the table. He knew she was keeping something from him. But she said nothing and he stood to go.

He returned to the Mill the same way he had come and stood for a moment at the top of the steps in the rock to look over the bay. The tide was out and the low winter sunlight reflected on wet mud. Two figures were on the shore, quite separate and engrossed in their own activities. The boy, Timothy, was digging for lugworm, struggling with a spade that was too big for him. Aidan Moore sat on Salter's Spit. Through binoculars George saw that he was still drawing. As he watched, the man collected his gear and walked back to the Mill, presumably on his way to lunch.

What keeps him here? George thought. He seems a solitary chap who'd rather be on his own. The painting? He must have enough sketches now to complete the thing at home. Some imagined obligation to Meg, because Jimmy had been kind to him? Neither explanation

84

seemed quite satisfactory. He watched Aidan progress over the shingle, his head bowed so he could see none of the splendour around him.

8

In the afternoon they drove into the town together. Molly had made an appointment to visit Grace Sharland at home. In a telephone call to the health centre Molly had found the nurse distant, obviously suspicious.

"I'm looking into the death of one of your former patients on behalf of his widow," Molly had said. "James Morrissey. He died quite recently. There are some circumstances surrounding his suicide that she finds hard to accept." She hoped that she sounded like a social worker. After years of trying not to, it came as a bit of a strain.

"I don't think I should talk to you," the woman said abruptly. "All that information is confidential. I've nothing to add to the evidence I gave at the inquest." The voice was young, rather county, the sort you'd expect to hear at a hunt ball.

"I don't expect to see any medical records," Molly had said. "It's a matter of your impressions, your judgement of his state of mind. I think it would help the widow to come to terms with her grief . . ." She was rather proud of that. It was the sort of jargon workers in the caring professions like. "If you're anxious about being put into an awkward position ethically I'd be quite happy for someone else to sit in on the interview—

James's GP perhaps. I could talk to him first if you'd prefer."

"No," the woman said immediately, "that won't be necessary." Then there was a silence. "Look," she said at last, "if you feel it will help Mrs. Morrissey I'll spare the time to talk to you, but I'd rather you didn't disturb me at work. I suppose I can arrange to finish early today." She gave her address. "I'll be there at three." There was another pause and she seemed to regret her earlier impulse. "I really don't think this is a good idea," she said.

Molly had pretended she had not heard and hung up.

George had decided to drive with Molly into the town because he wanted to make a surprise visit to Phil Cairns at work. He wanted to talk to Phil before Cathy could tell him about George's visit to Salter's Cottage, before they could concoct a story between them. There was a possibility, of course, that Cathy had telephoned the factory—she had been sufficiently shaken by the visit—but still, George thought, he would get more out of Phil if he saw him alone.

The town was lit by a red sun already low over the wooded hills to the west. As they approached it from the river, it seemed a grey place, fortified, with blank stone walls and steep slate roofs. It was famous because of its connection with the woollen industry—Mardon Wools sweaters were recognized in expensive stores from New York to Tokyo and the history of the town featured heavily in the marketing. The town had been founded on wool, said the publicity leaflet attached to each garment, settled first by the Romans and becoming a thriving centre of trade throughout the Middle Ages. In the sixteenth century, boats had sailed up the river to dock at the town's quay and wool from the area had been shipped out to the rest of Europe. The industrial revolution had almost passed it by—the River Marr was too shallow for the new steam boats and there was no coal for mass production. It could not compete with the mills and factories in Lancashire and Yorkshire. So it had always specialized in a high-quality, hand-finished product. Now, said the leaflet, Mardon Wools was the only firm left in the town to carry on that tradition. In the days of the green consumer they believed small was beautiful. They were still committed to the town and as a symbol of that relationship had chosen one of the famous Mardon swans for their logo.

Molly and George had never visited the town before, had only heard of it in connection with Mardon Wools. Molly remembered a television advertisement of the products that involved a misty aerial shot of the town, set amid rolling hills with the river winding from it to the sea, but there had been no close-ups. The reality shocked them. Because of the quality image of the clothes they had expected Mardon to be smarter, more up-market. They had not expected the shabbiness, the air of decline, the boarded-up shops in the High Street and the unemployed teenagers squatting in groups on the pavement. The town centre was dominated not by a woollen mill but the prison-like bulk of the tannery.

"I suppose the recession has hit the luxury market, too." George said. "There must have been redundancies, suppliers not paid on time . . ."

"I think it's rather reassuring," Molly said. "It makes me feel almost at home. I'd expected county ladies in cashmere sweaters on their way to the tennis club or a game of golf."

They drove slowly through the town centre looking for someone to direct them to Grace Sharland's address. The streets were narrow and already in shadows. It was very cold; people wrapped in coats and hoods hurried past, ignoring George's request for help. They stopped outside a small café with steamed-up windows. A young mother was manoeuvering a pushchair and a bag of shopping through the narrow door. Molly got out of the car and the cold with its sharp, metallic smell of ice took her breath away.

"I wonder if you can help me," she said. "I'm looking for Penn Walk."

"On the other side of the river," the girl said. "It's that posh new development they put up where the infants' school used to be. You can't miss it. Estate agents' notices all over the houses. Don't know how they have the nerve to ask those prices. Not at times like this." She looked at Molly's scruffy and dishevelled clothes with sympathy. "If you're looking for somewhere to buy," she said, "there are lots of places on the market much cheaper than that. My husband says you're only paying for the fancy name and who wants a view of a load of stinking mud when the tide's out, anyway?" She lifted the plastic carrier bag of shopping on to the pushchair behind the baby and walked on down the street.

Molly returned to the car. "I can walk from here," she said. "I'll meet you in the café later. We can compare notes then."

Penn Walk had only recently been completed. A large notice described the development as architect-designed, "old-fashioned quality combined with modern comfort." It was a terrace of three-storey houses, faced with local stone. There were landscaped lawns stretching down to the river, fake concrete cobbles, and mock Victorian lamps. Most of the houses were still for sale. The prices on the large notice board seemed astronomical and Molly wondered how a health service worker could afford to live there. Perhaps she had a well-paid husband. She sensed that her progress along the Walk was being watched. The occupied houses had fancy net curtains or vertical blinds and she imagined the inhabitants' disapproval. In her schoolboy's parka and disintegrating sand shoes she did not fit in.

It became clear, as soon as Molly entered the house, that Grace Sharland did not fit in there either. For one thing she was young—in her early thirties. And she was obviously single. Amid all the clutter there would be no room for anyone else.

She opened the door immediately and made a striking figure. The light in the house was on and she stood framed by the doorway, glowing like a pre-Raphaelite painting. She had a cloud of fine red hair and wore loose and richly coloured clothes that must have been chosen, Molly thought, to give just that effect. Over it all she had a Mardon Wools mohair cardigan draped across her shoulders like a cape. Molly recognized the swan logo on the collar, remembered again the television advertisement, and thought it had probably cost her more than a week's salary.

"Yes?" The young woman looked out with curiosity but not disapproval.

"Molly Palmer-Jones. We have an appointment."

"Oh yes, of course!" Molly was not what she was expecting, but she was too polite to express surprise. "Of course. Come in."

There was a small hall and then they stepped into a long, narrow room with doors at one end that led out on to the lawn and the river. The room was as highly decorated as she was. There were shawls thrown over chairs and hung on walls, rugs, and cushions in gold and chestnut and red. In one corner stood a big bowl of dried flowers. Two cats slept on a velvet cushion next to the fire. Even they were orange and white and fitted in with the colour scheme. Grace Sharland did nothing in half measures.

Molly's response to the room was uncertain. What did it reveal about its owner? A romantic and extravagant nature perhaps. What had Jimmy Morrissey made of that?

"I don't know what you expect from me," Grace said.

Molly looked through the double-glazed door across the river, where the light had almost gone. Six mute swans like white ghosts took off and flew away. She thought Grace Sharland was used to getting her own way, but this encounter was making her nervous.

"I don't expect anything from you," she said mildly. "I just wanted the chance to talk to you about James Morrissey so I can persuade Meg that there was nothing suspicious about his death." She sat on a low sofa, felt her knees creak, thought she was getting old.

"Does she believe there was?"

Molly nodded. There was a silence.

"That's quite natural," the woman said eventually. "It's normal in bereavement to need to blame someone for a loved one's death. It's a phase everyone goes through."

She squatted by the fire and stroked the cats. Molly thought the words lacked professional detachment. Had Jimmy Morrissey exerted his charm on Grace Sharland, too?

"Are you a friend of the family's?" she asked.

"Yes," Molly said. It was almost true. "I used to be a social worker so Meg thought I could help."

"Did she ask you to see me?" The words came quickly and without thought.

"Not exactly. She said that you and James had been close and that you'd visited him on the day that he died."

"I always had the feeling that she resented me." Grace Sharland said slowly. "I never meant that to happen."

"Wouldn't it have been usual to include the wife in your work in a case like Mr. Morrissey's?" Molly spoke carefully. She did not want to imply criticism of the woman's methods. "If he were depressed, wouldn't he need the support of the whole family?"

"Of course," Grace said, "if he were depressed . . ." She leaned forward, eager to explain. "When I first visited I wanted to do joint interviews, but James made it clear he didn't want her there. 'If you see her you don't see me,' he said. 'She's part of the bloody problem. She only makes things worse.' By then I was intrigued by his case. I really thought I could help. So I saw him alone."

"What do you mean 'if he were depressed'?" Molly said. "Weren't you happy with the diagnosis?"

Grace shrugged. "I'm only a nurse," she said. "I'm not competent to say."

"But you must have had an opinion?"

"He'd been prescribed anti-depressants by his doctor in London," she said. "I don't know what he was like then. When the GP I work for asked me to see him he was apathetic, miserable, slightly doped up, but I wouldn't have said he was clinically depressed."

"Yet you continued to see him?"

She nodded. "I saw it as a preventative measure. It was interesting. Most of our work is reactive after the crisis has occurred and then drugs really are the only answer. I thought if we could discover what lay behind the unhappiness we could prevent him becoming seriously ill."

"And did you discover what lay behind the unhappiness?" Molly asked cynically. Grace was young and idealistic. In her experience things had never been that simple.

"There was the death of his daughter, of course," Grace said. "At first I thought that was the trigger. He obviously felt responsible. . . ."

"Meg saw that as the cause of his illness," Molly said.

"Yes," Grace said. "I know, but in the end I wasn't convinced." She looked up at Molly. "Meg didn't help, you know. She enjoyed having him dependent."

"What was it then?" Molly asked impatiently. "What was making him so miserable?"

She saw at once that she should have been more careful. Grace shook her head angrily.

92

"I'm sorry," she said. "That's confidential information. Between the patient and me."

"He's dead!" Molly said. "It can hardly matter to him now."

"I'm sorry," she said again. "It matters to me."

There was a pause. Molly tried again.

"You encouraged him to write his autobiography," she said.

"Yes," the woman said, strangely self-mocking. "That was my doing."

"How did you think that would help?"

She did not answer directly. "Do you know," she asked, "what Mrs. Morrissey intends to do with that? Will she still publish?"

"She can't," Molly said flatly. "It's disappeared."

"Did Jimmy destroy it before he killed himself?" The notion seemed to excite, even to please, her. Molly thought again that she might have been more involved with the man than she was letting on.

"I don't know," she said. "I suppose it's a possibility. That had never occurred to us." She looked at Grace Sharland and asked again: "How did you think the autobiography would help?"

This time the nurse seemed more willing to answer. She seemed to have forgotten about her commitment to confidentiality.

"Soon after meeting James I thought it more likely that his sudden lack of self-confidence and self-esteem had to do with his professional rather than his private life," she said. "Work always mattered to him more than personal relationships. He defined himself by his work. For some reason he thought that he'd failed. I saw the autobiography as a way of remembering all the successes."

"What do you mean 'he'd failed'? Was there some specific incident?"

She was cautious again. "Yes," she said. "I believe that there was."

93

"He didn't tell you about it?"

There was a silence. "No," she said. "He told me I could read about it in the autobiography."

Molly did not quite believe her. "You must have been surprised when he committed suicide," she said at last, "if you didn't consider he was clinically depressed."

"Of course I was surprised," she said. "It was dreadful. I'd been so wrong about him. . . ."

She turned away from Molly and looked into the fire.

"You went to his memorial service," Molly said. "Why did you do that?"

"To say goodbye, I suppose."

"Do you get so involved with all your patients?"

"What do you mean?" She looked up sharply, blushing.

"Jimmy had something of a reputation with women, you know," Molly said gently.

"Did he?" she said sadly. "I suppose he must have done."

"What happened?" Molly asked.

"Nothing happened!" She was shocked. "He was a patient!"

"I suppose he fell in love with you," Molly said matter-of-factly. "He was always doing that. And it's not unusual, is it, for a patient to form a romantic attachment with someone caring for them. A sort of gratitude."

Grace smiled gratefully. "No," she said. "It's not unusual."

"What about you?" Molly said. "Did you fall for him?"

There was no reply.

"Why wouldn't you?" Molly went on. "He was charming, a celebrity. At the very least it must have been flattering to receive his attentions."

"I never encouraged them!" she said defensively.

"Of course not," Molly said.

"I'd never met anyone like him," she went on. "Even when he first arrived and he was so morose you couldn't help being impressed by him. He was so *intelligent*. And then, as you say, when his mood improved I felt that I'd really achieved something. It gave me such a buzz! And I was flattered by his admiration. It was only later that I saw he was using me. . . ."

"In what way?"

But she shook her head and would not answer.

"Tell me what happened on the day he died."

"He phoned me and asked me to visit," she said. "I'd only seen him the week before and I said I wasn't sure I could fit him in. He insisted. During the previous meeting we'd had a . . . misunderstanding. I thought perhaps he wanted to apologize, so I agreed to go."

"What sort of misunderstanding?"

Again she refused to answer, and Molly continued: "And did he want to apologize?"

"Of course not!" She laughed. "I should have known him better than that. He wanted to let off steam, that was all. Meg had done something to annoy him. He didn't say what it was. I expect it was something trivial. He said he couldn't stand it at the Mill any longer. He'd had enough." She smiled again. "He even suggested moving in with me. Can you imagine him in here? He said if I'd just get rid of my hang-ups we could make it work. He claimed he was desperate, but I didn't take him seriously. He was always saying that he had to get out of the Mill, leave Meg and the bloody circus behind. But for some reason he never did."

"Why do you think that was?"

Grace Sharland shrugged. "Perhaps he still didn't have the confidence to break out on his own. Perhaps it was the kids. He was fond of them in his own way. Especially Caitlin."

"How did he take it when you refused to let him move in with you?"

"I don't think he ever thought I would agree. He was trying it on. He said: 'Well, sod off then, Sharland. If you won't help me I'll find my own way out.'" She paused and stared blankly into the fire. "I thought he intended to go off on his own, down to London perhaps. If he found the courage to leave at all. It never crossed my mind that he meant to kill himself."

Molly made no attempt to comfort her. The only way to relieve her sense of guilt would be to prove that Jimmy Morrissey hadn't taken his own life.

"You didn't mention all this at the inquest?" she said.

Grace Sharland shook her head. "What would be the point? Meg had enough to cope with without having to face the fact that her husband was chasing another woman."

She stood up and her voice was calm and unemotional. "I've told you all I can," she said. "Perhaps you'd leave now."

"Of course," Molly said. "But there is one thing . . . When you visited James that afternoon did you see him in his office?"

The woman nodded.

"Was he working on his autobiography?"

"Yes," she said. "When I arrived he was writing frantically. When he saw me he shut the notebook. He was always very secretive. He never showed me anything he wrote."

"Yes," Molly said, "I see."

On the doorstep they paused. Outside it was quite dark and very cold.

"I'm sorry to have troubled you," Molly said.

"That's all right." Grace seemed reluctant now to let her go. "It was good to have someone to talk to. It was hardly the sort of thing I could discuss with my friends." She shivered, but still she did not shut the door.

"I'm staying at the Mill." Molly said. "If you think of something else, perhaps you'd ring."

"Yes," she said gratefully. "I will."

Molly turned and walked back towards the town.

9

Mardon Wools had a square brick and glass factory on a trading estate inland from the town. It was larger and more solid than the other units on the estate, but George was disappointed. He had expected something massive and gothic: a dark, satanic mill. That was ridiculous, of course. They wouldn't be spinning or weaving at Mardon now, just putting together the finished garments and machine knitting. He parked neatly in a space marked VISITORS and got out of the car. It was almost dark. As he approached the main entrance to the factory, one of the shifts must have ended because a group of women still wearing overalls under their outdoor clothes spilled out of a small door at the back, almost falling over each other in their eagerness to leave. A bus drove slowly down the hill on its way to town and they ran, giggling, towards the stop, waving their arms and shouting for it to wait. They climbed aboard, the bus drove off, and the estate seemed suddenly quiet and deserted.

The reception area was spacious, with a shining block-wood floor and a forest of potted plants. Beyond it was the factory shop where seconds and end-of-range garments were sold at a discount. A few well-dressed women browsed through the rails. A middle-aged woman in a camel coat and suede boots lifted out a sweater and held it against her. The inevitable swan

98

was embroidered on the chest. She looked at the price, shook her head, and replaced it.

In glass cabinets in reception more of the company's designs were on display reflecting the fashion of the past. There were twinsets from the forties, fifties' short-waisted cardigans, little knitted suits. In the last cabinet was a display of chunky sweaters that had been popular several years before when green consumerism had first taken off. The colours were bright and the designs were of tigers and elephants and whales and stitched underneath were simplistic exhortations to save the planet. Cathy had mentioned that her first work had had an environmental theme and he supposed these were her designs. He recalled that there had been a sponsorship deal with the International Wildlife Fund that had attracted a lot of publicity. It had made George uneasy. He had always thought that increased consumption and conservation were incompatible. Now, in the depths of a recession, people were more concerned about saving jobs than the rain forests and the jerseys had gone out of fashion. They were preserved as a relic of a more optimistic time, when the Green Party were considered electable and politicians thought they could save the world by banning hair spray.

A receptionist sat behind an impressive curved desk made, he suspected, from imported South American hardwood. She was operating a switchboard and finished dealing with a call before turning to him.

"Yes?" she said with a bright, almost natural smile. "Can I help you?"

"I wonder if it might be possible to see Mr. Cairns. I'm a friend. I'm afraid I haven't an appointment, but if he's busy I'm quite prepared to wait." He gave his name.

"Just a minute, Mr. Palmer-Jones. I'll see if he's free. She pressed some buttons on the switchboard and added confidentially: "I know he's been in a meeting for most

99

of the day because he asked me not to put any calls through to him, but I think his visitors have just left."

She spoke into the telephone, then gave George another of her professional smiles. "Mr. Cairns says if you'd like to take a seat he'll be with you in a minute."

It was extraordinarily lucky, George thought, that Phil hadn't taken any calls. Cathy wouldn't have been able to tell him what to say.

George had known Phil since he was a teenager. They had met at annual ringing and migration conferences, then bumped into each other at bird observatories where they both went to increase their ringing experience: at Portland in the sixties when you still slept in the lighthouse tower and the warden's wife cooked an evening meal for three shillings and sixpence; on Lundy where they had shared a squalid, rat-infested dormitory; and on Cape Clear off the southern point of Ireland where they drank Guinness together in Paddy's Bar. They still met up at the Swanwick Conferences and it was hard to believe that he was now middle-aged. There was some grey in his beard. He had put on weight. But the enthusiasm that had had him up at dawn every morning on Lundy even though the best migrant was a willow warbler remained with him.

A door beyond the reception desk burst open and Phil bounded across the floor towards George, beaming.

"What are you doing here then?" he said. "Meg said you'd be at the Mill, but I didn't think you'd waste time by coming into town. There's not much to bring a keen birder to this place. I thought you'd be out on the shore making the most of the light. But, eh, man, it's great to see you." He turned to the receptionist. "See if you can rustle up some tea, Helen, and some of those chocolate biscuits that only come out at directors' meetings." He clapped George on the shoulder. "Come on through, and you can tell me what this is all about."

His office was on the second floor and there was a large plate-glass window with a view of the river.

"I have to sit with my back to that," Phil said, "or I'd not work at all. Not that there's much to see, of course. It's not like the view from the cottage."

"There are always the swans," George said.

"Oh, there are always the bloody mute swans. But I sometimes think they're more bother than they're worth. We have coach trips in the summer, guided tours around the works, and hope they spend a fortune in the shop. You know the sort of thing. If there are no swans about they ask what we've done to them and if they're here they feed them with leftover sandwiches." He smiled broadly. "I don't mean all that, of course. The swans have really captured the public's imagination. They're spectacular—the biggest gathering in the north of England—and Mardon Wools wouldn't be the same without them. Sometimes I think they're symbolic of our success, like the apes on the Rock of Gibraltar, and if anything were to happen to them the company would go down, too. But they can be a nuisance all the same."

He took a seat behind the desk and motioned George to sit opposite. Helen brought in a tray with tea and a selection of biscuits. He thanked her and she blushed with pleasure. He would be popular with his staff.

"What's all this about then?" Phil asked. "What are you doing at the Mill? You're not just there for the winter birding."

"No," George said. "Didn't Meg tell you why she wanted us to come?"

Phil shrugged. "I haven't seen much of her since the memorial service. I don't know what to say to her and I don't like to intrude. She's got her family with her and Cathy feels awkward about going there."

"But you had heard that she's not happy with the inquest verdict of suicide?"

"I'd heard," he said. "You don't keep many secrets in a place like that."

"What's your feeling about it?" George asked.

"My feeling is that it should be over and forgotten. It

does no good going through it all again. The inquest should be the end of it." He paused. "Cathy's been a nervous wreck since it happened," he said. "I hate to see her like that. It brought back all that business with Hannah, the talk of inquests. I wish Meg would leave well enough alone."

"You don't think it matters how Jimmy died?" George asked mildly.

"Not much. Accident, suicide, what does it matter? It'll not bring him back."

"But murder? What if it were murder?

There was a brief silence. "So that's what Meg's saying, is it?" His voice was compassionate but disapproving. "You can understand her cracking up under the strain. I always thought she'd taken on too much. She's run the Mill almost single-handed, you know, since it opened and she teaches all those kids at home. She's a wonderful woman."

"You don't think there can be any truth in her allegations?"

Phil gave a sharp laugh. "Of course not," he said. "Who would want to kill old Jimmy? Everybody liked him."

"Meg's hired us," George said. "Professionally. To find out if James was murdered."

There was an awkward silence while Phil Cairns poured tea.

"I would have thought better of you than that, George," he said at last. "You and Molly can't be so hard up that you need to take advantage of a bereaved woman."

George was shocked. Was that really what he was doing? Not for the money, of course. That had no relevance. But out of curiosity and a fear of boredom? There must be more to it than that.

"I wouldn't have come to the Mill," he said, stung into a reply, trying to convince himself, "if I could have

102

believed that Jimmy committed suicide. You knew him, Phil. You can't think he took that way out."

"What are you saying?" Phil demanded. "That he was really murdered? You spent too long working next to the police, George. You can't believe anyone at the Mill capable of violence."

"It's almost easier," George retorted, "than thinking Jimmy capable of suicide."

They stared at each other across the desk. George had not expected this reaction from Phil. He had thought of him as an ally, someone who would look at the facts with an open mind. This hostility surprised him.

"Did you know that Jimmy was writing an autobiography?" George asked.

"Of course," Phil said carefully. "He'd been full of nothing else for months."

And yet, George thought, Cathy claimed to know nothing about it.

"It seems that it's disappeared."

"What do you mean disappeared?" Phil's voice was impassive.

"We think it's probably been stolen."

"Look," Phil said, "are you sure Meg hasn't hidden it away? She was never keen on it being published. She wanted Jimmy remembered as an established figure in the conservation world and he was hardly that. There were bound to be a few skeletons hidden somewhere." He grinned boyishly as if he were trying to re-establish good terms with George. "More than a few. Some of the tales he had to tell about his life!"

"I suppose it's possible Meg took it," George said, "but I don't know why she should. She'd inherit it naturally with the rest of Jimmy's estate. She could do what she liked with it then. Was there anything specific she might have objected to?"

"Any number of things, I should imagine," Phil said. "Jimmy was no saint, was he? There were certainly other women. Meg used to give the impression to the press that they were a perfect family. It wouldn't do her credibility much good if he gave a list of his lovers since they were married."

"No," George said. "Was there anyone recently? Since he moved to the Mill?"

Phil shrugged. "When did the autobiography disappear, anyway?" he asked.

"Presumably on the night of his death. He was working on it earlier that day."

"He'd nearly finished it," Phil said. "He was hoping to get it done by the end of the weekend."

"How do you know?"

"Because he told me. He came to see me on that Saturday and he told me then." He paused and added reluctantly: "He'd made an appointment to give it to his agent. He was going down to London on the following Wednesday. 'He can arrange to have the bloody thing typed,' he said. 'Let him earn his ten percent for once. I want it out of the Mill. I've seen enough of it.' "

"Surely he wouldn't have made an appointment like that if he intended to kill himself!"

"You wouldn't know with Jimmy, would you? Logic never played much of a part in his make-up."

"Do the police know that Jimmy came to visit you that day?"

"Yes. They sent a fat slob called Porter to talk to me. I knew him when he was a kid and I never liked him then."

"But you answered his questions?"

"Of course I answered his questions. He asked about Jimmy's state of mind and if I'd noticed anything unusual. I said no. Then he went away."

"You didn't tell him that Jimmy had an appointment to see his agent about his book?"

"No," Phil said. "Porter never asked."

"Can you tell me what happened when Jimmy came to see you that day? Perhaps you'll convince me that he

104

killed himself, then I can go away and leave Meg alone."

"I don't blame you really, George," Phil said uncomfortably. "I suppose you're only doing your job."

"But you will tell me?"

Phil nodded. "Of course," he said. "Cathy was out. She'd gone into Mardon to do some shopping. She knew I'd not want to go. Especially in the winter I like to spend all the daylight on the shore. It was one of my wildfowl and wader count days."

"Were you out when Jimmy came to the cottage?"

"I'd just come back for a spot of lunch. He'd probably waited until he saw me walk in from the saltmarsh. You can see the whole shore from the common room in the Mill. I made him a sandwich and we drank a couple of bottles of beer."

"What did he want?"

"Nothing, probably. An excuse to get away from the Mill. He couldn't stand the visitors, you know. He could be quite rude." There was a brief silence. "He talked about Timothy first. He was really proud of the lad. Said he was a chip off the old block. If he didn't turn into a scientist he'd eat his hat. 'He's got quite a sophisticated lab set up in the schoolroom. I help him, of course, but he knows what he's doing.' Then he told me the autobiography was nearly finished. I asked him what he'd find to do with his time then. I was a bit worried. He'd been so wrapped up in it that I was anxious he might find it a bit of an anticlimax when he didn't have it to work on any more. Do you know what I mean?'

George nodded. "You thought the depression might return if he didn't have the project to take his mind off things."

"Something like that."

"And was he depressed?" It was an explanation, perhaps, for the suicide.

"He said not. He just winked. 'Don't worry about

me, Phil, old boy,' he said. 'If things work out as I hope, I'll have plenty to keep me busy.' "

"And you thought that had something to do with the book?"

"I didn't think anything," Phil said with a trace of irritation. "If you must know I just wished he'd go, so I could get back to my count."

"But he seemed excited?"

Phil shrugged non-committally.

"Weren't you surprised then when you heard he'd committed suicide late that night?"

"I suppose so, but Jimmy was never predictable, you know. I could imagine him finishing his book, drinking most of a bottle of whisky, then thinking his life's work was completed and there was nothing left to live for."

"Yes," George said. "Perhaps that would be possible . . . Did he come back out on to the shore with you in the afternoon?"

"No, he said he had an appointment at the Mill. He winked again. 'Wish me luck, old boy,' he said. 'I'm hoping for a bit of comfort in my old age.' "

"Did you know what he meant?"

"Didn't have a clue," Phil said frankly. "But I didn't understand most of what he said. It was all jokes and riddles."

"He had an appointment with the community psychiatric nurse that afternoon. Does that make sense to you?"

"I suppose it was just a joke then. She's a pretty little thing. She was at the memorial service and I thought so then."

There was a silence. Somewhere in the factory a hooter sounded.

"Jimmy made some jokes about the book, too," George said. "He talked about exposing secrets, causing embarrassment. He might not have meant it just in a personal sense. He'd have access to all sorts of information through his work at *Green Scenes*. He didn't mention anything like that to you?"

"No," Phil said. "Why should he? It would have nothing to do with me." He must have realized that he had sounded abrupt because he added: "Besides, if he'd come across anything like that, wouldn't he have made it public at the time?"

"Yes, I suppose he would." George spoke almost to himself. "Perhaps I should ask Aidan Moore."

"Aidan?" Phil said sharply. "What would he know about it?"

"Oh," George said, "he worked for Jimmy on the magazine before he made enough to support himself as an illustrator."

"Did he? I didn't realize . . ."

"You didn't see Jimmy again that night," George asked, "the night he died?"

"Of course not," Phil said.

"Did you or Cathy go out that evening?"

"I think Cathy went to see a friend in the village for half an hour." He stopped suddenly, seeming to realize the implication of George's questions. "What are you saying, George? That one of us went to the Mill and forced a handful of tranquilizers down his throat?"

"No," George said uncomfortably. "Of course not."

Phil Cairns sat for a moment, apparently lost in thought.

"You really think that Jimmy was murdered," he said suddenly. "Don't you?"

"I don't know," George said. "Not yet."

But Phil shook his head as if he did not believe him.

Molly was the only customer left in the café. She was sitting in a corner hunched over a mug of tea as if she belonged there and had been at the same table all day. The proprietor was making a big show of cleaning up, but when George asked for tea she could not quite find the courage to refuse him. She handed it over the counter ungraciously and retreated to a stool by the microwave to read the *Sun*.

"Well?" he said. "What was your nurse like?"

"Very exotic," Molly said. "And rather clever."

"Are we any further forward?"

"Jimmy Morrissey thought he was in love with her," Molly said. "On the afternoon of his death he told her he wanted to leave the Mill and move in with her." She looked up. "You don't seem very surprised."

George shrugged. It was hard to explain that Jimmy Morrissey had usually been in love. There had been nothing particularly tawdry about his affairs and quite often the object of his infatuation was hardly aware of his passion. He was a romantic and women were delightful creatures to be worshipped. He had experienced the strange sheltered upbringing of an English gentleman and even after two marriages he had still lived in hope that one day the magic would last.

"I'm not surprised," he said. "If anything it's another indication that he was returning to normal."

"So you don't think he would have killed himself because Grace turned him down?"

"Of course not. There was nothing he liked better than admiring his beloved from afar. And a challenge."

"She's afraid she might have driven him to suicide," Molly said. "She didn't say anything at the inquest because of Meg."

"No," he said, quite certain. "That's impossible." He drained the strong, brown tea and leaned back in his chair. The café proprietor got up expectantly, hovered, waited for them to leave, then returned, disappointed, to her paper. "Did you get anything else?"

"Grace thought there was something in his past that was troubling him, something that she could have told me more about if she'd wanted to. He defined himself by his work, she said. She thought work mattered more to him even than the death of his daughter. I wondered if he intended to put the record straight in his autobiography."

George remembered his last meeting with Jimmy. Perhaps the diffidence and the lack of confidence had more to do with some error of judgement, some opportunity missed in the conservation field, than Hannah's death. It made sense.

"Yes," he said. "It's certainly a possibility."

"And if we find out if anyone else was involved in his mistake we have a motive for murder?"

George nodded slowly.

"But there's no one at the Mill who could have had anything to do with his environmental work. That was based in London."

"There's Aidan Moore," George said. "He worked on *Green Scenes* for a while." He got to his feet, clattering his chair on the tiled floor, bringing the woman rushing out to shut and lock the door behind them. "I wondered, you know, what kept him at the Mill after all his students had left."

"You'll talk to him about it?" Molly asked.

He nodded again. He was already starting to lose enthusiasm for this case. It was too messy and perhaps, as Phil Cairns had said, Jimmy Morrissey would be better left in peace, remembered by his family and friends as a hero.

In the High Street a Mardon Wools lorry was negotiating its way past a double-parked car and blocking the traffic. By the time they returned to the Mill it was almost dinner-time.

10

Dinner that night was a quiet and gloomy affair. Apparently there had been a family row in the afternoon because Timothy had run away to the shore without permission and the cloud of Meg's disapproval hung over the place. Even Rosie and Jane communicated in whispers and arch silent gestures.

Ruth, who had been filling in university application forms, looked forward for the first time with enthusiasm to leaving the Mill. She had always shared her mother's love of the place and had believed it would be a dreadful wrench to leave, but now the anonymity of a crowded student residence seemed appealing. Since James's death she had felt obliged to take on some of the responsibility of keeping the family happy—in her grief Meg could not be expected to do it alone. Now the strain was beginning to tell and she looked forward to living in a place that made no demands on her—somewhere red brick and vulgar that she could leave at the end of the degree without sorrow.

She looked across the table secretly at George and Molly. She was trying to pick up some clue about how the investigation was moving, fascinated despite herself, but she only discovered that they had spent the afternoon in Mardon. What would they find out about James there? He hardly ever went near the place, said it was a miserable dump, that it reminded him of one of those grey towns in the Eastern bloc he had visited when he was still some use to the world.

Meg, too, had been watching the couple closely and when the meal was over she said: "George! I'd like to see you in the flat, please." She turned to Rosie. "Perhaps you'd bring us coffee."

The invitation was not extended to Molly. George would have protested, but Molly shook her head. This was no time to make a fuss and he was welcome to a tête-à-tête with Meg. She could think of nothing more tedious.

"You may watch television for an hour if you like," Meg said to the children, and Molly was astounded that there was no rude retort, no sarcasm. Her own teenagers' response would have been: "Well, thanks a bundle, Mum. How will we ever survive the excitement?" Didn't Caitlin and Ruth crave discos, parties, boyfriends? Or did they get all those things on the sly? Perhaps the model behaviour was a front and they were growing cannabis on the schoolroom window-sill and slipping out after dark to all-night raves. The idea made her smile, but there was something about Caitlin's demeanour as she left the room that did not make it seem quite so ridiculous.

With the departure of the children to the schoolroom and Meg's summons of George to the flat, Molly was left alone in the dining room with Aidan Moore. Rosie and Jane had cleared the pudding dishes, brought coffee, then disappeared with relief into the kitchen. Molly heard the buzz of laughter. Aidan made to go, too, but Molly engaged him ruthlessly in conversation. George had intended to talk to him. Surely she could do it just as well.

"You must have known the Morrisseys for a long time," she said. She poured him another cup of coffee so he would be obliged to stay at least long enough to drink it.

"I first met Jimmy when I was sixteen," he said. "But

111

not Meg, of course. He was still married to Cathy then. Officially."

"Of course." She drank coffee. "He must have been an exciting person to work for.

Aidan Moore was suddenly animated. "Oh, he was. Wonderful. I only worked on the magazine in my spare time and it paid peanuts—hardly more than expenses, really—but I learned so much from him that I'd have done it for nothing." He blushed.

"But not an easy man," Molly said. "Surely he could be unpredictable . . . unreasonable?"

"Certainly. But teenagers don't like their heroes clean-cut, do they? At the time it was part of the charm."

"And later?" she asked. "When you were more mature did you still find him charming?"

"Oh yes," he said. "He was always that."

"What exactly did you do at *Green Scenes*?" she asked.

He shrugged. "Everything from making tea to working on some of the really big stories. There was only one full-time reporter. I was useful because I was an unlikely journalist—spotty and adolescent."

"Why was that useful?"

"Once the magazine got well known we'd get tip-offs from members of the public about environmental issues—toxic waste being transported in unlicensed trucks, an animal-feed wholesaler who was flogging poisons to farmers to control pests, a dodgy building firm dumping asbestos on a patch of wasteland used as a playground by local kids. You know the sort of thing. Before the magazine committed the time and resources to a proper investigation I was sent out to look into it, chat to local people, make a few discreet enquiries with the authorities. Quite often the complaint was unjustified—the result of a personal vendetta or a misunderstanding. Sometimes it was worth following up. Then the big boys would move in."

112

Molly considered him with astonishment. It was hard to imagine this shy and indecisive man as the great boy detective. He seemed to guess what she was thinking and grinned.

"I couldn't do it now," he said. "I wouldn't have the bottle. But then we thought we could change the world. James's inspiration, I suppose."

There was some irony in his voice and she thought: He became disillusioned with James. Not enough to stop him admiring the man but enough to make him stand back and be more critical. What caused that?

"Did you have many successes?" she asked.

"Sure. We tracked down the owner of a fleet of small tankers that were regularly rinsing out their tanks at sea. It didn't cause a major oiling incident, but a series of small ones, serious enough to wash up hundreds of oiled auks on to North Sea beaches." He paused. "We got an award for that," he said proudly. "Campaigning magazine of the year."

"But there must have been occasions when the issues weren't quite so clear cut, when it was impossible to prove who was behind the pollution or that a company had been negligent," Molly said. "Wasn't there a danger of libel action? You must have been the *Private Eye* of the conversation world."

"There was one case when we alleged corruption in a planning enquiry," Aidan said. "I'm not sure of all the details. I think it was for an open-cast mine and several councillors were suddenly able to buy big cars and fly off to the sun. The jury found in the council's favour but must have been convinced that there was some truth in the story because they awarded only nominal damages. *Green Scenes* had to pay the costs though and the magazine almost went under. If there hadn't been a large donation from a well-wisher to keep it afloat the whole thing would have collapsed. After that the board made James clear all the copy with a solicitor."

"Who was the well-wisher?" Molly asked.

"I never knew," Aidan said. "It happened not long before James sold up. Ironic, I suppose."

"Do you think there were other scandals that went unexposed because of a fear of litigation?"

"I suppose so," he said. "Without really strong evidence that danger was always hanging over us."

"Was there anything specific?" she asked.

"What do you mean?" He was the nervous, prematurely middle-aged man again. The enthusiastic teenager who had fought beside James Morrissey had disappeared.

"Was there one case that you felt should be tackled in the magazine but that James or the board felt was too risky to be published?"

He hesitated and for a moment she thought he would confide in her, that he would find the nerve to disagree openly with a decision taken by Jimmy Morrissey. But in the end he shook his head and mumbled, "I don't know. I was never party to those sorts of decisions."

"Because," Molly continued, "Grace Sharland, the community nurse, thought that his lack of faith in himself was caused by some trauma in his professional life. If he'd allowed himself to be persuaded to play it safe, not to tackle, for example, a really big pollution incident. If he'd been paid off or frightened off a story . . . That would matter to him, wouldn't it?"

"Yes," Aidan said. "At one time it would have mattered more than anything else."

"At one time?"

"Look," Aidan said, persuading himself as much as her, "perhaps he just grew up. Learnt to compromise."

"So there was a story that was that important?"

"I'm not saying that," Aidan said. "I wasn't there all the time. Painting kind of took over. I lost touch."

"But you heard that Jimmy wasn't going in as hard as he had in the past?"

There was no reply.

"Or perhaps you were sent off to do a preliminary investigation only to find out later that the case had been dropped?"

She was convinced that she had struck home and waited for a reply. But he only shook his head. He could not betray his hero so lightly. Like everyone else who had admired Jimmy Morrissey, he had a vested interest in maintaining the myth of Jimmy as honourable schoolboy, incorruptible fighter for the planet. It gave him something to believe in.

"Well, there must have been *something*," she said lightly. "Something he wasn't particularly proud of. He was going to expose it in his autobiography. Confession, as they say, being good for the soul. You're sure you have no idea what he had to confess?"

He shook his head again, unhappily.

"I wonder why the autobiography disappeared," she said, almost to herself. "Perhaps someone else had something to confess, too."

Meg Morrissey sat, regally upright, in her chair by the fire.

"I want to know, George," she said, "what you've achieved. Have you spoken to the Sharland girl?"

Perhaps the argument with Timothy had annoyed her because she seemed less inclined to make the effort to be pleasant.

"I'm sorry," he said. "I really can't discuss the case until it's completed." He was not sure what they had achieved and until it was straight in his own mind he wanted to keep the information he had obtained to himself.

"But, George," she said, "I'm paying you to do this for me."

"Of course," he said, "but if the people I'm talking to can't be assured of the confidentiality of the interviews, they won't tell me anything significant. Then the investigation won't get anywhere. I might as well give up now."

"I *see*." He thought she must have been practising at mimicking the queen. The resemblance in tone and inflection was remarkable. "But you are getting *somewhere*?" Again the emphasis was on the last word. "I don't have to feel that I'm wasting my time and my money? You don't, for instance, think that I'm completely mistaken and that James did take his own life?"

"No," he said, "I don't think that."

"Well," she said, "that at least is something. And the autobiography? Are you any closer to finding that?"

"I'm not sure that it's available to be found," he said. "If it was stolen because the murderer was frightened of what James intended to reveal in it, I should think it's probably already been destroyed."

"I suppose it has." Her voice gave away nothing of what she felt about that possibility.

"Was James going to talk about his depression in the book?" George asked.

"I'm sure not!" she said definitely, as if George had made an improper suggestion. "It was to be positive. That was the idea behind it."

"I'd like to know more about how and why the illness started."

"Why?"

"For the background," he said, realizing the explanation sounded limp.

She gave him the look of a mother indulging an exasperating child.

"It started after Hannah died in the car accident," she said. "Not immediately afterwards. At first he seemed to take the whole thing very well. He was upset, of course, and angry with himself but determined to get on with his life. I understand that's quite a common reaction and it's only some time after a crisis that depression sets in. He became listless. He couldn't be bothered to go in to work. His sleep pattern was disturbed and he'd prowl around the house all night. That was when I sent for the doctor."

"And he diagnosed clinical depression?"

"I don't know what he diagnosed," Meg said crossly. "They never will tell you, will they, doctors, not straight out. But he prescribed anti-depressants. They didn't seem to do much good. James went into the office for a couple of weeks but usually came home early. He said it was too 'stressful' there. That's when I saw that something would have to be done."

"Was there anything particular causing the stress?"

"No." Her voice was dismissive. "At around that time the magazine was under financial pressure because of a libel settlement against it, but the accountants were handling that and it wasn't the first time that had happened."

"So he didn't confide in you?"

"Of course he confided in me. He was very dependent at that time. It was rather touching. But there was nothing specific to confide. Then I remembered the Mill, how we'd said what potential it had. I made some enquiries and we decided to go ahead."

"It can't have been quite that easy," George said. "You must have been very determined to see it all through."

"I could see what was best for him," she said finally. "I knew I would have to get him away from that office."

There was a silence. She stood up, smoothing her skirt. It was clear she considered the interview to be over. "Well," she said. "I suppose I shall have to trust you and wait until you get a result."

"Yes," he said. There was an almost irresistible urge to add "ma'am." "I'm afraid you will."

He began to walk out of the room, then turned back to her. "There is one thing . . ." he said. "In James's study I noticed a collection of bound copies of *Green Scenes*. You wouldn't have any objection to my looking at them?"

"No," she said. "Of course not." But the tone of her

117

voice implied that she thought he would have better things to do with his time.

Molly and George went through the copies of *Green Scenes* together. They sat in James's study with the door closed. The only light came from an anglepoise lamp on the desk. The place still smelled of cigarettes.

Molly told George about her conversation with Aidan. "Perhaps you would have got more out of him," she said. "I think he has something to tell. He seems rather confused, uncertain ... But I thought it was worth a go. It seemed a good opportunity with the two of us left at the table. That he might give more away if he thought I was just a nosy old woman wanting to know what it was like to work for the great Jimmy Morrissey."

"Is that what he did think?"

"At first," she said. "I'm sure he was more suspicious in the end."

George shrugged. "I can't see that there's any harm done," he said. "If you think he'll be more forthcoming I'll talk to him tomorrow."

He began to pull the copies of *Green Scenes* from the shelves. Each black binder contained a year's copies of the magazine and they were arranged on the shelf in chronological order. George thought that they must have been a gift from the board when he resigned. Jimmy would never have had the patience to collect them and arrange to have them bound.

"I think we must be looking for something that happened at around the time Hannah died," George said. "Meg said he seemed stressed and indecisive a couple of months after. She put it down to the accident, but there might have been something else. . . . This is the volume for that year: 1991. Let's start with these."

Molly would have rushed through them, looking for something dramatic and obvious to connect a story from the magazine with someone at the Mill, but George was meticulous. He started at the January issue and read everything on each page. The inside cover of each magazine was devoted to advertisements. There were holiday companies specializing in natural history tours, binocular and telescope retailers, wild-bird feed suppliers. He worked steadily through February and March, becoming engrossed for five minutes in a paper about wheatear identification. Halfway through April he stopped at a page devoted to readers' letters.

"There's a note here from Phil Cairns about the decline of roseate terns in the country," George said. "But I don't see how that could be relevant to Jimmy's autobiography."

On the inside cover of the May magazine there was a full-page colour advertisement for the Mardon Wools' SAVE THE PLANET sweaters. "A percentage of all profits goes to Nature Conservation," said the text. Then: "Individually designed by Catherine Morrissey."

"Those were pushed very heavily at one time," Molly said. "I've not seen them around for a while."

"Perhaps the International Wildlife Fund saw sense and stopped taking commercial sponsorship," George said. He continued turning the pages slowly.

On the inside cover of the last page there were more advertisements, including one for future issues of the magazine. "In *Green Scenes* next month," it said, " 'The Reintroduction of the Sea Eagle in Scotland—an evaluation of the project to date.' Coming later in the year: 'An investigation into the newly privatized water companies and their regulatory body. Can they really be expected to put pollution control before profit?' "

"No," George said out loud in response to that question. "Of course not." And he turned to the remaining copies of the year's *Green Scenes* with interest, wondering what Jimmy Morrissey had done with the topic. He scoured the magazines with the same intensity as before, even studying the wanted ads for back copies of *British Birds* and requests for "Single vegetarian guy

119

with a love of the countryside," to get in touch with Donna from Peckham.

"It's not here," he said at last.

"What's not there?" Molly had already lost interest in the venture. She wanted a drink and was wondering whether the Lord Nelson would still be open when she finally dragged George away from the magazines.

"The piece on the water companies and the regulatory body—the National Rivers Authority."

"Does it matter?" she asked. She looked at her watch. "What connection could it have with the Mill? No one here works for the NRA."

"It might matter," he said, "if Jimmy was put under pressure to drop it. That article would have been written just after the water authorities were privatized. There was lots of publicity about it. If he had evidence of corruption, or the NRA not properly carrying out its function, all the national newspapers would have picked it up. And if he'd decided to tell the story in his autobiography, it would still cause embarrassment. . . ."

"How would you find out?" Molly asked. "If the article was written, would there be some record of it at *Green Scenes* headquarters in London?"

George thought of the disorganized office, the piles of paper, important messages taken on the backs of envelopes and immediately lost.

"Probably not," he said. "But Aidan Moore was working there then."

"Why not ask him now?" Molly said, looking at her watch again.

They might just make it to the Dead Dog before closing time. And surely most country pubs had flexible opening hours, anyway. In the village where they lived even the local policeman drank after hours as long as the curtains were drawn and the door was shut. "Let's take him to the pub and talk to him there."

But when they knocked at his door there was no reply, and the next day, when they asked for Aidan at breakfast, they were told that he had decided to leave. He must have arranged for a taxi to take him to the station for the early London train. Only Molly noticed that Ruth, who was passing on this information, seemed disproportionately upset.

11

Timothy woke early. Since his father's death his sleep had been disturbed, not by morbid thoughts but by memories. In the month before he died his father had seemed suddenly to recognize his presence, to see him in some way as a kindred spirit. Timothy had been aware that his father had been pleased with his interests, without quite understanding why. "You'll carry on the Morrissey name," the man had said as they worked together at the makeshift lab in the schoolroom. "What will you be, do you think? Marine biologist, chemist?" Timothy had never known what to answer. "I want to be like you," he had said, thinking his father would like that. "Oh no," James had said. "You don't want to be like me."

Timothy woke suddenly with the memory of his father's words in his mind. It was just getting light, still very cold, but overcast. The weather forecast had predicted snow. The tide was out and from his window he saw the grey expanse of mud, merging on the horizon with the grey sky. He lay still for a moment, thinking he might go back to sleep, but his brain was too active, analysing already the results of the day before's experiments, and he got out of bed and began absent-mindedly to dress. His mother would ask if he had washed, but he was finding it increasingly easy to lie to his mother. Standing at the window, watching the lightening sky, feeling a child's excitement at the prospect of snow, he suddenly saw a white shape on the mud where the River Marr entered the bay.

That's strange, he thought. He knew the shore so well that anything new was of interest.

"Investigation," he heard his father say in his head. "That's the basis of all good science. If there's something you can't explain, investigate it."

He pulled on an extra jersey and a thick pair of socks and padded quietly out of the flat and down the wooden stairs. At the kitchen door he paused—even scientists had to eat and Rosie was grilling bacon.

"Can I have breakfast now?" he asked. "I want to go out on to the shore." Then, thinking that it wasn't quite a lie, "Mother doesn't mind."

"What about a bacon butty to take out?" she said. "Like in a transport caff."

"What's a transport caff?" he was going to ask, but he was in too much of a hurry, so he took the doorstep sandwich and went outside, expecting all the time to hear his mother call him back.

It was a mute swan and it had been washed down the river and left stranded by the tide on the mud. It was waterlogged, bedraggled, and spattered with wet sand. When Timothy approached it he thought that the creature was unable to move, that he could scoop it up in his arms and despite its weight carry it back to the Mill. But when he reached out to pick it up it turned on him and struck out with its beak and scratched him with its sharp claws.

"You frightened him off," George said in a low voice. "He's run away." He was talking about Aidan Moore. Molly was stung by the unfairness of the accusation. Last night he had said that she could have done no harm.

"That's impossible," she said. "Perhaps he just got fed up with the place and went home."

"Like this?" he demanded. "Without telling anyone or saying goodbye?"

They were sitting at the breakfast table. Everyone else seemed preoccupied and drained. The meal was over—there were sad scraps of toast, dregs of coffee—but no one made the effort to leave. Opposite to George, Ruth sat with her elbows on the table. Since telling them flatly that Aidan had decided to leave she had been silent.

"Where was Aidan going?" George asked conversationally.

She shook her head. "Home, I suppose," she said. "He's got a flat in Deal. He moved out of London when he started making a living from his illustrations."

"Have you got his phone number?"

"Yes," she said listlessly. "Somewhere."

"Did he tell you why he was going so suddenly?"

She shook her head again.

"When did he tell you?"

"We went out for a drink together," she said. "To the Dead Dog in the village." Ruth blushed as she remembered her excitement. He had asked her to go with him. Not the gang. Not Rosie and Jane and Caitlin. Just her. They had walked there in the moonlight down the deserted lanes, and when occasionally a car went past he had pulled her with him into the hedge, putting his arm around her to keep her safe. And then, almost as soon as they had arrived, after they had ordered their drinks from Cedric and taken them to the small table in the corner, he had dropped the bombshell. He had come to a decision, he had said. There was something he had to see to. He couldn't afford to spend any more time at the Mill.

"Were you there all evening?" George asked.

"No," she said. "We had a couple of drinks and then came home. Aidan was restless. He said he had a lot to do before he left."

"What did he mean?"

124

"I don't know," she said resentfully. "Packing, I suppose. He certainly didn't tell Mother he was going. She was really cross when she found out about it this morning."

Meg's crossness had been apparent as she raised her voice, interrupting their conversation from the end of the table.

"Where's Timothy?" she demanded. "I haven't seen him this morning. Has he been in to breakfast? Rosie, have you seen Timothy?"

Rosie appeared from the kitchen with a fresh pot of coffee.

"He came down early," she said, "while I was laying up. I gave him a sandwich, then he went out. He was in a terrible hurry. I think he'd seen something on the marsh that had excited him. I thought he'd cleared it with you."

"No," Meg said with ill-disguised fury. "I haven't seen him. Where is the boy?"

Almost on cue he appeared at the door. His hands and his arms were smeared with blood and there was a cut on his forehead. He was crying and the tears ran through the dirt on his face.

"You've got to come," he cried. "Quick. Before it's too late."

But by the time George followed the boy out on to the marsh, the swan was already dead and seemed nothing but a pile of rubbish washed up by the tide.

The boy was hysterical. He screamed in a way that he had not done when he heard of his father's death. George stood awkwardly and waited for the noise to stop.

"Look," he said at last. "There was nothing you could do."

But Timothy was remembering again what his father had told him. The swan and his father had somehow become confused in his mind and he felt equally guilty at the death of both.

George tried to phone Aidan Moore all morning, but there was no reply from his flat. This only confirmed George's feeling that the man had for some reason gone into hiding. At last he gave up and on impulse phoned *Green Scenes*. He asked to speak to Christabel Burns, who had been Jimmy's secretary for years. He presumed the magazine's new proprietors would have kept her on. Her knowledge and skill would be invaluable to them. Jimmy had always said, without exaggeration, that she really ran the publication. She had been an unlikely employee of *Green Scenes*; smart, respectable, and middle-aged, she had started there first as a temp when her children had become independent. Before caring for them she had had some high-powered job in insurance, but when she tried to return to a similar post she found that she was considered too old, out of touch. She made no compromises to *Green Scenes*. The other staff and volunteers might wear jeans, sweaters with holes in the elbows, but she was always immaculately made up and turned out.

"Do you know," Jimmy had once said to George in awe, "I think she even votes Tory."

George was put through to Christabel immediately. George had always been a favourite. She had seen him as an ally, a supporter of her sanity amid the chaos of the magazine.

"George," she said. Her voice was Essex flat, modulated by years of impressing clients and employers. "What can I do for you?"

He knew that he would have to be straight with her. She was as perceptive as they came, had been able to detect a fraudulent insurance claim after two minutes on the phone.

"I'm investigating Jimmy's death," he said.

"What's that, George? I thought you'd retired from that sort of thing years ago."

"Meg doesn't think he committed suicide. She's

asked me to look into it. It's nothing to do with the po-lice."

"Ah," she said. "Meg." She invested the word with all the disapproval she could muster.

"You didn't get on?" It was hardly relevant, but George was intrigued.

"I only met the woman once. Didn't think she was right for Jimmy."

Had Christabel been jealous? George wondered. She had always treated Jimmy with affectionate irritation, but perhaps he had worked his charm on her, too.

"I can't explain now why it's important," George said, "but I'm interested in a story he was working on just after water privatization. Probably something about the new NRA. He'd obviously reached some conclusions about it because it was advertised for publication later in the year, but I couldn't find any record of it. I don't suppose there's any chance you remember it after all this time?"

"Yes," she said slowly. George imagined her removing her spectacles from her nose, letting them hang by the chain around her neck, then shutting her eyes and waiting until the computer efficiency of her memory began to work. "Yes, I remember. It raised a great deal of excitement. The magazine was dead against water privatization. We'd campaigned against it for months. You know that, George. Jimmy thought that the regulatory body would end up in the pocket of the private water companies and he was looking for a story to prove that he was right. It was the big subject of the moment."

She paused as someone obviously came into the office with a query.

"Sorry about that George," she said. "This place is still run by children straight from college. They can't find a thing without asking me first."

"What happened?" George asked. "Did he get the evidence he was hoping for?"

"I don't know about evidence," she said. "But there

127

was a letter, all very mysterious, alleging corruption between a polluting business, the NRA, and the water company."

"Who was it from?"

"Don't know. It was anonymous. I wouldn't have taken it seriously. It was obviously from some crank, all very John le Carré. A meeting was arranged in some pub and he even suggested that he'd be carrying a copy of *Green Scenes* under his arm."

"He?" George said. "Was it a man?"

There was a pause while she considered. "I'm really not sure," she said. "Perhaps I just made that assumption."

"Where was the pub?" George asked. "London?"

"No, not London. Somewhere in the wilds, up the A1, Yorkshire? Humberside?" She had a southerner's ignorance of the north. It was all the same to her. "Jimmy couldn't make the meeting. He was filming for the BBC. He even wanted to cry off, plead illness, but I made him see that wouldn't do. So he sent young Aidan, Aidan Moore. Anyone less suited to be a spy it would be hard to imagine."

"What did he find out?"

"I don't know," she said. "Jimmy wouldn't tell me." Even after all those years George could tell that it still rankled. Perhaps that's why she remembered the incident so well. " 'It's not that I don't trust you, Chrissie, old girl,' he said, all flattery and trying to get round me, 'but this is the big one, the scoop that goes down in the annals. I don't want some Fleet Street hack getting wind of it before we're ready to publish.' He was quite paranoid about it, talked even of government moles. Nothing was written down. Then there was a phone call for him. I took the message. The caller wanted another meeting but with the big boss. He left his number. Jimmy rang back then left an editorial meeting halfway through. High as a kite, loving the drama. You know

128

how he was. That meeting was in a pub, too. Typical Jimmy."

"Where did he go?" George asked. "Did he ask you to make the travel arrangements, book a hotel room?"

"He drove himself," she said. "I asked him about a hotel room. It was the start of the holiday season. I thought he might have problems finding somewhere. But he said not to bother. He had somewhere to stay."

"You remember it all very well," George said.

"Of course I do," she said. "I went over it all in my mind hundreds of times. That was the weekend of the accident, the weekend Hannah was killed. Nothing was the same again."

"Is that why the article was shelved?" George asked. "Because Jimmy was in hospital and he wasn't able to put it together?" Perhaps the explanation was that simple and this was a wild-goose chase.

"No," she said. "Not entirely. No one else could have put the story together, of course. Jimmy was the only one with the facts. But it wasn't as if we'd missed some deadline—it could have gone out at any time. None of our rivals had got hold of it so far as I could tell. I assumed that as soon as Jimmy got back to the office he'd start working on it."

"But he didn't?"

"Yes, he did," she said. "He was obsessed with it. He wrote it and rewrote it, all in longhand. And he was still terribly secretive. None of us was allowed to see it. Not even Aidan Moore, who'd been in on it from the beginning. But he couldn't come to any decision about whether or not to publish." She paused. "It was so unlike him," she said. "He was always so *certain*."

"But he must have come to a decision in the end."

"Oh yes," she said. "And even then we had to have a Morrissey touch of drama. I had to watch him feed all his drafts through the shredder."

"Did he give any explanation for his change of heart?"

"He said that he didn't have the stomach for a fight. One person had died already. 'It's no good, Chrissie,' he said. 'I'm not up to it. I'll admit defeat now.' "

"What did he mean that one person had died? Was he talking about Hannah? What did she have to do with the pollution case?"

"I don't know," Christabel said. "He was confused, under stress . . ."

George's imagination was firing in all directions. Had Jimmy's car been tampered with? Had he been the intended victim? Was his death so many years later just a fulfilment of the earlier murder attempt? Would it be possible after all this time to find out? Christabel had continued speaking and he had to ask her to repeat what she'd said.

"Soon after that he told me that he was resigning from the magazine," she said with some impatience.

"Were you surprised?"

"I was bloody angry," Christabel said, surprising him with her vehemence. "Meg had always resented the time he spent on *Green Scenes*. She wanted him home, playing the model father. Still in the public eye, of course. She liked the reflected glory. A few bits of telly that weren't too demanding or controversial. But not the commitment that *Green Scenes* involved. She got him to resign when he was at his most vulnerable. He regretted it almost immediately after, but he'd given his word then and he felt he ought to go along with it. He was quite honourable, you know, in a silly upper-class way." She paused. "I still don't know how she persuaded him to do it," she said bitterly. "She must be some sort of witch."

"And he never mentioned the article again," George said.

"No, and after it went through the shredder, nor did I."

"What about Aidan Moore?" George asked. "He

130

must have had some idea what it was about. Couldn't you have asked him?"

"I could have tried," she said, "though I'm not sure he would have told me. But it would have been a sneaky sort of thing to do. Jimmy didn't want me to know and I suppose he had his reasons. Besides, Aidan wasn't here much after that. At around that time he got his first big commission illustrating a prestigious new field guide. He never came back to *Green Scenes* to work again."

"I see," George said. "Well, thanks very much for your help." He was about to replace the receiver when he had a sudden thought. "Did Jimmy shred the original letter? The one that started all the excitement, giving information on the pollution incident and arranging the meeting in the pub?"

"No," she said. "He didn't shred that."

"I don't suppose you've still got it in your magnificent filing system?"

"Flattery won't do you any good, George," she said. "I had kept the letter. But Jimmy sent for it when he first started writing his autobiography. And there was no copy."

"I see," he said slowly. "Yes, I see."

He found Meg in the schoolroom. She was reading Gerard Manley Hopkins to the children.

"I'm sorry to interrupt you," he said when she had finished. "I was hoping for a word. . . ."

"Of course," she said graciously. She turned back to the children. "Why don't you try something of your own? In a similar style? There's inspiration enough here. You only have to look out of the window to understand what the poet felt about nature."

Caitlin raised her eyes to the ceiling, implying that she could think of nothing more tedious. Meg judiciously ignored her and swept from the room.

"We'll talk in the flat," she said. "We'll be more comfortable there."

In the flat she offered him tea, made sure he had the best seat by the fire, gave him her full attention.

"I need to ask you about the weekend of James's accident," he said. "Can you remember the circumstances surrounding the car crash?"

"Of course," she said. "It was a nightmare. Though I don't know what it can have had to do with his death."

"Please bear with me," he said. "I do think it's important."

She nodded indulgently. He sensed she was definitely more well-disposed to him without Molly.

"What would you like to know?"

"What was James working on at the time?"

"Oh," she said dismissively, "as to that I don't know. How would I? I was never involved in his work."

"He never discussed it with you?"

"He may have discussed it," she said. "And of course I listened. But it didn't mean very much to me." She watched his reaction closely. *She wants to see if I believe her,* he thought in astonishment. *But why should she lie?*

"If work took him away from home, you must have asked where he was going and how long he would be away."

"Of course," she said. Then tartly: "But he didn't always tell me. 'I'll go where the story takes me,' he would say. It was rather inconsiderate." She paused. "I suppose brilliant men often are."

"Had he been working away from home before collecting Hannah on that Friday night?"

"Yes," she said. "I rather think he had." She appeared to give the matter further thought. "Yes," she said. "He left home on the Wednesday. He never phoned if he was away and I was worried that he would become so engrossed in whatever he was working on that he would forget to pick her up."

"Had Hannah's visit been arranged a long time in advance?"

"No," she said. "Just the day he went away. It was James's idea to invite her. He said it would tie in very nicely with his plans. He did love his children, George, but only when it was convenient."

"So you had the impression that he was working here in this area and he would be able to collect Hannah easily?"

"No," she said sharply, "I didn't say that at all." Then: "I don't mean to be rude, George, but I don't think this is relevant to your enquiry. If I were you I would leave it alone."

He had the feeling that he was being warned off, but he persisted.

"Did he ever give you the impression that the car crash might not have been an accident?"

"Whatever do you mean, George?"

"That there had been some deliberate attempt to cause the crash, that the car had been tampered with in some way?"

"No," she said. "That's impossible. Who would do such a thing?"

But as she spoke he suspected that she was considering the matter and that she found the idea interesting.

"No," she said again, less certainly. "I'm sure there was nothing like that."

12

While George was with Meg, Molly sought out Rosie and Jane. She had been intrigued by the phone call to Christabel Burns but was still interested in the emotional relationships in the case. She especially wanted to find out more about Grace Sharland. The girls seemed to have opinions about everyone connected with the Mill. What had they made of the nurse and her visits to Jimmy Morrissey?

The housekeepers accepted Molly into their realm behind the dining-room door and treated her as if she were a favourite eccentric aunt. They thought she was escaping from Meg and the family and that amused them. Most of their jokes were at Meg's expense.

When Molly found them they were in the laundry, which backed on to the kitchen. They were working together as if performing some elaborate dance, pulling bedspreads out of a large tumble-dryer then facing each other to stretch and fold them ready for ironing.

"Meg thought we needed something to do," Jane said. "She came into the kitchen first thing: 'I know it's a bit early for spring-cleaning, girls, but as it's quiet we might as well get on with some of those jobs that usually get left until the end of the season.'" She mimicked the voice with surprising accuracy, catching the pretension, the hint of Welsh. "So we're washing all the curtains and bedspreads from the dormitories. As if we

134

hadn't got anything better to do. No peace for the wicked, I suppose."

"I think she's got worse since James died," Rosie said, bending to pull another quilt from the dryer. "I can't stand being bossed around. It reminds me of being in care, in that bloody children's home. That nearly drove me round the bloody bend. I'm not getting screwed up like that again just for Meg Morrissey."

"I don't know," Jane said. "It probably wasn't much worse than that ghastly school I went to."

"Don't you believe it," Rosie said bitterly. "A building like a workhouse run by sadists . . ."

"Like I said, just the same as my school."

"At least you got to go home at night." But some of the bitterness had dissipated, and as she leaned forward to take the bedspread from Jane she added: "They taught me to cook, so I suppose they were doing me a favour. They thought they were fitting us best for adult life by giving us domestic skills. But since then I haven't been able to stand being pushed around."

"I didn't mean to laugh," Jane said. "I hadn't realized it was so bad."

"No," Rosie said. "Well, I try not to let it get in the way. It's only at times like this when Meg decides to play the high-and-mighty lady that it bugs me. And then she gives us all that crap about struggling to keep the family together. It's easy enough for her, isn't it? Even with James gone. She's got money, a bloody lovely house, and folks like us to do the skivvying for her." She slammed the dryer door shut. "I'm sorry," she said. "I must be having a bad day. Let's forget about the wonder mother and get the kettle on."

"You should talk about it more often," Jane said. "Not keep it all bottled up."

"Nah! Who'd want to hear about it?"

"I would," Jane said gently. "I would." She lifted the laundry into a basket and set it on the floor. "No one ever talked to me at home. They were all too busy with their careers and their smart friends. You shouldn't be jealous of the Morrisseys. Would you like Meg as a mother?" She grinned and mimicked her again. " 'We have great *expectations* of you all.' "

"I suppose so," Rosie said, smiling. "You're right. It can't be a bundle of laughs living with that."

She led them into the kitchen, made tea, and set out chocolate biscuits. "Come on then, Molly," she said when they were settled at the table. "Tell us how the investigation's going. Do you have any idea yet whodunnit?"

"Not yet," Molly said, ignoring the flippant tone. "George thinks it might have something to do with a story Jimmy was working on at *Green Scenes* just before he retired. He never mentioned anything like that to you?"

"We're only the hired hands," Rosie said with a return of the old bitterness. "Why should he talk to us about his work?" She paused. "Have you found the autobiography yet?"

Molly shook her head.

"And you?" Jane asked her quietly. "What do you think?"

"Oh," Molly said. "I rather think it might be something more *personal*, you know. Murder's seldom a calculated crime." She paused. "I met Grace Sharland yesterday. . . ." An unspoken question hung in the air.

"And you think she might be the personal element in the investigation?" Jane seemed glad of the change of subject. Perhaps she thought the gossip would distract Rosie and cheer her up.

"She's a very attractive young woman," Molly said. "I wondered if there was ever any talk . . ."

"About her and James?"

Molly nodded. "He was obviously close to her."

"He fancied her like crazy," Jane said. She looked at Rosie, hoping to involve her in the scandal and lift her gloom. "Didn't he, Rosie? Anyone could see that."

"I suppose so," she said, but she still seemed preoccupied.

"Of course he did. Don't you remember that time when he went for a walk on the beach with her? Everyone else was out but us and they must have thought we couldn't see them. But there's a pair of binoculars in the common room and we watched them through those. They were walking side by side like an old married couple."

"Oh, Jane, that's outrageous," Rosie said, roused at last from her brooding. "Those binoculars have been out of focus since Tim dropped them on the floor. And they were miles away. All you could see was a couple of shapes. They were probably talking. Or perhaps he was upset and she was comforting him. It was some sort of therapy."

"I bet it was!" Jane said. She rolled her eyes and made them laugh. "Grace might live in splendid isolation in that posh new house, but you know what a reputation she's got."

"You know her socially?" Molly asked.

"We do get let out of this place occasionally," Jane said. "It's not quite a prison, whatever Rosie might tell you. When I moved up here my parents gave me a second-hand Mini. A sort of consolation prize for being a failure. At least it means we can escape during our times off. Usually we just go to the pub in the village, but sometimes we go to Mardon for a change. The night life isn't terribly sophisticated, but there's a folk club in one of the pubs and a group of us meet up there once a week. I suppose you could say that Grace is one of the gang. Or she was. She hasn't been around much lately."

"Tell me about her," Molly said.

"Duckie, where shall I start?" Jane was enjoying herself enormously. "Her mother died when she was little, but she certainly didn't have a deprived childhood.

137

There was loadsa money. Her dad was a director at Mardon Wools till he retired."

"Was he?" Rosie was definitely interested now. "I didn't know that."

"Didn't you, dear? You can't have been listening to the right people. She was always a bit wild. In the end she got sent away to one of those progressive boarding schools where you only have to work if you feel like it. She was an only child and spoilt rotten. Daddy hoped she'd do some sort of business management course and follow in the family footsteps, but she surprised him and opted for nursing. Daddy thought that was a bit beneath her. What would *she* do with a bedpan? But when she decided to go in for psychiatry he was horrified. He hated the idea of his little girl being mixed up with those loonies. For years he kept up a determined campaign to persuade her to change her mind. In the end he bought her that smart house by the river just before he retired. Perhaps it was a final attempt to get her to join the family firm. Obviously it didn't work, but they say he became resigned to the idea of her nursing in the last few months, and he's almost proud of her now."

"They?" Rosie interrupted in astonishment. "Who are they? Jane, where did you get all that information?"

"By listening," Jane said, suddenly serious again. "I'm always telling you that I'm a good listener." She turned to Molly in explanation. "Look, I'm not very good in company. Shy, I suppose. My parents always left me with the impression that I had nothing worth saying. So in the pub when the music's finished and Rosie's being the life and soul of the party I'm usually sitting in a corner eavesdropping. I live a sheltered life and get all my excitement second-hand. You'd be amazed at some of the things people say when they think they can't be overheard."

"And in those conversations, did the subject of Grace's boyfriends come up?"

"All the time," Jane said. "As you say she's a very

138

attractive woman, very sought after. And getting on now. Thirty-five next birthday. Her name must have been linked with most of the eligible men in the county. Though if they were after her money they must have been disappointed."

"And in all this gossip there was never any talk about an intimate relationship with Jimmy Morrissey?"

"No, but then there wouldn't be. James was something of a local celebrity, of course. Most people had seen the repeats of his programmes on the telly. But he was quite a recluse. And no one would have considered him Grace's type. He was so old, for one thing. Besides, she always went for the flash and the irresponsible, usually the younger sons of county families. The rural equivalent, I suppose, of the yuppie."

"But nothing serious?" Molly asked. "There was no prospect, for example, of marriage?"

"Definitely nothing serious," Jane said. "At least not since we've been here. I heard her say once that she saved all her emotional involvement for her work. Everything else had to be fun. There was only one man in her life and that was her father."

"What about before you lived here? In her past?"

"She was engaged once," Jane said. "Apparently she was mad about the bloke. Besotted. He was a conservationist. A bit like James, I suppose. Perhaps she had a thing about green wellies. He dumped her six months before the wedding and went off to Malawi to do a research project into fish for an aid agency. I think that's the story, anyway. No wonder she was put off serious commitment."

"Fish," Molly said. "I suppose that would have made him a marine biologist?"

"What? Yes, I suppose so." Jane was losing interest. This was all past history.

"I don't expect you ever knew his name," Molly said casually. "Or who he was working for?"

Jane thought hard. It was a challenge. "He was called

Nick," she said at last, triumphantly. "I never knew his surname. And he was working for the water authority. Apparently he spent a lot of his time up to his thighs in the river taking water samples. It didn't sound much of a job."

Molly changed the subject as if Grace's ex-fiancé held no interest for her.

"When did it first occur to you that Grace and Jimmy might be emotionally involved?" she asked.

"It never occurred to me," Rosie said quickly. "It's all in Jane's imagination."

"When James started to shake off his depression something had to be giving him an interest in life again," Jane said. "And it certainly wasn't Meg."

"You don't think it was starting to work on the autobiography then?" Molly said. "That seems to have been most people's opinion."

"No," Jane said. "It was sex. Nothing like sex to buck you up. Wouldn't you say?"

It was so unlike her to be worldly wise, so outside her own experience, that they began to laugh again.

When Molly left the kitchen she found Ruth in the schoolroom. It was almost lunch-time and the others had drifted away. Their scraps of poetry were scattered over the table. Ruth was reading and was concentrating so hard that she did not hear Molly come in. Only when the door closed behind her did she look up.

"If you're looking for your husband I think he's with Mother," she said. "They're probably still in the flat."

"No," Molly said. "I wanted to talk to you. About Aidan. You must have some idea why he left so suddenly. You were friends, weren't you?"

"I thought so," Ruth said.

"When did you first meet?"

"Ages ago. Soon after Mother married James. He won a painting competition and James invited him to the house for supper. I was very young, but I remember

140

how shy he was. It must have been a terrible ordeal for him. Mother was pregnant with Emily and Tim was just a toddler. It was a big house full of toys and children, terribly embarrassing, don't you think, for a teenage boy to cope with. He dropped his fork during the meal and blushed like a turnip. I thought he was quite grown up, but I still felt sorry for him."

"You remember it very well," Molly said.

"I suppose I do. Probably because he was kind to me. Perhaps I was feeling a bit left out. Mother was all tied up with Tim and being pregnant. She was writing pieces then, too, for women's magazines on family life, child care, you know the sort of thing." Molly nodded. "But that was all . . ." she paused, not wanting to be disloyal but trying to explain, ". . . abstract, theoretical. She liked the *idea* of our being a big family, but I think quite often Caitlin and I just got in the way. Babies were easier. They went to bed early. Caitlin probably resented it more than me." She paused again. "James was enormous fun but hardly ever there."

"So when Aidan gave you some attention you remembered it," Molly prompted.

"He read to us," Ruth said, "and drew pictures to go with the stories. And sometimes, when James was away, he came to babysit so Mother could go to the theatre with her friends. We always looked forward to that. We said he was the best babysitter in the world. Much better than the childminders who came in occasionally to give Mother some time to herself."

So Meg wasn't a wonder mother after all, Molly thought. Just human and selfish like the rest of us.

"Aidan went to work for your father, didn't he?" she said.

Ruth nodded. "When he was at art school. During the holidays."

"You must have been a bit older then. Did he ever talk to you about the work?"

141

"I don't think so. He still treated me as a kid even when I began to wish he wouldn't."

"And James?" Molly asked. "Did he talk about his work at all?"

"All the time. It was the only thing he thought about. It was all plans, dreams, schemes—ideas for a new television series, for an article for the magazine. I don't think it was what Mother expected when she married him. She thought, somehow, it would be more of a partnership."

"Do you remember the weekend Hannah died?" Molly asked.

"Of course," Ruth said.

"How did you get on with Hannah?"

"Very well. We were about the same age. I could talk to her, you know, about things you could never discuss with your parents. I know Mother thought she was doing the right thing by teaching us at home and she always made sure there were lots of other children around. But they were children of *her* friends. It wasn't like being in a big class and being able to choose for yourself. I suppose I was always quite lonely and that's why I looked forward so much to Hannah coming to stay."

"Did you ever come to visit her in Salter's Cottage with Phil and Cathy?"

"Once," Ruth said. "It was the Easter holidays. I loved it. Phil took us out ringing with him and let us hold the birds though that wasn't really allowed. I was only thinking of it this morning because we found a dying swan on the shore, just like Tim. Phil took it back to the cottage and tried to clean it up, but it died in the night. Hannah cried for it."

"When was that?" Molly asked gently.

"The same year. The year that she died, too. July 1991."

"Can you remember what arrangements were made that weekend, the weekend she was going to visit you?"

Molly half expected the girl to demand some explanation, to ask where the questions were leading, but she answered readily enough.

"It was a spur-of-the-moment thing, right at the start of the summer holidays. James said he had to go north anyway for work and he might as well bring Hannah back with him."

"Did he tell you what the work was about?"

"Not really, but I heard him discussing it with Mother." She paused, wondering why she found it so easy to talk to this old lady. She was trusting her with memories she'd not discussed with anyone else. "They were arguing," she said. "That's why I remember it so clearly, I suppose, and because everything that happened around the time of the accident seems very sharp and immediate because of the shock. They didn't argue much. James sometimes tried to provoke a fight—I think he would have quite enjoyed it—but Mother didn't respond. She usually walked away."

"But that day there was a row?"

"Yes. I didn't hear it all. I came in, I think, at the end of it. Mother didn't want him to go away. I suppose there was some event they'd been invited to. She liked to be seen out with James. He was famous then. She was shouting: 'But what will people think?' Then he said quite quietly: 'Does it really matter?' "

"Did you ever find out what the argument was about?"

"No," Ruth said. "I couldn't ask Mother. But James came to find me later that night before he went away. I was in my room reading and he knocked on the door and came and sat on the bed. He'd never done that before. He was always in so much of a hurry. He talked about Hannah. He asked what I'd like to do when she was staying. I said ice-skating, bowling, the usual things. Then he said: 'You and Hannah must stay friends whatever happens. Even if the grown-ups fall out you must stay friends.' "

"Did you understand what he meant by that?"

"Not at the time. I suppose I thought then he was sorry for having rowed with Mother. But later I wondered if he was meaning to leave her, that he was saying that even if they separated Hannah and I could still see each other."

"Yes," Molly said. "I suppose he could have meant that. But he never did leave your mother, did he?"

"No," Ruth said, "and after the accident he wouldn't have had the courage."

They sat for a moment in silence. "What's this all about?" Ruth asked at last. "I thought you wanted to talk about Aidan. I can't help you, you know. I don't have any more idea than you do where he's disappeared to."

"But you might know *why* he left," Molly said. "You seemed very close."

"I think I scared him away," Ruth said bitterly. "I wanted him to notice me, to see that I'm not a kid any more. But he wasn't interested and I scared him off. That's why he ran away in such a hurry."

"Oh no," Molly said. "I don't think it was like that at all."

13

They told Meg that they would be out for lunch and drove instead to the Dead Dog, where they ate limp ham sandwiches and drank glasses of flat beer. The place was empty except for Cedric, who stared at them mournfully from behind the bar. They seemed to have gained a lot of information during the morning, but it was all vague and unsubstantiated. George especially felt he needed a fact, something concrete to work from.

"What are we saying then?" he demanded. "That Jimmy hadn't fallen for Grace at all? That he pretended to be close to her because he wanted to find out about a boyfriend she'd had, who happened to work for the National Rivers Authority?"

"We don't know that it was the National Rivers Authority," Molly said. "Jane wasn't that specific."

"Of course not!" George said crossly. "Nothing in this case is that specific."

"It's an odd coincidence, though, isn't it?" Molly went on. She was accustomed to George's frustrations. "Grace did tell me that she felt she was being used. And I don't think one thing precludes the other, do you? Jimmy could have fallen for her and still used her to get information for his story. Surely he was never bothered about mixing business and pleasure . . ." She paused in thought. "Perhaps the article Christabel told you about was never quite completed, the facts never checked. When Jimmy decided to write the autobiography and set the record straight he might have needed to talk again to the people involved. The boyfriend of Grace Sharland's would have given him access to those. Especially if the incident happened locally."

"But it's so *uncertain*," he said. "There's no evidence that the story Jimmy was working on originated from this area. He could have been based farther north during that week before the accident. Even if he were driving back from Scotland it would have been convenient to pick up Hannah on the way."

"Then we'll have to find out," Molly said. Her calm only provoked him more.

"But how?" he demanded. "Aidan Moore's disappeared and all we know about this Nick is that he went to work in Malawi. We haven't even got a second name for him."

"There can't be that many British-sponsored aid projects in Malawi," Molly said. "Even fewer employing a marine biologist. Don't you have any contacts in the Overseas Development Administration? One of your pals from the civil service? All those working lunches and endless seminars must have had some use. . . ."

"There was someone," George said. "He transferred from the Home Office not long before I retired . . ." He lapsed into silence, already framing the question in his head, planning an excuse for needing to know.

In the end it was easy. His chum remembered him immediately. George, he always felt, had been the one to really swing his promotion, and he owed him a few favours. He didn't even ask why George needed the information and the prepared lie about wanting to trace a distant relative was never needed. The only problem was in getting the information quickly. Sandford wanted to chat, to discuss office politicking that George had long forgotten. As he tried to contain his impatience George thought that his final appraisal of the man had been over-generous.

"We're only sponsoring one research project in Malawi," Sandford said at last. "It's a study into the viability of commercial fishing on the lake. Based near Salima."

"Yes," George said gratefully. "That would be it. There's no guarantee, of course, that the chap I'm looking for will still be there. Don't you employ most of your scientists on short-term contracts?"

"Yes," Sandford said slowly. "But I've got a feeling that this scheme's overrun and quite a few of the contracts have been renewed. It happens that way sometimes . . ."

There was a distant sound of computer beeps.

"Here we are," Sandford said. "The list of staff. The only one with the initial *N* is the freshwater biologist Lineham. Nicholas Lineham. Do you want a home address for him?"

"Please," George said casually.

"It's a place in Mardon," Sandford said, unaware of the excitement he had caused. "If you've got a pen I'll give it to you."

"I was hoping to get in touch with Nick," George said. "Could I get a message to him through you?"

"No need, old chap," Sandford said. "Why don't you phone him direct? You can get straight through to the lab. We've got quite a sophisticated set-up out there, you know. It's not all mud huts and bush telegraph. I'll give you the number."

But when George finally got his call to Salima connected he couldn't speak to Nick Lineham. The project's research manager was very helpful. Over a crackly line he said he would get Nick to contact George when he returned. But he had just started a rou-

147

tine three-week cruise up the length of Lake Malawi on the project boat, collecting samples, and there was no way of getting a message to him there.

The address Sandford had given for Nick Lineham turned out to be a sub post office and general store on the outskirts of Mardon. It was on the main road west out of the town and now, at five-thirty, the traffic was heavy. As they sat in a queue of cars at traffic lights George's impatience increased. He had convinced himself that this was a wild-goose chase. The suburb was unprepossessing. On one side of the road were a series of red-brick terraces, on the other a grey, 1950s council housing estate that sprawled up the hill. They came at last to a small row of shops, built into a terrace. Most were still open, hoping perhaps to attract commuters on their way home. George drove past them and parked, then walked back past the launderette, the newsagent's, and the Chinese takeaway to get into the Lineham's shop by the front door.

There was a post office counter at one end but that had been closed and covered by heavy metal shutters. The rest of the cramped space was set out like a miniature supermarket with goods piled on shelves in the middle of the room and along the walls. Everything was faintly grubby. A young woman sat on a stool behind the till next to a rack of ageing vegetables. Molly and George stood just inside the door, taking their bearings.

"It's self service," the young woman said aggressively. "You'll have to help yourselves." She did not move from the stool but nodded towards a pile of wire baskets.

"We were hoping to talk to Mr. and Mrs. Lineham," George said. He had assumed from the beginning that Nick had given his parents' address to the Overseas Development Administration. "They do live here?"

"Why do you want to know?"

"Perhaps I could explain that to Mr. and Mrs. Lineham," he said firmly.

"I'm not sure," she said. There was something protective in her attitude and he thought she must be Nick's sister. "They've just gone into the back to have their tea. It's the only break they get." She paused but could not control her resentment. "They used to close at six, but they have to stay open till ten now to make any sort of living. I've got better things to do than mind this bloody place after a full day's work, but what can you do? They should have sold it when the market was better. You couldn't give it away now." She regarded them with hostility as if they were to blame for the recession.

"We'd like to talk to them about Nick," George said carefully. He did not want to provoke another outburst of anger.

"Oh well, if it's about their precious Nick I'm sure they'll want to see you."

Still she did not move from her stool, but she shouted towards an open back door: "Mum! There's someone here to talk to you." She turned back to Molly and George. "You'd better go through."

The Linehams were in a small scruffy living room at the end of a short passage. The passage and much of the room had been used as storage space and they sat surrounded by cartons of washing-up liquid and baked beans. The place had all the comfort of a warehouse. There were two upright armchairs and a large television set, which dominated their attention. They had trays on their knees and were forking food into their mouths while they watched an American soap.

George hesitated in the doorway and coughed, but the television was too loud for them to hear.

"Mr. and Mrs. Lineham?" he said, and they turned in unison, surprised and frightened. They were small, slight, grey, so alike that they could have been brother and sister.

"I'm sorry to disturb you," George said. "Your daughter said it would be all right."

Mrs. Lineham jumped to her feet, gathered the half-full plates together, and scuttled into the kitchen. Her husband stood, too, but his mouth was still full and he could not speak. The woman returned empty-handed and muttered a shamed apology about the mess. It was as if she, not they, were intruding.

"We're really very sorry to disturb you," George said again. He wanted to put them at their ease. How could they confide in him when they felt so obviously threatened? "It's about Nick. I'm interested in some work he was doing before he went to Africa. He's out on the boat now and I can't get in touch with him. I thought you might be able to help."

"Oh!" she said, relieved, relaxing into a smile. "You'll be from the university." She spoke in a hushed tone as if the place had some sort of religious significance and he was a high priest. "They were still interested in his work even after he finished his Ph.D." She turned towards the mantelpiece where a framed photograph of the boy in cap and gown flanked by his parents had pride of place. It was hard to tell from the photo what Grace had seen in him. To George he just looked very young.

"So you're from the university," she said again, enjoying saying the word.

George did not contradict her. If she thought he was a professor following up her son's research, she was more likely, surely, to help him.

"Sit down," she said, moving boxes to reveal two more chairs. "What must you think of us living like this. Do sit down. Ernie, this gentleman's from the university. Switch that rubbish off at once."

Ernie leaned forward and reluctantly switched off the television.

"Now," she said. "How can we help you?"

"Was Nick living here when he was working for the

150

NRA?" George said in a chatty tone, hoping that was where he *had* been working. He wanted to start with simple, unthreatening questions.

"No," she said. "Not really. Not then. He was living at home when he first started with the Mardon and District Water Company, but when the National Rivers Authority was formed after privatization he'd already moved out."

"So he started with the NRA right from the beginning?" George said.

"Oh yes. It was what interested him most, you see, the conservation side."

"And where was he living then?"

She blushed and lowered her voice to a whisper. "With his girlfriend," she said. "She's moved since, but she had a flat then in one of those big houses just off the High Street. I can't say I was happy about the situation. You had to wait in my day. But they were engaged so that was something. And he kept in touch with Ernie and me. He always came for his Sunday dinner." She lowered her voice even further. "I don't think *she* was much of a cook. I don't suppose she had to learn where she came from."

"Oh?" George said. It was all the encouragement she needed. As her daughter had said, she was glad of any excuse to talk about her precious Nick.

"Grace Sharland she was called," Mrs. Lineham said. "The Sharlands were a big family in Mardon. No shortage of money there. Her dad was something high up in Mardon Wools. Nothing came of it in the end and I can't say that I'm sorry. Despite all her money our Nick could have done better for himself than her."

There was a pause and Ernie Lineham stood up. Perhaps he had heard it all before and was embarrassed by his wife's boasting. "Look," he said awkwardly, "I'd best go and relieve our Linda in the shop. She works the early shift in the tannery and she only comes here to oblige. She's got her own husband's tea to see to.

151

May'll be able to help you better than me, any road." He nodded and disappeared. Mrs. Lineham turned to them expectantly.

"It must have been a shock when Nick took off for Africa," Molly said gently.

"Not really," Mrs. Lineham said stoutly. Her devotion obviously included the self-sacrifice of giving up his company without complaint. "You see, he'd wanted to go to Africa ever since he was a lad. The wildlife pro grammes on the telly were always his favourites. You know, *Zoo Watch* and Johnny Morris, all the elephants and lions.

"I could tell he was bright right from the start," Mrs. Lineham went on. "I said to him, 'You work hard, son, and you'll be out there some day working with animals, too.' " She paused reflectively. "It doesn't seem the same, does it, fish? Not so glamorous somehow. But Nick explained it all to me. Fish are just as important in the scheme of things. It's all to do with . . ." She paused again groping for the word. ". . . the ecology."

"And he was working on fish here in Mardon, too?" George was finding it hard to contain his impatience. Molly would be prepared to sit here all night, listening to the woman's reminiscences. She had no sense of urgency. But he needed some sign that the investigation was moving forward.

"Not just fish!" the woman said, as if George should have known. "He was the regional conservation officer for the National Rivers Authority. It was his job to stop the rivers getting polluted."

"Of course," George said. He leaned forward. "Did Nick leave any notes from work with you before he went to Africa?" he said. "That would really be most useful to our research."

"He did," she said. "A great pile of files and paper. He made a joke about it. Half a rain forest, he said. I put everything in his old room for him. 'It'll all be here for you when you get back, son,' I said."

"Would you have any objection if we looked through his notes?" George said. He was allowing himself to become excited. For the first time he started to believe that this might lead somewhere. He tried to sound professional. "We would acknowledge his contribution, of course, if anything was published."

"What a shame!" she said. "I'd let you have them if I could, but they're not here any more. Grace Sharland, the one I was telling you about, came here a couple of months ago." She paused for dramatic effect. "With James Morrissey, the chap who was always on the television. He asked if he could see Nick's work. Grace had been talking about it and he thought it would help with a programme he was planning. Of course I gave him everything. He said he'd bring it back when he'd finished. He was such a nice man, older than he looks on the telly, but lovely, interested in what Nick was up to. I knew Nick would be thrilled to help. It was James Morrissey that made some of the wildlife programmes that got him started as a kid."

"And was he thrilled when you told him what you'd done?" George asked.

"No," she said, still surprised and disappointed. "Not really. He just said: 'Well, I suppose it won't do any harm after all this time. It's got nothing to do with me any more.' "

George wanted to go then. He thought they had got what they had come for, but the woman was obviously keen to chat and Molly only encouraged her.

"Why did he go to Africa so suddenly?" Molly said. "Was it because Grace broke off the engagement and he. felt he needed to get away?"

"Grace didn't break off the engagement," Mrs. Lineham said. "She was broken-hearted about it." She hesitated, then ventured a mild criticism of her son. "I

153

think he could have handled it better. It wasn't kind to run away like that without a word. She deserved some sort of explanation. More than the note he left her."

Molly nodded sympathetically but said nothing. There was more to be told. Who else did the woman have to talk to? Her family and friends would be bored crazy with the stories of her son.

"He was offered the job in Malawi before," Mrs. Lineham said at last, "when the project was first thought up. They knew he'd be the best man for the job. But he'd just got the post with the National Rivers Authority then and he didn't think he should risk leaving. There was no guarantee, you see, that he'd get it back again."

"But something made him change his mind," Molly said. "Something persuaded him to go after all."

There was a pause. "He never told me about it," the woman said.

"But you must have guessed."

There was another silence. She had been carrying the burden of the information for years and the temptation to share it was suddenly too great to resist.

"He came into money," she said suddenly. Molly remained silent.

"We don't have a lot to spare," Mrs. Lineham went on. "At one time everyone on the estate used this shop. Now they all have cars and go into town. . . ." She was postponing the moment when she would have to put her suspicions into words. "But I wanted to save something for him. I thought if I put something into his building society every month it would mount up in the end. And when he came back it would be a nice surprise for him."

She lapsed into thought.

"And when you saw the building society pass book you realized he'd been given some money," Molly prompted.

The woman nodded. "Ten thousand pounds," she said. It was too much for her to contemplate. "Ten thousand pounds. That would tide him over, wouldn't it, if he came back from Africa and couldn't find a job straight away. That's why he decided to go."

"Where did the money come from?" Molly asked gently. "Did it say in the building society book?"

Mrs. Lineham shook her head.

"But you know where it came from, don't you?" Molly said. A clever and perceptive woman like you would know, she implied. A mother would have some idea.

"I think he was paid to go away," Mrs. Lineham said quietly.

"Who would do that?" Molly asked. George forgot his impatience and leaned forward to listen for the answer. Was *this* the story Jimmy Morrissey was following: the pay-off of a corrupt official? But he was disappointed.

"Mr. Sharland never thought he was good enough for his daughter," she said. "He was against the engagement from the start. I think he gave Nick the money to break it off and go as far away from Mardon as possible."

She looked up, shocked that she had given so much away but relieved because Molly did not seem horrified by the revelation.

"You can't blame him for taking it," she said. "You see what it's like here. You can't blame him for wanting something more exciting. Grace was a pretty enough lass, but he'd dreamed of Africa all his life. He couldn't turn down a chance like that."

"No," Molly said. "Of course not."

They walked out through the shop. Ernie Lineham was selling a packet of cigarettes to an elderly woman in carpet slippers. They were talking about the weather forecast. Everyone was predicting blizzards, they said.

Molly thanked him for his help and they went outside. Perhaps it was auto-suggestion, but George thought the air smelled of snow.

14

The snow started as they drove through Mardon on their way back to the Mill, but at first they hardly noticed it. There was so much to sort out. Again there was the sense that they were swamped with information without any way of knowing what was important or relevant.

"If there was a major pollution incident and Nick Lineham had found out, wouldn't we have heard of it?" Molly asked. "After that leak of toxic chemicals into the Camel in Cornwall the papers were full of nothing else for weeks."

"I'm not sure," he said. "It's not something I know enough about. I'm not sure how easy it would be to keep a thing like that secret." It was the ignorance that was so frustrating, he thought. Jimmy Morrissey with his background in the biological sciences would have known what to look for. "It would help if we could find those notes of Nick's, but they must have been stolen with the autobiography. They're certainly not in the study. I went through everything in there yesterday."

"But if the pollution incident was serious enough to attract Jimmy's interest, wouldn't there have been some environmental damage?" Molly said. "I don't know— dead fish floating to the surface, a sudden build-up of algae, something like that." She was even more vague about the science than George.

"I haven't got a clue!" he said angrily. "I need to talk to an expert. Nick Lineham must have a successor at the NRA. I'll try to get in touch with him tomorrow."

The snow was heavy now and he was forced to slow almost to a walking pace. Ahead of them a gritting lorry with lights flashing was taking up almost the width of the narrow road. George flashed his lights and hit the horn, but the lorry would not pull in to let him past. A shower of grit clattered against the windscreen.

"What about swans?" Molly asked suddenly.

"What do you mean?"

"Could swans be an indicator of pollution?"

"I suppose so. Why? Are you thinking of the bird Tim found this morning?"

"It's not only that," Molly said. "Ruth told me that she came to stay with the Cairnses during the Easter holidays before Hannah died. Phil found a sick swan on the shore."

"It could be a coincidence," George said uneasily. "If Phil had any worries he would have had it analysed. Unless . . ."

"Unless?" she said.

He shook his head. A suspicion had been gnawing at his mind since the visit to the Linehams', but he told himself that the idea was preposterous. At least he should discuss it with Phil before it went any further. If he could get past this bloody lorry he'd have time to call in at Salter's Cottage and clear the matter up before dinner. It would be useful to talk to Phil, anyway. Of all people he would know if any of the rivers in Nick Lineham's patch had been polluted.

But when they got to the cottage it was ten to seven and Molly would not let him stop. Meg would see it as an unforgivable discourtesy if they missed dinner, too, she said. There was nothing to prevent George coming out after the meal and talking to the Cairnses then. The cottage lights shining through the falling snow seemed to taunt him, but he did as he was told and drove past.

It was the first of a series of setbacks and set the tone of the evening.

At dinner he made sure he was sitting next to Tim. It came to something, he thought, when he had to turn to a ten-year-old boy for help.

"Have you ever found sick mute swans on the shore before?" he asked.

Tim shook his head. The memory of his lack of control that morning still upset him.

"What about other species?" George asked.

"There's sometimes a botulistic gull in the summer," the boy said. "Dad thought they picked up the infection by feeding on the rubbish tip outside Mardon. There's nothing you can do to save them."

"Anything else?"

Tim shrugged. "Some little auks were blown inland after a really strong north-easterly gale one November. We picked up one in a cattle grid by the farm up the road. But they were just exhausted. And occasionally we find oiled guillemots and razor-bills. We're part of the beached bird survey and we get called out if there's been an oiling incident."

George continued his meal in silence. There was nothing there to excite interest. It was what you would expect on any coastline in Britain. Why then had Nick Lineham been so eager to leave the country? Was it, as his mother suspected, that he was considered an unsuitable husband for a cherished daughter? The more George thought about it, the more unlikely that seemed. Something had provoked Jimmy's interest. The suspicion that had been niggling all evening grew stronger.

As the plates were cleared and Rosie brought in cheese George found it increasingly difficult to sit still. The family talked about the weather, about the time the Mill was cut off from the main road by heavy snow and a farmer had to come with a tractor to dig them out, but the chatter seemed distant and irrelevant. Jimmy must have felt like this, George thought. He must have felt

159

that compared to the work on his story the family were unimportant. He was convinced now that Jimmy had intended to leave Meg. It would be a tidying up, too, a completion of the process that must have started when he had talked to Ruth about her and Hannah staying friends, even after the grown-ups had argued. Then another explanation of those words occurred to him and he got to his feet, although he had not finished the meal, and said abruptly that he had to go out.

Molly telephoned Grace Sharland several times that evening. Despite the snow she wanted to speak to her and would have gone into Mardon if the nurse had been in. She was sure she could persuade Grace to talk about Nick and the broken engagement. She must know why he had disappeared to Africa. She, after all, had taken Jimmy Morrissey to the Linehams' house to collect his notes. Or had Jimmy charmed her into doing that without giving her a real explanation? Each time she phoned Grace was out. She left messages on the ansafone, then sat in the common room with the door open so she would hear the pay phone in the lobby if it were to ring. But the phone rang only once and then it was a well-spoken woman asking for Jane.

'That'll be Mother doing her duty,' Jane said when Molly called her from the kitchen. "Checking that the black sheep's alive and well. And not intending to embarrass her by returning to London."

When she had finished on the phone Jane sought out Molly in the common room.

"We're just going to open a bottle of wine," she said. "Only cheap plonk, but you're welcome to a glass. If you hang around here there's a danger that you'll get invited to the flat and that's a fate worse than death. We'll go into Rosie's room. Mine's like a pigsty."

She took it for granted that Molly would go with her. They seemed to have taken Molly under their wing, to feel that she was a kindred spirit who needed protect-

160

ing. Molly was grateful to be asked. She thought perhaps they were right and she was downtrodden, too. George had rushed off without consulting her, without asking if she would like to go with him. He had tried to treat her as a partner, but if there was an emergency his natural arrogance took over. Perhaps he and Meg were two of a kind.

The girls' rooms were at the end of a bare corridor at the back of the Mill, on the ground floor, so there was little natural light. The corridor was used to store crates of mineral water, boxes of bleach, and packets of toilet paper and Molly was reminded of the Linehams' house.

"Just a minute," Jane said. "The wine's in my room." She opened a door and Molly saw an unmade bed, a heap of clothes on a hard-backed chair. It was like a room in a students' hall of residence. There were posters, a pin board covered with photos, even a pile of chemistry textbooks, dusty and unopened on the narrow window-sill. Jane saw Molly looking at them and laughed. "I tried to persuade myself that if I did some work on my own I'd be able to catch up enough to go to college," she said. "Not the university, of course. They'd never have me back there. But I thought some institution might be daft enough to give me a second chance. I shouldn't have bothered. I haven't opened one of them since I arrived."

"What will you do when you leave the Mill?" Molly asked.

"Oh," Jane said lightly, "I don't suppose I'll ever leave. I'll grow old in the service of the Morrisseys like a Victorian governess."

She laughed again and took a bottle of red wine from the bottom of her wardrobe. They continued down the corridor. Rosie's room was identical to Jane's but immaculately tidy. There were no books or posters and only one photograph: a family group shot with people who all looked very like Rosie sitting on a beach and smiling into the camera. When they went in she was sitting at the dressing table, using it as a desk, and seemed to be writing a letter. Jane had knocked at the door but not waited for a reply and Rosie appeared for a moment to be irritated by the interruption. Jane seemed not to notice.

"I've brought Molly with me," she said. "I knew you wouldn't mind."

"No," Rosie said absently. "Of course not."

"Sorry," Jane said. "Are you busy?"

"Just writing to Mum," Rosie said. She turned to Molly in explanation. "She's ill again. Severe depression. They've taken her back into hospital. I feel so bloody helpless up here. I know she'd be better if we could move her back to her friends. She'd never been ill in her life until we moved away and Dad died. All they can suggest is pills and ECT. . . ." She was lost in thought for a moment, then set the letter aside and turned to face them, determined, apparently, not to impose her gloom on them.

"Come on then," she said cheerfully. "Where's the wine? Why don't you put on some music? Did Jane's information about the lovely Miss Sharland lead to anything?"

Molly drank the wine and shared the second bottle Jane brought from her room. In the company of the young women she felt quite at ease and for the rest of the evening she forgot the investigation.

Ruth, too, spent the evening waiting for the telephone to ring. She sat in her room. Her mother had said that they should have a quiet family evening together.

"What about a game of Scrabble before the little ones go to bed?" she had said brightly.

In the old days Ruth would have agreed meekly. Caitlin was the only one who had dared stand up to Meg. But since James had died Ruth thought she, too, had learned to be more assertive. Meg didn't seem quite so indomitable. So tonight she had excused herself without a fuss. She was sorry, she said, but she had work to do. Then she had sat in her room with her books open and unread in front of her, staring out of the uncurtained window, watching the big flakes of snow blow against it and slide down the pane. She wondered if Caitlin were playing Scrabble and thought it would not hurt her to do her bit for once.

George had decided to walk along the road from the Mill to Salter's Cottage and by the time he rang the front door bell his hair and clothes were covered with snow. He had walked past the uncurtained living-room window that faced the road and saw Cathy sitting at a large knitting machine. She was pushing a ratchet back and forth over the metal keys with a muscular ferocity, as if it were a piece of gymnasium equipment and making her fit. The yard where the Land Rover was usually parked was empty and there were tracks in the snow. It occurred to him that he should go away and come back when Phil was there, but then he thought that Cathy would do just as well.

"Phil's out," Cathy said abruptly when she opened the door. "A directors' dinner. Black tie and too much to drink. Phil will hate it."

"Weren't you invited?"

She shook her head. "They don't bother any more. They know I'll not go."

She stood aside to let him in. She was not surprised to see him. It was almost as if she were expecting it. He took off his boots and shook the snow from his waterproof jacket.

"We need a drink," she said in a voice that allowed no contradiction. "Something to fend off the cold. What will you have, George? Whisky?"

He nodded.

"To what do we owe the pleasure then, George?" she said in a hard, tight voice. "You didn't come out on a night like this because you felt like some fresh air. Or

163

perhaps that's it. Perhaps you're finding the Happy Families atmosphere at the Mill a bit stifling."

"I was hoping to speak to Phil," he said.

"Well, as you see he's not here."

She poured two large glasses of whisky and carried them through to the living room. She sat on the stool in front of the knitting machine but with her back to it so she was facing him. He settled into a low armchair and felt immediately at a disadvantage.

"Aren't you going to ask any questions?" she said. "That's not like you."

"It's probably not important," he said. "As I said, I wanted to talk to Phil. He keeps records of his bird counts?"

"Oh yes," she said. She nodded to a shelf where a pile of notebooks were neatly stacked. "Help yourself, George."

"I wanted to talk to him about swans," he said. "To know if he'd noticed any decline in the mute swan population over the years."

Again he thought she was not surprised by the question.

"You'll have to ask him," she said without interest.

"The young Morrissey lad found a dying swan on the shore this morning. It seemed to have lost the water-proofing on its feathers. Ruth said there'd been a similar incident when she was staying here with Hannah, the summer of '91. I wondered if it happened very often."

She did not ask him why he wanted to know and he thought that was more suspicious than her earlier aggression. She shrugged.

"It happens occasionally," she said. "The mute swans gather in big numbers up the Marr near the town bridge. The river's more polluted there though it's still tidal. I think cooking oil's usually the culprit. Restaurants flush the oil down their drains."

"And it would be enough to kill a swan like that?"

164

"Not by itself, apparently. It leaves them without proper waterproofing, then they lose weight because they can't feed properly. And that lowers their resistance to disease ..."

It was all too much like a prepared speech for him to be quite convinced.

"Look," she said. "The NRA took a fish-and-chip shop to court a few years ago. If you're interested, there must be some record of it."

"Yes," he said. "I suppose there must." Still she had not asked him what the questions were all about.

"What about Mardon Wools?" he asked, hoping to shock her into a reaction.

"What about them?" Her voice was easy and controlled, even slightly amused.

"The company's never been prosecuted for polluting the river?"

"Of course not." She gave a short mocking laugh. "With Phil involved?" She looked outside. The flakes were falling more slowly. "He's pure as the driven snow."

There was a silence. George felt as if he had shown his hand too early and been beaten. She sensed, too, that she had won and pushed home her advantage.

"If that's all, George, I'd like to get back to this knitting. It's a new venture for me designing for home machines."

"Yes," he said. He drank the last of the whisky and stood up. "I think that's all. For now."

She led him out to the kitchen and watched him pull on his boots. At the door he stopped and looked back at her.

"Nick Lineham," he said. "Does the name mean anything to you?"

She shook her head. "Never heard of him," she said.

"Phil's never mentioned him?"

"I'm sure he hasn't."

He pulled on his jacket and went outside, convinced

165

that she was lying. It was impossible that she could have retained all that information about sick swans and not remembered the name of the conservation officer who must have worked on some of the cases. But what did it all mean? And was it relevant, anyway, to Jimmy's death?

Outside the snow stopped suddenly and a pale moon appeared through the clouds. George remembered his own children's excitement at the arrival of snow. It was one of the few clear memories of their childhood he had. He had always been busy, concerned with other things. They had been there in the background but not really a part of his life. Weekends had been for birding and for catching up with paperwork from the office. He had acted, he supposed, much like Jimmy Morrissey, who was now being made out to be such a monster. George, like Jimmy, had taken it for granted that that was how things were. He had no excuse for his blindness.

The time he remembered the snow had been too thick for him to get to the office and the children had been sent home from school. It had started snowing the day before and during the evening they had rushed out every half hour into the darkness with a ruler to measure how deep it was. The next day they had built snowmen and he had pulled them around the garden on a sledge. Had he felt then that he was missing out? he wondered. Probably not. But he could appreciate how disappointed Tim Morrissey would be that the snow had stopped. He imagined him looking out of his bedroom window, willing the clouds to gather and the moon to disappear.

Because there was a moon George decided to walk back to the Mill along the shore. It was quicker and he was already very cold. Old age, he supposed, creeping up on him. So when the cottage door was shut behind him he walked back through the garden past the charred remains of Cathy Cairns's bonfire down the steps in the rock to the beach. His eyes were soon accustomed to the pale moonlight. It was reflected on the water. The tide was past the turn and there was still a sprinkling of snow on the shingle farthest away from the sea. It was not such a bad place, he thought, for Jimmy Morrissey to have ended his days.

He walked briskly, hoping the movement would bring some feeling back into his feet, keeping his eyes on the ground just ahead of him so he would not trip on loose shingle or a boulder. He stopped for a moment to get his bearings and catch his breath, to make sure that he was taking the shortest route to the Mill. At the high-water mark he saw a pile of rubbish, a pale shape caught in the moonlight. He thought it might be another swan and he went to investigate. But as he approached he saw that it was too big to be a swan. It was Aidan Moore, drowned, and washed up by the tide.

15

The police came with a portable generator and spotlights, though it seemed to George that the inspector in charge was just going through the motions. He seemed to find nothing sinister in Aidan Moore's death. It was happening all the time, he said with indecent enthusiasm. Though you wouldn't normally expect the corpse to float as quickly as that. He looked at Aidan Moore's body with something approaching disappointment, as if he were sorry it was not more decayed. George thought he was the sort who took delight in watching a young constable vomiting over a particularly unpleasant body. It would show how tough he was.

"This looks fresh enough," the inspector said. "Not like the one we had last summer. He'd been in the drink for weeks. That was some moron mucking around on a glorified lilo and thinking he was Francis Chichester. Perhaps this poor sod never got carried out into the open sea."

"It should look fresh enough," George said tartly. "Mr. Moore was still alive yesterday morning."

"Mr. Moore," the policeman said. "Staying at the Mill, was he?" He led George away from the body, and even that small exertion caused him to breathe heavily. He was nearing retirement, running to fat, with a smok-

168

er's wheeze. His name was Porter. George had taken an instant dislike to him. He was too cocky, too full of himself.

"Yes," George said. "He was a lecturer. He taught the course on illustration."

"Of course!" Porter said. "I should have recognized him. I talked to him after Mr. Morrissey committed suicide. He was a nervy sort of chap."

"You're not suggesting that he committed suicide, too!" George was provoked to sarcasm.

"I'm not suggesting anything." Porter grinned, showing gold-filled molars and fanglike canines. "Keep an open mind. That's what we're told in those Home Office guidelines that land on my desk every five minutes. But I'd bet you anything that this was an accident."

He stamped his feet and thrust his hands into the pockets of his sheepskin jacket. George thought, with a touch of snobbishness, that there was something of the used-car salesman about him. He was flash, quick, and not entirely reliable. An open mind was the last thing he possessed.

George, who had drafted many of the Home Office guidelines of which Porter complained, spoke slowly. "You don't think it's more than a coincidence—two sudden deaths in a month?" And shouldn't you be treating it more seriously? he thought. I found the body, but you haven't even asked my name.

Porter did not answer directly.

"You must be Palmer-Jones," he said, speaking casually but watching George with the look of a conjurer who has just pulled the rabbit from the hat. "I'd heard you were around. I was going to get in touch anyway to see if you fancied talking to our Rotary Club. This month's speaker's dropped out. 'My Life as a Private Eye,' something like that. They wouldn't be interested in the Home Office stuff."

He obviously wanted to show off how much he knew

about George, but still the suggestion seemed entirely serious. George looked at him in horror. Porter appeared not to notice.

"Think about it," he said genially. "You don't have to let me know now. There'll be a tenner in it and a fancy lunch."

"How did you know I was here?" George asked. The scene was slipping into the surreal and he needed something to hold on to.

"Hm?" The policeman's attention had been caught by a group of uniformed officers who slithered over the shingle, carrying canvas screens to shield the body. "Daft buggers. What do they want to bother with that for? By the time it gets light enough for any nosy parker to see, the tide'll be in again and we'll have to move the poor sod anyway. It's a lot of fuss about nothing. I told the governor it would be an accidental death and we wouldn't need all that palaver." He turned back to George. "What did you say?"

"I asked how you knew I was here."

"Oh." Porter could tell that George was impressed and wanted to make the most of the story. "It's a small place, Mardon. There's not much goes on that we don't hear about. We don't need a pile of paper sent from the Home Office to tell *us* about community policing. You and your good lady are staying at the Mill because Mrs. Morrissey doesn't want to believe that her old man committed suicide. That's all right by me. We had a full coroner's inquest, but you can ignore the verdict if you like. I'm a believer in private enterprise. How can they expect anyone to survive on a pension these days? I might take up the same line when I retire. Perhaps a bit more up-market. If I were you I think I'd call myself a security consultant. You've got to think of image these days. Make much of a living at it, do you?"

The sudden question was meant to offend. George ignored it and made an effort to keep his voice even.

"That's very impressive," he said. "All the same I'd like to know how you found out we were here."

"That's easy." Like a child playing a game, the detective had lost interest in the teasing. "My wife's a local girl. Born and reared in Markham Law. Her aunty's Florrie Duffy, who does the cleaning at the Mill. She helps out those two lasses who do all the work in the place. She heard you were coming. Probably knew before you did. She's that sort. I thought I recognized your name from all those bloody circulars, so I looked you up, made a few enquiries."

He stamped his feet again. "I don't know about you," he said, "but I'm bloody freezing." George saw that he was wearing polished leather slip-on shoes, quite unsuitable for the shore. "I think I can leave this to the troops now. It's time to get home to a hot toddy and my bed. The wife'll be wondering what I'm up to." He grinned lewdly. "I'll probably see you in the morning. I'll be in then to tie in all the details."

"Don't you want to see Aidan Moore's room?" George asked in disbelief. "Or talk to the other residents?"

"Why would I want to do that?" The cheery good humour disappeared quite suddenly. "I've told you. As far as I'm concerned this was an accidental death. The chap wasn't a local. He couldn't be expected to know the tides. It's a treacherous bit of coast, especially if you go wandering about after dark. He probably tripped on a slippery rock and knocked himself out. Then the tide came in and drowned him. Or he might have gone out to Salter's Spit and not left himself time to get back before high water. It's not the first time it's happened and it'll not be the last."

"But there's that cut on the side of his forehead."

"Of course there is!" Porter made it clear he was losing patience. He knew what he thought of civil servants who'd never done a day's practical policing in their lives but tried to tell the men what to do. "He'd been in the water for twenty-four hours in a strong tide, then washed up on a rocky beach. What would you expect?"

"There are things you should know," George persisted. He could not believe that the man was taking it so lightly. Porter seemed not to hear him. He yelled something incomprehensible to his subordinates and began to march purposefully over the shingle. George was put in the ridiculous position of having to follow, scrambling to keep up. The detective ran out of breath before he did and he stopped, still on the beach, wheezing painfully.

"My investigation has thrown up a number of inconsistencies," George said. "Facts that make me believe that Jimmy Morrissey was murdered."

The policeman turned crossly, still struggling for breath. "I suppose you've passed on these facts to the police," he snapped.

"No," George said defensively. "Not yet. I wasn't sure ..."

"Well, wait until you're bloody sure then," Porter interrupted, "before you bother me with them." He stared furiously at George and continued quietly: "Look, Mr. Palmer-Jones, I don't mind you playing at policeman. We've all got to have a hobby in our old age. I don't even mind you ripping off a daft old widow who's got more money than sense. But I do mind you coming along and telling me that I don't do my job properly. I enquired into Mr. Morrissey's death. With an open mind. He committed suicide. I will enquire into Mr. Moore's death. But unless the post mortem shows that he died from anything other than drowning, I'm telling you now that it'll go down as an accident!"

He took another gulp of air and launched himself over the shingle towards his car. George watched him go.

* * *

They were waiting for him in the living room of Meg's flat. He was reminded rather of an audience waiting for the show to start. There was no shock or excitement, hardly any conversation. Molly must have passed on the news of Aidan Moore's death. He had met her in the lobby on her way back from Rosie's room when he had come into the Mill to phone the police. She must have told Meg and arranged to gather everyone together. They must all know by now that Aidan was dead, could have seen the police in the spotlights through the window if they had bothered to pull back the heavy curtains, but they seemed blank and unengaged. They did not want to think of the tragedy until he was there to make sense of it for them. When he came into the room they looked at him expectantly as if he would have all the answers.

Only Emily and Tim were absent. They must have slept through the fuss. Rosie and Jane were there, sitting together on the floor, leaning against the wall. They looked tired and ill at ease and it occurred to him that they had never been invited into the flat before. They had been there to clean, but not like this, as guests of the family. Rosie must have been preparing for bed. For the first time he saw her with her hair out of its plait and she looked quite different with it loose about her shoulders.

Caitlin was curled at the end of the sofa, her bare feet tucked beneath her. She was wrapped in a striped towelling robe and her hair was still wet from the shower. She watched him as he entered the room and her eyes became bright and feverish, as if she could hardly wait for what he had to say.

What is wrong with them all? he thought. Don't they care that Aidan's dead? Then he saw that Ruth was crying. She made no sound, but tears were rolling down her cheeks. The family were staring at him and did not notice and it was left to Molly to try clumsily to comfort her.

"Well?" Caitlin said. "What's happened, George? What's going on?" She ran her tongue around the outside of her lips.

"Aidan's dead," he said angrily. "Drowned."

"When?" Meg demanded. "When did it happen?" Like everyone else in the room, George's presence had made her more attentive and alert.

"Some time before high water last night. The police think he was cut off by the tide."

"No!" Meg said. "Not Aidan! He knew the shore like his own back garden."

"Did anyone see him yesterday evening?" George asked quietly. "I know he went to the pub in the village with Ruth straight after dinner. But later? After that? He must have been killed before this morning's high water. When was that—six? Six-thirty?"

"I saw him last night," Jane said. "He was using the pay phone in the lobby."

"What time was that?"

She shrugged. "Nine. Half past. Perhaps even later than that."

"Did you hear what he said?"

She shook her head. "I don't think he wanted to be overheard. He turned his back to me and he was speaking quite quietly. I think I had the impression that he was making an appointment or arranging to meet someone. This morning when Ruth said he'd intended to leave I presumed he'd been calling a taxi."

"Wouldn't you have heard a taxi arrive?"

"Not necessarily if he'd been waiting up on the road."

"Did you see where Aidan went when he finished on the phone?"

She thought for a moment. "He went out," she said. "Yes, he definitely went out. I remember because when he opened the front door there was a blast of cold air and I thought: Why would anyone want to go out on a night like this? I didn't know then that he was thinking of leaving."

"Didn't he give any explanation for going out in the dark?" George asked.

"I don't think he saw me," Jane said. "By then I was on my way to the kitchen."

"He didn't go upstairs first?"

"No. I don't suppose he needed to. He was still wearing his coat after coming in from the pub."

"Are you sure he made the phone call?" George asked. "It wasn't an incoming call that he answered?"

"It might have been," she said. "I'm sorry. I can't remember."

"Did you see which way he went?"

She shook her head. "I didn't take much notice." She paused. "He just seemed to disappear into the darkness."

"Did anyone see him after that?" George asked. "Did you see him come back?"

They stared back at him in silence.

The room where Aidan Moore had always slept was on the first floor. It was bigger than the other single rooms, with a polished wood floor and a large window. An easel was still propped against the wall, but otherwise it was empty and bare. The bed had been stripped and there were no curtains.

"Meg asked Rosie and Jane to start spring-cleaning," Molly murmured. "They must have been in here this morning. They'd have assumed like everyone else that Aidan left early without telling anyone."

"Not much point worrying about fingerprints then," George said. He pulled open the wardrobe door. There were no clothes on the metal clothes-hangers, but a large rucksack stood on the floor and a portfolio of watercolours and sketches was leaning against the wall.

"So he did intend to leave," George said. "He was already packed and ready to go. If he'd left all his stuff where Rosie and Jane would have seen it they'd have called the alarm earlier."

"Is that significant, do you think?"

"I don't know," he said. "It could just be coincidence." He lifted out the rucksack and set it on the bed. "I'm more interested to know why he decided to leave yesterday. He obviously wasn't happy at the Mill, but he'd put up with it for this long. What happened recently to make him change his mind?"

"Ruth thinks it was her fault," Molly said.

George shook his head. "He must have known for ages that she had a crush on him. He didn't have much else of a love life, did he? You'd think he'd have welcomed her advances, not run away from them."

"He was very shy," Molly said.

"Not so shy that he couldn't act as Jimmy Morrissey's snoop on the water pollution story," George said.

"Do you think that's relevant?"

"It's another coincidence, isn't it? If Jimmy was killed to stop the story getting out ... Perhaps somebody recognized Aidan, realized that he was here all those years ago asking questions ..."

"And you think Aidan was murdered, too?"

"I don't know!" he said. "Isn't that the problem? We don't even know where to look."

He picked up a small plastic book, which turned out to be a compact photograph album, and flicked through the pages. Aidan's own family hardly seemed to feature; there was one snap of a middle-aged couple who might have been his parents. The other pictures were all of the Morrisseys. There were Ruth and Caitlin as children, swinging from a climbing frame in a leafy garden, the whole family standing outside the Mill before construction had started, with Jimmy, leaning on his stick, looking miserable. And at the end of the book there was a posed photo of all the *Green Scenes* staff, with Aidan

176

himself looking very young and Christabel Burns looking over her spectacles out at the camera.

George carefully folded up Aidan's belongings and replaced them in the rucksack. He took the album and stood by the window and stared out. The scene was still lit by spotlights, but there was no sense of urgency. A group of men stood caught in the bright light drinking coffee, which they poured from one large thermos. The tide was out. Two men appeared on the shingle carrying a stretcher. The body was lifted on to it and carried unceremoniously away.

George turned back to the photo of Aidan's parents. Porter, presumably, would have arranged for them to be informed. Would they want to come here and see where their son had died? At least they would be spared the indignity of this—the joking policeman who only wanted to be home, the scramble with the stretcher over the shingle. Suddenly the lights went out. The portable generator must have been switched off. The faint hum that had penetrated even the double glazing had stopped. The men cleared the rest of their equipment and left, swearing as they tripped. Then there was silence and the shrouded moonlight reflected in the mud.

"What did Aidan see," George asked almost to himself, "that frightened him so much?"

"Perhaps he wasn't frightened," Molly said. "Or not so much that he decided to leave. Ruth said that he had important things to do. Perhaps he had made up his mind that Jimmy's story had to be told after all. We've only his word that he never read the autobiography. He was painting the jacket, so Jimmy could have consulted him. . . ." She stopped abruptly and fetched the portfolio from the wardrobe, opened it up, and spread the paintings and drawings over the floor.

They saw the jacket design develop from a pencil sketch to a completed painting, from a few grey lines that set the Mill in the landscape to a detailed watercolour. The final version was the last in the series and differed from the rest: in the foreground, lying on the shingle of Salter's Spit, was a mute swan. Its feathers were delicately drawn and it was obviously dead.

16

Ruth woke with the same detachment as she had experienced at James's memorial service. If anything, she was more numb, more clearsighted. She thought nothing could touch her or hurt her again. Is this what it's like to be ill, she wondered, what they mean by a breakdown? She remembered newspaper stories of a battered wife who had killed her husband. After years of putting up with bruises and beatings, she had planned, quite calmly, to stab him. The judge had been unusually sympathetic and had found her guilty only of manslaughter. The defendant was not in her right mind when the crime was committed, he said. The woman had been battered not only by fists but by an excess of emotion. Her calm was unnatural, a reaction, an illness. That's what's happened to me, Ruth thought, a touch melodramatically. I've been emotionally battered, too.

At breakfast Meg tried to fuss over her. The night before Ruth would have welcomed the comfort, but today she could not stand it. She was not even sure the concern was genuine.

"Leave me alone!" she said, too sharply, so Meg looked at her oddly, as if she thought her daughter might be ill or mad, too. "I'm fine. Really. Fine."

I should get away, she thought, but where would I go? She had long ago lost touch with her old friends from Putney. She went to the schoolroom and read Thomas Hardy. The uncompromising bleakness of *Tess* suited her mood.

Molly saw that Ruth needed help but was not sure if it was her place to offer it. Besides, George was making his own demands. He needed reassurance, to be convinced that he wasn't a miserable failure. He felt responsible for Aidan's death, was wallowing rather in self-pity.

"Of course we'll sort out what happened," Molly said. They were in their room with its view of the shore. The tide had already washed away the traces of the police presence the night before: the scuff marks in the sand, the discarded sandwich wrappers. "We're close to it already. You're right about one thing though. We need some facts. We need to know exactly what Jimmy's story was *about*. That's the only way to find out who was implicated."

"The local newspaper might be a place to start," he said, allowing himself to be distracted. "There might be an environment correspondent with specialist knowledge. At least we can look in the files for a story about pollution involving mute swans."

"You're sure the swans are important?" Molly asked.

"Certain. Cathy Cairns had her tale about discharged cooking oil too well prepared. And then there was Aidan's painting. Jimmy hadn't asked for the Mill to be on the jacket because he was specially fond of it. The Mill and the dead swan were there for a purpose. To shock. And as a pointer to the revelation inside." He paused. "I'll get in touch with Nick Lineham's successor at the National Rivers Authority, too. It's their responsibility to monitor water quality. . . ." He left her staring out of the window and went to phone.

The woman on the switchboard at the *Mardon Guardian* said that they kept copies of all past issues and that they were available to the public by appointment. He made an appointment for two-thirty that afternoon.

The conservation officer at the NRA was a woman, young by the sound of her voice, certainly pleasant. "I'll be tied up for most of the day," she said. He had given his name and she had recognized it. She said she had read his papers in the *Ibis*. "I'm free late this afternoon. Why don't you come to the office then?"

George returned to Molly in their room. He was restless and impatient because he could not follow up the leads immediately. What would they do for the rest of the day? In this mood he could not stand meeting the detective, with his cocksure certainty that Jimmy was a depressed lunatic and Aidan an incompetent fool. He had to find an excuse to be away from the Mill.

"Why don't we start from the beginning?" Molly said patiently. "From where Jimmy started."

"What do you mean?" He suspected that she might be trying to humour him. She was jollying him along as if he were a child.

"How did it start?" Molly said. "We know that Jimmy had an anonymous letter that disappeared with the autobiography. Aidan was sent to make enquiries and to meet the correspondent in a pub. He's dead, so we can't ask him what it was about. Then Jimmy had a phone call from the same man and similar arrangements were made. Isn't that what Christabel Burns said?"

"Yes," George said. He considered Molly with respect. He thought she seldom had such clarity of thought. "Christabel said it was all very theatrical. "He'd be carrying a copy of *Green Scenes* under his arm." He paused. "If it was a man . . ."

"If we can find that anonymous correspondent," Molly said, "we'd know what Jimmy knew."

"We've no way of tracing him."

"Wouldn't Jimmy arrange to meet the person in a place he knew? He'd been here before, to Salter's Cottage, to see Hannah. Wouldn't he have suggested that they meet in a pub close to here, somewhere he could find easily?"

"The Dead Dog!" George said. "You think they met there?"

"It's worth a try," she said.

"It's a long shot," he said, "after all this time."

"Surely it's worth asking though. Jimmy would have been a celebrity. His programmes were on the television then. Someone might remember who he was with. The regulars in that place can't have changed for twenty years."

"Yes," he said again slowly, repeating her words. "It's worth a try." He was not really persuaded, but anything was better than waiting there, hiding from Porter in his room. He looked at his watch.

"It's not eleven yet," he said. "It won't be open."

"We can walk," she said. "Slowly."

The hamlet of Markham Law was a gathering of unimposing buildings on the crossroads between the main road to Mardon and the lane to the Mill. On the lane there was a terrace of single-storey cottages with long front gardens separated from the road by a white-washed wall, and nearer the coast two pairs of shabby semi-detached houses. But for the unkempt gardens and the peeling paintwork they would not have been out of place in a suburban street. The Dead Dog was on the main road opposite a big farmhouse with gaping empty barns and an overgrown farmyard.

As George and Molly approached the crossroads an elderly man came out of one of the cottages and walked slowly but purposefully ahead of them, unbothered by the snow still lying on the road. He knocked on the door of the pub with his walking stick and yelled angrily through the letter box that it was bloody cold here and why couldn't Cedric pull his finger out. When they caught up with him there was the sound of bolts being pulled back and the door was opened.

Inside it seemed dark and warm. Instead of the calor

heater there was a fire banked up in a small grate. The old man sat in the chair nearest to it and shouted to Cedric to be served. He glared at the Palmer-Joneses as if challenging them to complain about his taking first turn.

"I'll pay for that," George said. Molly had sat on a stool near the bar. The man turned to him, his eyes glittering greedily. Usually you only got fools like that in the summer, fools who'd stand the drinks all night for what they'd call local colour. He'd give this chap all the local colour he wanted so long as the beer kept coming. Cedric poured a pint of mild, which George delivered to the old man by the fire. He nodded and gave an unpleasant grimace that was the nearest he could come to a smile.

"Staying at the Mill, are you?" he said. Most of the fools who bought him drinks stayed there.

George nodded, took a chair beside the old man.

"I'd get out of that place while you can!" the old man said, licking the froth from his lips. "I heard they lost another one, washed up by the tide. There must be something about it that makes folks feel like topping their selves."

"He was drowned," George said. "They think it was an accident. He was cut off on Salter's Spit."

"Is that what Reg Porter says?"

George nodded.

"Well, what could you expect from a bloke like that?"

"You don't think it's likely then?"

"Not unless the chap who drowned was a fool."

George was pleased that someone else shared his theory that Aidan's death wasn't an accident, but this was hardly conclusive. The old man would say anything just to be contrary.

"Why do you say that?" he asked.

The old man shook his head as if it were obvious to anyone but a lunatic. For a moment George thought he

183

would refuse to answer. "Smallest tide of the year this week," he said at last. "Even if you got cut off you'd be able to walk back. If you wanted, like."

There was a silence while he drank his beer. All the whorls and lines that formed his fingerprints were stained brown and his nails were filthy. He smelled faintly of manure and tobacco.

"But if he'd slipped," George said, "the currents could have taken him out."

"Oh aye." The old man spoke dismissively. "Like I said, if he was a fool, anything could have happened." He drained his glass noisily.

"Did you know Mr. Morrissey?"

The old man gave a reluctant nod of his head. He thought he had done enough now to pay for one pint of beer. "Aye," he said pointedly. "He was always one to stand his round."

"Did he come here often?"

The old man gave a loud cackle. "When his old lady would let him out. Or when he ran away from her. She came in here one dinner-time spitting blood and dragged him back as if he were a lad. Don't know why he put up with it." He looked slyly to the bar where Molly was drinking her beer. "Never married myself," he said. "Couldn't see the point."

"It must have been a shock when he bought the Mill," George persisted. "It must have caused a bit of a stir locally."

The man sniggered as if to admit surprise was a weakness. *Nothing* could shock him.

"Oh aye," he said. "It had the old biddies 'round here chattering like a flock of hens on lay. They'd all seen him on the telly. You'd a thought he was royalty when he first came in."

"When was that?" George asked.

"What?" He was concentrating on his empty glass as if will power alone could refill it. He looked at George dolefully, then returned his stare to the glass. George got to his feet and went to the bar. Cedric poured another pint of mild without a word.

"When did James Morrissey first come to Markham Law?" George asked again.

"I don't know," the old man said unhelpfully. "When he first moved to the Mill, I suppose. When was that, Ced? Easter '92?"

"No," Cedric said, then realized he had interrupted and began to blush. "I saw him before that."

"Oh?" George said casually. "Was he a regular visitor to the area, then? Is that how he came to buy the Mill?"

"Not regular," Cedric said. "You wouldn't call it regular." There was a pleasure in being taken seriously by this gentleman with the cultivated voice. "He came in once with Phil Cairns."

"Oh?" George said again, trying to sound interested. Phil Cairns couldn't have been the anonymous correspondent. What would have been the point? Jimmy could have recognized him as soon as they met.

"Yes," said Cedric with his precise, rather fussy voice. "Mr. Morrissey was married to Mrs. Cairns years ago and he came up to see Hannah, his daughter. He and Phil always seemed friendly enough."

"Really?" George said, as if it were news. "Was that the only time he came in before he bought the Mill?"

"No," Cedric said definitely. "He came in one other time. I remember because it was the weekend his lass died, the lass from Salter's Cottage." His expression became mournful again. Before Caitlin had become the object of his dreams, Hannah had starred in his fantasies. He still remembered her in her school uniform climbing out of the bus that dropped her outside the pub.

"Was she with him that weekend?" Molly asked sympathetically. "Did he bring her here? You must have been one of the last people to see her."

"No," Cedric said, sad that he could not claim that

185

distinction. "She never came in here. Her mother didn't like it. She was still under age, you see."

"Right." There was a silence while Molly tried to think of some pretext for asking if Jimmy had been with anyone else on that occasion. Cedric interrupted her deliberations.

"He was with some other chap," he said. "I'd never seen him before."

"That's some memory you've got!" Molly said. He glowed with the unaccustomed praise. He could not resist the temptation to show off.

"Mr. Morrissey was here first," he said. "You could tell he was waiting for someone. He was sitting where he could see the door and looked up every time someone came in."

"Almost photographic!" she said admiringly. "I bet you can tell me exactly what the man looked like."

Cedric screwed up his face in concentration.

"He was middle-aged," he said. "Fifty-odd. Big build. Sandy hair."

"What was he wearing?" Molly asked.

"Suit and tie," Cedric said immediately. "As if he'd dressed up specially for meeting Mr. Morrissey. Though I must say the suit looked as if it had seen better days. Not the height of fashion, if you know what I mean. What I'd call a wedding and funeral outfit."

"So he wasn't the sort of person who'd normally wear a suit," Molly said. "He wouldn't wear one for work, for example."

"No," he said, pleased that she'd understood. "That's exactly what I mean."

"Well!" she said. "To come up with all that detail after such a long time. I am impressed."

"I probably wouldn't have remembered," he said modestly, "if it wasn't the weekend Hannah died."

Molly pushed forward her empty glass and he filled it. His face lit up.

"I can remember something else!" he said. "The man

was carrying a copy of *Green Scenes*, you know, the conservation magazine. I was interested in horticulture then and I used to take it myself. . . ." His voice faded as he recalled a more optimistic time. There was a pause and he continued. "Mr. Morrissey ran the magazine," he said. "It seemed a peculiar coincidence."

"Yes," Molly said cheerfully. "I can see that it would. Have one yourself," she said, handing him a five-pound note. She watched carefully as he poured orange juice into a glass. "I don't suppose you've seen that chap again?"

This time he was less certain. "I don't know, I'm not sure." He wanted to impress her again. "You know, I think I might have seen him," he said. "Someone came in quite recently and I thought their face was familiar. But I can't for the life of me think who it might have been." He looked at her pitifully, sorry to disappoint her.

Two men in suits came into the lounge then with a lot of noise, banging the door, shouting to each other in loud Midlands accents. Molly guessed they were reps, early perhaps for a meeting in Mardon. Cedric went through to serve them and across the bar Molly heard them order whisky "to keep out the cold." She set down her empty glass and climbed off the stool. She wanted to leave while Cedric was distracted. She thought he was so lonely that he would want to prolong the conversation, might even invent stories about Jimmy Morrissey to gain their attention. As it was she was convinced he had told them the truth. George stopped at the door and looked at the old man by the hearth, intending to say goodbye to him, but he turned his back to them deliberately and spat into the fire.

There had been no fresh snow overnight, but it was still too cold for a thaw and in the lane where there had been little traffic it still lay on the road. Everywhere was unnaturally quiet. There was no birdsong, no distant sound of cars or machinery, only the dense thud of their feet compacting the frozen snow. George walked quickly, already making plans for the afternoon.

"Well?" Molly said, scampering to keep up with him. She was annoyed because he did not seem more pleased. "Didn't I say it was worth a try? At least we've got one fact now. We know that Jimmy did meet his anonymous correspondent in the pub and we know what he looked like."

"It doesn't help much though, does it?" George said. "The description doesn't tie in with anyone at the Mill." He must have realized how churlish he sounded because he added: "Look, it was a good idea and you handled that barman splendidly, but I don't see that it takes us very far forward."

He half expected her then to accuse him of being patronizing, but she said nothing. She was thinking that somewhere, recently, she had seen someone who fitted Cedric's description of the stranger in the Dead Dog. But like Cedric she could not quite place him. She was to worry at it for the rest of the day, but the elusive memory that had seemed so within her grasp on the walk back from the pub would escape her completely, so she had to give up the struggle.

In the garden of the Mill Timothy in Wellingtons and duffel coat was aimlessly shying snowballs at a small, round snowman. Molly thought that he must have been waiting for them. As they approached he continued the repeated action of stooping to collect the snow, crushing it between chilled red fingers, and flinging the ball away from him, but he watched them intently from the corner of his eye, waiting, she thought, for the right time to make his move. He waited until they were on the porch, taking off their boots, then he wiped his wet hands on his trousers and joined them, too.

"I've got something to show you," he blurted out to George. He had his hand on the man's elbow to make sure of his attention. "There's something you should see."

George was mentally preparing his questions for the afternoon's interviews and was irritated by the interruption.

"I've seen your snowman," he said, trying to sound kind. "It's very nice."

"No!" Timothy said. "It's not that. Em made that. It's in the schoolroom. Come and see."

George sighed unobtrusively. He supposed he would have to go along to see the model or the painting, whatever masterpiece the boy thought he had created. Molly would only make a fuss if he refused. He was saved, however, by the lunch bell, a large ship's bell that hung in the lobby and that Jane was ringing by the string attached to its clapper.

"Later," he said. "Remind me to look at it later."

But after lunch he was worried that they would miss the appointment at the local newspaper office and he put the boy off again.

17

The offices of the *Mardon Guardian* were dusty and old-fashioned. The editor seemed to have an aversion to all modern technology and past editions of the newspaper were kept not on micro-film but in files on shelves in a long, windowless room. There was one large desk of the sort found in reference libraries and the whole procedure was supervised by a strict woman with horn-rimmed spectacles and a peculiar bouffant hair-style that might have been fashionable in the nineteen-fifties. There had always been stories, Molly remembered, of insects breeding inside the lacquered thatch, and while George read steadily through the newspapers she looked with fascination at the construction, which seemed to stay in place without pins or clips, imagining an ants' nest underneath.

The newspaper was weekly and the story of the swans took the front-page headlines on and off over a period of a couple of months during the spring before Hannah's death. "Massacre" said one, and even allowing for a small newspaper's natural hype, George thought the incident must have been more serious than Cathy Cairns had led him to believe. There was more here, surely, than a couple of swans with plumage damaged by cooking oil. The columns that followed were high on melodrama but short on facts. There

190

were no numbers of casualties, though there was one reference to the danger that "the whole of the River Marr's famous swan population could be wiped out."

A grainy photograph in a later edition showed a line of volunteers in waders passing the distressed birds down a human chain to the bank. There, apparently, they were cleaned and cared for by the RSPCA in an animal rescue centre until they were fit to be released. Again, no figures were given for the number of birds that survived this treatment, though there was an interview with an RSPCA inspector who said that the incident would be a test for the new National Rivers Authority. "We expect them to find the culprit quickly and for a prosecution to follow," he said. "It's in the spirit of the new act that the polluter should pay."

"It did hit the national press," Molly said. "I remember now. May '91. We were on holiday with Jonathan, Mary, and the kids in Suffolk and it rained all week. There were pictures of the rescue on the television news. Jonathan was very sniffy about the expert they got to comment."

Jonathan, their son, was inclined to be sniffy about many things.

"Yes!" George said. "Then there was the piece in the business section of the *Observer*, speculating whether Mardon Wools would profit from the public's sympathy for the swans, or whether its image would suffer through being associated with such a misfortune. Why didn't we remember before?"

"Old age I expect," Molly said cheerfully. "It was the picture that triggered my memory. And then the story went out of the news so quickly."

In the local paper, too, it seemed, the story had soon faded into oblivion, overtaken by news of more redundancies from the tannery and a visit by the Princess of Wales to open a new wing in the general hospital. It was not until the autumn of the same year that the case had come to court and then it had warranted only one column on an inside page. The swan population had recovered, apparently, and without pictures of dead and dying birds the story had lost its impact. The case had been brought by the National Rivers Authority under the Water Resources Act against a fast-food restaurant and take-away outlet known as the Flying Fish. The owner had admitted emptying his fryers into the drainage system but claimed that he had not been aware that the oil would find its way into the river.

"It could happen to anyone," he had said.

The magistrate had called for more education for local catering businesses and householders and ordered the owner of the Flying Fish to pay a five-hundred-pound fine.

That was the end of it. George and Molly split between them the work of checking intervening copies of the newspaper, but there was no further reference to water pollution in the Marr or dying swans.

"Is that it then?" Molly said. "Is that the story Jimmy was working on?"

"In a way," he said. "But, don't you see, there's been a cover-up? The chap from the chip shop probably *did* flush waste cooking oil down his drains and it might have had some effect, but it didn't cause the extensive damage to the birds reported in the paper. He was made a scapegoat. Otherwise, why would Nick Lineham disappear to Africa and why would Jimmy Morrissey be so keen on getting hold of his notes? Lineham must have sampled the water near the outfall where the swans were feeding. He must have known who the real polluter was."

"You know, too, don't you?" she said.

"Oh, I know," he said, and he explained his suspicions to her in full, whispering to escape the disapproving gaze of the horn-rimmed librarian. "But I've no

192

proof at all. And I still can't quite believe that it had anything to do with Jimmy Morrissey's death."

They left the newspaper office and went out into the cold, grey afternoon.

"We'll walk, shall we?" George said. He did not want to face Mardon's unfathomable one-way system in the car and he thought the walk would clear his thoughts. He could see why Jimmy had dropped the story of the river's pollution after Hannah's death and why he had considered it important enough to take up again when he needed to restore his faith in himself. He could see where Aidan Moore fitted into it all. But he could not reconcile his knowledge of the people involved with cold-blooded murders. Molly, too, was silent. As she tried to make sense of George's suspicions, the man Cedric had described in the pub that morning came again fleetingly into her mind. She knew she had seen him but had no idea where they had met.

The National Rivers Authority had a smart office in a small block on the other side of the river from the town centre, close to the houses where Grace Sharland lived. They crossed the Marr by a narrow foot bridge and in the darkening gloom saw the white shapes of swans farther upstream. George stopped for a moment to look at them and wondered if it was only in his imagination that they seemed unusually sluggish.

"You won't want me there while you talk to the conservation officer," Molly said suddenly. "I'll see if Grace Sharland's at home and try to surprise her with the information that we know she took Jimmy to the Linehams' house." If anyone knows what was going on, she thought, it will be Grace. She's the one who links it all together.

"Won't she be at work?"

"I don't know," Molly said. "She finished early on

the day I visited her before. Perhaps she works some sort of shift or flexi-time."

But he hardly seemed to be listening and she walked off without trying to explain that she felt Grace had been under so much strain that she might not even have been at work.

The NRA had the ground floor of the office block that was built of yellow, cheese-coloured stone with brightly painted fittings. It looked as if it had been made from a child's construction kit. Inside there was the usual jungle of shiny-leaved plants and a secretary with a hang-dog expression who said that Sue wasn't back yet actually from her meeting, but she definitely was expecting him and would he like to take a seat?

He sat. There was a low table with some newspapers and magazines and he picked up a recent copy of *Green Scenes*. He had stopped subscribing more than a year before and it seemed to him now that the publication was even more bland and undemanding than it had been then. There was a feature on birdwatching holidays, an article entitled: "A Day in the Life of an Environmentally Sensitive Gamekeeper," and an interview with the new secretary of state for the environment that concentrated on the interior decoration of his home and his love of King Charles spaniels. He thought Jimmy Morrissey must be turning in his grave. Had he seen these recent issues? George wondered. That alone would have provoked him to take a stand on the pollution question. He must have felt some responsibility for his brainchild's decline into mediocrity.

The heavy outside door with its red, lollipop-shaped handles was swung open and a young woman came in. She was carrying a briefcase and a pile of files and seemed flustered. She exchanged a word with the secretary and joined him. "Mr. Palmer-Jones!" she said. "I'm so sorry to be late. Do come in!"

He followed her to her office, muttering that it was quite all right, but the sight of her had depressed him. He had hoped for someone organized, someone who could give him the facts he needed in a clear and orderly way, and she gave only an impression of disorder with her rushing and her armful of tatty files and the mud on her shoes. And she seemed so young to him, hardly more than a child.

Perhaps because of that, when she sat behind her desk and asked him how she could help him, he told her the truth. He thought there would be no danger in telling her what he wanted. She seemed so young and inexperienced that she would not grasp the implication of it or see how serious a matter it was.

"It's rather sensitive," he said. "I'd like to ask some questions about Nicholas Lineham, your predecessor. I think it's possible that he removed sensitive information from this office and kept it at home. Did you meet him before he went to Africa?"

"No," she said. "He only gave a month's statutory notice and left even more quickly than that in the end because he had holiday owing to him. There was quite a gap before I started." She looked at him carefully. Her face was still flushed after hurrying to get there. "As I said on the phone, I know your reputation and I'm flattered that you think I can help, but you do realize that I have to know what this is all about before I answer any more questions."

He saw then that he had underestimated her.

"It's very complicated," he said slowly.

"You'd better spell it out then," she said with some sarcasm, "so I can understand."

He felt awkward. This wasn't going as he had planned.

"Do you know why Mr. Lineham left the authority so suddenly?" he asked.

"I don't think there's any mystery about it," she said.

"He'd been interested in working in Africa for ages and the chance came up, so he jumped at it."

"He was able to jump at it," George said, "because he was paid a considerable sum of money."

"What are you saying?"

"I believe he was working on a water pollution incident," George said. "He'd reached certain conclusions about the nature of the pollution, had probably identified the likely polluter. Somebody thought it would be more convenient if his findings weren't made public. As you say, he'd always been fascinated by Africa, but he was reluctant to give up the security of a permanent job with the NRA. Somebody gave him a little extra persuasion to go."

"I don't understand why you're interested. After all this time." He had her full attention. She looked out at him through a wildly permed fringe.

"Jimmy Morrissey, the local naturalist, was writing his autobiography," George said. "I believe that he was approached with information about the pollution incident at the time it occurred, but for a number of personal reasons he didn't follow it up. Later he regretted it. It wasn't a simple case, you see. There were implications of corruption. He wanted to use the autobiography to put the record straight, and, less altruistically, to signal his return to centre stage in conservation matters. I know that he went to the Linehams' house and removed papers and records that had been kept there." He paused. "You may have seen on the news that since then Jimmy Morrissey has died. The police think he committed suicide, but I don't think that's true. You see, all the notes and the draft autobiography have disappeared."

"You think he was murdered?" she said calmly. He nodded, impressed. "How do you think I can help you?"

"We need the information that Nick Lineham had put

196

together to prepare his case. After all this time it's the only way to track down the polluter."

"I don't see how that's possible if he took all the files away with him."

"The office is computerized. Wouldn't a copy of all that material be kept on disc?"

"It probably would now," she said. "But you have to realize that then the whole set-up was new. The NRA was working from a couple of rooms in the old water-company building. Staff were still being appointed. I don't think it was terribly efficient."

"Lineham must have had a boss," George said, "someone who would assign him work and follow up what he was doing."

"Oh, he had a boss," she said. "Of sorts. He was still here when I started. An old water-company scientist by the name of Jack Clough was transferred to the NRA to get him out of the way. Or because someone owed him a favour. There wasn't any other reason I could see for putting him in any position of responsibility." She pushed her fringe back from her eyes angrily. "He started drinking in his office at eleven in the morning, took three-hour lunch breaks in the Queen's Head, and was pissed as a fart by the time everyone else went home. He might have had a useful contribution to make when he was sober, but I wouldn't know. I never saw him in that state. He was persuaded to take early retirement six months after I started here."

"All the same," George said, "he might have had some idea what Lineham was up to. It would be worth talking to him."

"Perhaps it would have been," she said. "Though I doubt it. But he won't be any use to you now. His liver finally admitted defeat and he died last year."

"There wouldn't be any records that would have been passed on to the person taking over from him?"

She shook her head. "You must be joking. All they

197

found in his filing cabinet were enough empty Scotch bottles to fill Sainsbury's bottle bank."

"What about a secretary? Someone who did Lineham's typing and filing and took messages for him. Would she be able to help?"

"It's certainly possible. Nick's secretary is still working here. She's been here longer than any of us. She started with the place. Just wait there and I'll fetch her."

She returned with a nervous, middle-aged woman who hovered uncertainly just inside the door.

"Joyce, this is Mr. Palmer-Jones," she said. "He's doing some research, but our records from the early days aren't as good as they might be. We wondered if you might be able to help. Do you remember what Nick was working on just before he left?"

Joyce wanted to help them. She screwed up her face in concentration and muttered to herself, but it was clear from the beginning that she would be no use. George had known many typists like her. They could type flawlessly the work set in front of them but would have no idea at the end what the letter was about or even if it made sense.

"I'm sorry," Joyce said. "I'm really sorry." Then wretchedly: "I think there was something with numbers on it. A printout had come from the lab. Nick was very excited about it and asked me to type it up for the file. I can picture a table of numbers on the paper, but I can't remember what it was about."

When she had left the room George said, "Does that mean anything to you?"

She shrugged. "Not really. We send water samples to our own lab for analysis. If it's too complex for them to deal with, we have experts in local universities who help. But the lab copes with most things. I suppose that was what it was about."

"And if you discovered an unusual level of a toxic chemical in the water, what would be the procedure then?"

"We'd try to trace where it came from."

"Is that easy?"

"That depends on the chemical and the geographical area. Where there isn't much industry you can do it almost by a process of elimination."

He hesitated, then decided that he had taken her into his confidence so far that there was little to be lost by sharing his suspicions.

"Do you remember a court case in the autumn, three years ago? A chip-shop owner was prosecuted for discharging cooking oil into the River Marr."

"I remember reading about it when I arrived. It happened in the interim between me and Nick."

"Did anything about it seem unusual?"

"Yes," she said slowly. "I got a transcript of the case because it was one of the first prosecutions to be taken under the new act. I thought at the time that the prosecution solicitor was guilty of dreadful exaggeration. He didn't give any figures, but he gave the impression that all the wildlife on the River Marr was at risk. One discharge of cooking oil wouldn't have caused all that damage. Not on its own."

"Yes," he said. "That's what I thought."

"You think there was something else in the water?" she demanded. "Something that Nick had discovered? But he was shipped off to Africa before he could make a fuss."

"Yes," he said. "I think it happened rather like that."

"But what was the other pollutant?" she asked. "Where did it come from?"

He paused again.

"Is there anything used in the manufacture of knitwear that could be the culprit?" he asked.

She looked up sharply. "You're thinking of Mardon Wools?"

He nodded.

"That would put the cat among the pigeons, wouldn't it?" she said. "Mardon Wools killing off the bird that is

199

internationally recognized as their logo. Especially after they've spent thousands on giving themselves a green image."

"It would certainly give the company a motive for covering up the incident," George agreed. "Is there anything used in the manufacturing process that could be to blame?"

"I'm not sure without checking," she said. "But I can look it up." She took down a number of reference books from the aluminium shelves against the wall and spread them on the desk around her. George waited impatiently. He wished he could help but knew he would only get in the way. She worked quickly, moving from one book to another, flicking through the pages and writing notes in a fast, tight script.

"That's it!" she said at last, closing all the books with a flourish. "There's a knitwear drying agent called tetrachloroethylene, known as TCE. Used for dry cleaning, too. The maximum amount allowed in water for human consumption is ten microgrammes per litre."

"What would its effect be on the swans?"

"It would act as a degreaser—rather like the cooking oil, I suppose. It would cause the birds to look bedraggled, make them lose their waterproofing, become less resistant to cold and disease."

"Is there any way of finding out if Mardon Wools uses this chemical?" he said.

"I could ask them."

"No," he said slowly. "I don't think that would be a good idea at this stage. Not yet."

"I could do a discreet investigation," she said. "Take some samples from their outflow. Make it seem like a routine visit."

"Yes," he said. "Why don't you do that?"

He stood to go but hesitated. "We found a dead swan on the shore near Markham Mill yesterday," he said. "It would be interesting to find out if that's just a coincidence, or if there's been a recent, perhaps more minor, contamination of the river."

"I'll check," she said. "You can leave it to me."

He left her office quite confident that he could.

18

When Molly walked down the street to Grace Sharland's home it was dark enough for the lights to be on in all the houses but most of the curtains were still not drawn. Even from a distance she could see that the visit would not be wasted. The light was on in the first-floor sitting room and as she drew nearer she saw the silhouettes of two people in the room. Grace and an older man.

They stood facing each other and although the double glazing prevented Molly from hearing what was being said, they were obviously in the middle of a heated argument. With the light behind them Molly could see every gesture: Grace's mouth open to scream, the man, who with sandy red hair must surely have been her father, shaking his head in an elaborate mime of impatience. Even if they had not been so preoccupied they would not have made out Molly in the dusk, and when she rang the door bell they were shocked and stood still for a moment, caught like a photograph, framed, and when the door swung open Molly could see him, standing on the stairs behind her.

"I'm sorry to disturb you," Molly said lamely. "I was just passing . . ."

"Come in!" Grace said desperately. "Come in. I was going to phone you anyway. There's something you need to know." Then with an air of defiance: "Father, this is Mrs. Palmer-Jones. I explained that she'd been to see me."

"I don't think this is a good idea, Grace," he said quietly. He wore an open-necked shirt, a jersey, and jeans and looked too young, Molly thought, to be retired.

"I bet you don't," she said, beside herself with emotion. "I bet you don't."

"If you're busy I could always come back," Molly said, but she did not move.

"Grace!" the man pleaded. "Think about this. Think what you're doing."

"I've thought of nothing else all night," she said, "since I heard that Aidan Moore was drowned. If I'd spoken out before it might never have happened."

He said nothing. He must have realized that he would not persuade her. He turned and walked back up the stairs, followed by Grace and Molly. After the fury of the argument the silence was shocking. They sat on the richly coloured chairs staring at each other, unsure of where to start.

Grace breathed deeply and tried to regain control. "Did you know that my father is a director of Mardon Wools?" she said at last.

Molly nodded.

"Not active any more," he said sharply.

"The power behind the throne," she said.

She paused and started again more calmly. "When you were here last I told you that I felt Jimmy had used me."

"Yes," Molly said. "I remember."

"That feeling had nothing to do with the fact that he fancied himself in love with me," Grace said. "He wanted to know about Mardon Wools and Father."

"And Nick," Molly said. "I expect he was interested in Nick, too."

"Oh," Grace said bitterly, "that was a bonus. He hadn't realized I'd been engaged to Nick until I told him. He must have thought Christmas had come early that day. It gave him a connection, you see, between the NRA and my father. That was what he was looking for all along."

Sharland leaned forward with his hands on his knees. "It's not as bad as it seems," he said. "There was no damage done. Not really. It was a lot of fuss about nothing."

"Father!" Grace screamed, and Molly thought this must be a rerun of the argument she had witnessed through the window. "Two men have died. That's not a fuss about nothing."

"Accidents," he said. "Or suicide. That's what the coroner thought."

"Oh, for Christ's sake," she shouted. "Take your head out of the sand."

There was another silence. Grace got up and jerked the curtains together, then returned to her seat. They waited for her to speak.

"You'll have to tell someone," she shouted at her father. The hysteria had gone and she spoke with a quiet intensity, willing him to agree with her. "There'll be no peace for either of us if you try to keep it to yourself." Then when there was no response: "If you don't talk about it I'll go to the police myself."

Molly intervened diffidently. "It might look better, Mr. Sharland, if it came from you."

"Yes," he said. "I suppose I can see that." He turned to his daughter. "I wanted the business to be a success for you," he said. "It was a sort of security. It was all I had to pass on to you."

"Don't give me that crap," she said. "You always were an ambitious bastard, Dad. You always were a fighter."

"No," he protested. "Really. I thought all the bad publicity would reflect on you. I've only ever thought of your happiness."

"That's bullshit," she said, "and you know it. Were

204

you thinking of my happiness when you broke up my engagement?"

"He wasn't worth it," Sharland said. "He wasn't good enough for you. If he'd cared for you, it wouldn't have been possible to buy him off."

"No," she said. "I don't suppose he was much good, but that's not why you did it, is it, Dad? You sent him to the other side of the world to save your bloody business. Don't expect me to thank you for that."

There was another hostile silence.

"I'm afraid I'm a little confused," Molly said. "I don't want to interfere, but perhaps you could explain . . ."

"Go on," Grace said bitterly. "Why don't you do that, Dad? I could do with some explanation myself."

He sat still for a moment and then started speaking. His voice was detached and formal. He might have been presenting a report to shareholders.

"At the end of the eighties the company decided that it needed a new image," he said. "We were known for quality, but there was a danger, we felt, that as our customers got older we would lose a share of a potential growing market. Younger people were more affluent during that time of boom and we needed to attract them and still maintain our reputation for quality. We employed a new designer, Cathy Morrissey. Her work was bold and innovative. Perhaps even more importantly her husband was a famous conservationist and her name had just the image we wanted. It represented concern for the environment, value for money, commitment to our customers. The new range was successful right from the start."

He paused and collected his thoughts. "In 1989 we decided to take the concept further and a major sponsorship deal with one of the big wildlife charities was arranged. It was heavily promoted. There was a television and poster campaign. Again Cathy designed the clothes in the new range."

He looked at Molly. "This is all background to the incident that Grace thinks I should make public, but it explains why we took it so seriously at the time. We had invested thousands of pounds in advertising and donations to wildlife charities in promoting Mardon Wools as a concerned and environmentally sensitive company."

"Yes," Molly said. "I see that."

"Then there was an unfortunate accident," he said. "An individual error led to a quantity of degreasing agent being released into the river. The timing could not have been worse. We had just signed a new contract with the International Wildlife Fund. Exposure would not only have been an embarrassment to us but to them."

"Did they ever know about the pollution?" Molly asked.

"Of course not," he said, shocked. "What use would there be in telling them?"

"Besides," Grace added, "they might have pulled out of the deal, mightn't they? That would never have done. Someone could have started asking why."

He seemed annoyed by the interruption and returned to his lecture. "The timing was unfortunate for a second reason. It coincided with water privatization. The press was full of scare stories that the NRA would not be able to regulate the industry adequately. Any story of pollution would have been headline news. Our claim to be an environmentally friendly company would have made us an even greater target."

"I understand that," Molly said. "What did you do about the spill?"

"Nothing at first," Sharland said. "Phil Cairns, our managing director, made sure that the leak into the river was stopped as soon as we discovered what was going on. He's a sound man, Phil. And we tried to limit the news of it to as few people in the works as possible. But none of us thought it would cause much damage."

206

"Only there was damage, wasn't there, Dad?" Grace said. "And it couldn't have been worse. It wasn't just a few fish floating to the surface. Nothing as unobtrusive as that. It was the famous Mardon swans. And perhaps you know, Mrs. Palmer-Jones, that the swan's embroidered on every garment that leaves the factory, and when the punters come in their coaches to look around the works it's the swans that they really want to see. So it was bloody embarrassing all 'round."

"It was dreadful," Sharland said. "Not just embarrassing. I hated to see the swans like that, in such distress. I was as moved as everyone else. But by that time the damage had been done. It would have done nothing to save the swans to make our responsibility public."

"You must have known you'd be found out eventually," Molly said quietly.

"No," he said. "Perhaps it was naive, but really I never thought we'd be discovered. I should have known, I suppose, that the NRA would have sophisticated sampling techniques though it was a new body and we didn't know how it would operate. No, I thought if we kept our heads down, we'd get away with it. There'd been an incident the month before when the cooking oil had been blamed. I hoped, I suppose, that no one would look any further than that."

"But Nick looked further than that, didn't he, Dad?" Grace said. "Nick, the comprehensive boy who you'd never had a good word for. He tested the river water and found traces of TCE—twice the amount considered safe for human consumption. And then he came to the factory and in a bore hole there he found massive readings."

"What happened then?" Molly asked.

"Lineham came to the factory and spoke to Phil Cairns," Sharland said. "He wanted to check that we'd stopped the leak. It wasn't easy for Phil. He's well known locally as something of a conservationist. If the thing had been made public it would have been a personal embarrassment for him besides the damage to the company."

"So that's why you did it, Dad, is it?" Grace said, her voice loaded with sarcasm. "Out of the kindness of your heart. To stop poor old Phil Cairns being publicly humiliated. Nothing to do, I suppose, with profit, with selling more over-priced sweaters."

"The factory employs more than a hundred people," he said, provoked at last to anger. "I had a responsibility to them, too. The town's not as prosperous as it was. Where would they all find work?"

"What *did* you do?" Molly asked.

"I had the lad in and talked to him," Sharland said. "It wasn't hard to make him see sense. Grace had told me that he'd been approached by those people in Africa and he was keen on the idea of working there. She thought it was love that kept him here . . ." His sarcasm matched hers. "But love had nothing to do with it. He was a working-class lad with no security behind him. Bright, but even graduates aren't guaranteed a job these days. He didn't want to leave the NRA with no money to fall back on."

"So you paid him off, didn't you, Dad? You paid him to keep his mouth shut?"

"I gave my daughter's fiancé a gift," he said. "What could be more natural than that? He went off like a shot, engaged or not, when he had the chance. Of course once he resigned from the NRA he'd have no responsibility to follow the case through."

"And there was no one else to take it on," Molly said, almost to herself.

"Of course there was no one else to take it on," Grace said. "His boss was an alcoholic who hardly knew what day of the week it was, and it was months before they appointed someone else to replace Nick. Besides, how could anyone guess what he was working on? You suggested he take all his files out of the office, didn't you, Dad?"

208

"I suggested he destroy them all," Sharland said angrily, "and if he'd done as he was told we wouldn't be in this mess now."

"You must have thought you were safe then and it was all over," Molly said.

"Of course I did. I thought it was all sorted. Lineham disappeared off to Africa leaving Grace a pretty little note saying he wasn't ready to settle down. The RSPCA got a load of free publicity when they put the swans they'd cleaned up back into the river. The fish-and-chip shop owner was charged with pollution because of the previous incident and everyone assumed that the charges referred to the later time, too. I thought I could go back to making jerseys and keeping our heads above water."

"When did you realize that Jimmy Morrissey was suspicious about the incident?"

"It was around the time of the accident when his daughter was killed. I was bloody furious. I thought at first that Cathy had been telling tales, but apparently it wasn't that."

"How did you find out he was interested in the story?"

"Phil Cairns told me. Morrissey was at their cottage that day to pick up his daughter and he started asking questions about TCE. Some trouble-maker with a grudge in the factory had put him on to it apparently. It was obvious by then that he'd been sneaking around and he'd already dug up most of the story. Phil told him that the problem was sorted and that it wouldn't happen again, but that wasn't good enough for Jimmy Morrissey." Sharland paused. "Phil phoned me that evening as soon as they left for London. He was in a terrible state about it." He hesitated again. "We didn't know then about the accident. I only heard about that later on the radio."

There was a silence.

"Are you sure," Grace said uncomfortably, afraid almost to voice her suspicions, "that it was an accident?"

"What do you mean?"

"It seems a bloody strange coincidence. Perhaps someone tried to frighten Jimmy off the case and killed the girl by mistake."

"No," he said deliberately. "I've told you before. I didn't kill the girl and I didn't kill Jimmy Morrissey. What sort of monster do you take me for?" He looked at her with hurt and angry eyes. "If you want to know the truth you should talk to Cathy Cairns. They had a blazing row that night about the story. She tried to persuade him that it wouldn't be in anyone's interest to publish it. He worked himself up into a state of righteous indignation, accused her of censorship and trying to gag him, and drove off like a maniac.

"He couldn't wait, he said, to get south to have the thing written. It was his pride and impatience that killed his daughter. He couldn't blame anyone else for it."

"So the story was never printed," Molly said.

"No," Grace said. "He couldn't face it. He saw it as a matter of principle, but in the end his personal feelings won. He couldn't give Cathy any more grief. He'd killed her daughter. Even Jimmy Morrissey realized it wasn't the time to drag her husband's reputation into the mud."

But he hadn't had any qualms about ruining Cathy and Phil's reputation before the accident, Molly thought. When he'd told Ruth that she and Hannah must stay friends even if the grown-ups fell out, he hadn't meant that he intended to leave Meg but that Cathy would probably never forgive him for making the incident at Mardon Wools public.

"Did you realize that Aidan Moore had been in the area before that, asking questions on Jimmy's behalf?" Molly asked.

Sharland shook his head. "I'd never heard of the man

210

until Grace came storming up to my house in the middle of the night accusing me of murdering him."

"I wasn't," Grace said awkwardly. "Not really. I had to know . . . "

"It must have been a shock when Jimmy Morrissey bought Markham Mill," Molly said.

"It was a nightmare," Sharland said. "You can imagine all the publicity when the place opened. The papers were full of what a great man he was and how lucky we were to have him on our doorstep."

"And then you found out that I was nursing him," Grace interrupted. "I wondered why you were so interested when you found out he was a patient. I should have realized you weren't just attracted because he was famous." She hesitated. "And I suggested that he should write his autobiography," she said. "I thought that would be a way back to work for him. It's ironic, isn't it? If you'd taken me into your confidence then perhaps I would have advised him that it wasn't a good idea."

"Would you?" he asked. "Would you have done that?"

There was a silence and she gave a shrug. "Probably not," she said. "Jimmy told me about the chemical leak and the swans and I thought the whole story stank. I didn't see why it shouldn't come out into the open."

"Even if it meant I was ruined?"

"Come off it, Dad!" she said. "You wouldn't be ruined. You've always made sure your investments were widely spread. If Mardon Wools went bankrupt tomorrow you'd have enough to live comfortably for the rest of your life. It was all about pride and face. And not wanting to be thought a failure. You took the easy way out because you thought you'd get away with it."

"I made a commercial error of judgement," he said. "I admit that."

"A commercial error of judgement that led to two deaths!" she shouted.

"No," he said, "that had nothing to do with me."

They looked at each other angrily. Molly turned to Mr. Sharland.

"Did you know that Jimmy Morrissey was intending to write the autobiography?" she asked.

He nodded. "Grace told me about it. She was obviously fond of the man and she liked to talk about him. Of course I was interested."

"You must have realized there was a danger that the story would come out in his book," Molly said. "Had you decided on a strategy for dealing with any revelation?"

"I discussed it with Phil Cairns, but we didn't think the man would be able to find any proof after all this time. There was gossip and rumour in the factory, but that would only be hearsay." He turned bitterly towards Grace.

"I didn't know my daughter would introduce Morrissey to the Linehams and persuade them to hand over all Nick's material."

"When did you find out that Mr. Morrissey had detailed information about the pollution incident and the cover-up?" Molly asked.

He paused and she thought he would refuse to answer.

"It was the week before he died," Sharland said at last. "He'd been to see Phil Cairns. He said he thought Phil ought to know what would be in the book before it went to the publisher. Perhaps Phil would have some contribution to make. It was really very insensitive of him. He seemed not to realize what a devastating effect publication would have on Phil's personal life. And they were supposed to be friends!"

"Phil told you about the visit?"

"Yes, Sharland said. "He was very upset. He came to my house. It was the impact the publicity would have on Cathy that concerned him most. The story was all tied up in her mind with Hannah's accident. She'd always thought Jimmy crashed the car because he was in such a rush to get home."

"Did Cathy know Jimmy planned to make the leak public?"

"I suppose so. I presume Phil would have told her."

"What action did you and Phil decide to take?"

"Phil was going to see him and ask him to think again."

"And if that failed?"

"Then we'd have to face it out, hope that the national press wouldn't care after all this time about what had happened to a small woollen factory. We could show what a brilliant environmental record we've had otherwise. At least the sponsorship of the conservation charity had finished. That would limit the embarrassment."

"There might be criminal charges resulting from the corruption," Molly said.

"No!" he said. "Hardly! No crime was committed. As I said before, I made a generous gesture to my daughter's fiancé. That was all."

"Did Phil ask Jimmy to think again?"

"Yes, Morrissey seemed quite surprised that Phil was taking the matter so seriously. He said he'd think it over for a few days and let him know."

"And did he?"

Sharland nodded. "He went to Phil Cairns's cottage on the day he died. Phil phoned me that afternoon and told me all about it. The story was written, he said, and he wasn't prepared to change it now. It was an important issue, more important than his friendship with Phil and Cathy. If the National Rivers Authority couldn't be trusted to police the new act, then our waterways could be poisoned without anyone knowing. It was a matter of principle." He spoke almost to himself: "Pompous bastard. I think it was book sales he was after and a chance to be in the limelight again."

Molly felt some sympathy with that point of view but ignored it.

"How did you react?" she said.

"I suppose it was more or less what I expected. I got in touch with our PR people and told them to prepare a plan for damage limitation."

"Didn't you think it was more than a coincidence when James Morrissey killed himself that night?" Molly asked.

"No," he said. "Why should I? I'd always thought he was unstable. He wouldn't have needed the services of Grace here if he'd been sane. And I've explained already: In my view it was a business setback, serious enough but not more serious than other problems I've had to face in my career. It wasn't worth murdering for."

Molly felt inclined to believe him. He was a businessman. He had made a commercial error of judgement. And she was convinced that the murderer of Jimmy Morrissey had a less clear-sighted, more emotional relationship with the victim.

19

When they returned to the Mill, Tim was waiting for them in the lobby. He was sitting on the stairs pretending to read a comic, but Molly thought he had probably been there for most of the afternoon.

"You did say you'd come and look at my work," he said to George, but without much hope. He was expecting rejection again. Molly watched George hesitate and suspected he was dreaming up another excuse.

"Oh, go on," she said. "We've no time to talk to the Cairnses before dinner and I'm certainly not going to miss the meal. We'll see them later. Go and find out what Tim's been up to. You might learn something."

The schoolroom was dark and empty. Tim pressed a switch and the room was flooded with harsh light from a set of neon strips.

"Actually it's not what I've discovered," the boy said seriously. "It was mostly Dad's work. But I helped him and then when we found that dying swan I remembered what he'd said." He paused and was obviously struggling to find the word he wanted. "Dad *predicted* that there would be sick swans," he said. "He told me to look out for them on the shore. It was a sort of project. Like lugworms."

He led George to where two wide stainless steel sinks were set into a workbench. Above them, on a shelf, stood a row of glass jars, half filled with liquid and neatly labelled. ·

"I went with Dad to collect the samples," he said proudly. "He said we'd need to take them to a lab to find out the exact chemical composition, but this one speaks for itself. That's what he said. Look, you can see it's separated. The chemical's sunk to the bottom."

"Where were they taken?" George asked.

"In the River Marr, of course. At different points from here in the bay to beyond the town."

"And this one?" George pointed to the jar in the boy's hand. "Where did you find this?"

"Close to the outfall near the woollen factory," Tim said. "We went on a Sunday to get that one when the factory wasn't working. It was the weekend before Dad died. I was the look-out. We told Mum we were going to the swimming baths and we had to sneak Dad into the Mill because he was covered with mud." George gave him a moment to enjoy the reminiscence, then asked gently: "Why did your father take the samples?"

"I thought it was for me," Tim said. "Mum couldn't really teach me science properly. It was part of my school work. Like I said, a project."

No, George thought, it wasn't for you.

"And what was special about the sample," George asked, "the one taken from the Mardon Wools outfall? Was it just that the chemical separated from the water?"

"No," the boy said. "It was the smell. Dad said it hit him when he was taking the sample from the river. Here, see for yourself." He unscrewed the lid from the jar. George bent obediently to smell. He was transported immediately to a high-street dry cleaner's, where he went occasionally to have his suits cleaned and where the fumes from the cleaning process leaked through air vents into the shop.

"Did your father tell you what the chemical was?" George asked.

"Yes," Tim said. "He knew straight away. I can't remember the name, but I wrote it down in my note-book." He took a small, cloth-covered notebook from a drawer, licked his finger, and went through it a page at a time. "Dad wrote it down for me because I couldn't spell it. Here it is. But it's got a shorter name. It's called TCE."

"And your father said you should look out for injured birds?"

The boy nodded. "He said it was like an experiment. He thought the chemical would have an effect on the swans. We had to look for evidence to confirm our theory."

"Did your father tell anyone else about the experiment?"

"Yes," Tim said. "He showed Aidan." He paused and swallowed hard. "He said it had to be a secret between the three of us, but now they're both dead I thought that wouldn't count any more."

"No," George said. "You're quite right. But now it's our secret, yours and mine, at least until tomorrow."

George was quiet through dinner, preoccupied. So the TCE leak from Mardon Wools that had started the fuss years before hadn't been an isolated incident. Through carelessness or cost-cutting it had happened again. And Jimmy had been monitoring the river looking for just that sort of evidence to add credibility to his story. How would Mardon Wools' PR people deal with this second leak?

It occurred to George then that evidence of the recent leak raised the stakes considerably for the company. And that Sharland hadn't told Molly or his daughter the whole truth about his concern to keep Jimmy's story secret. He must surely have known about the recent incident. Even if the company didn't do their own regular monitoring, the dying swan on the shore would have alerted Phil Cairns that something was wrong. This was a far more serious problem than a story that had been

217

forgotten years before. It was topical, up to the minute, with the potential for photographs of bedraggled swans to be plastered all over the newspapers.

Then George wondered why Jimmy had done nothing about the discovery. He had known about the pollution almost a week before his death but had not gone to the NRA so the leak could be stopped and the damage limited. But he had told Aidan Moore. Why? The answer was obvious and rather disturbing. So the artist could add the drawing of the sick swan to the book's cover. Jimmy Morrissey might have been a concerned conservationist, but he was also vain, egotistical, and determined to launch himself back into a career he had loved. He had not told the NRA because he wanted to bring the story to the world in a way that would give him maximum publicity. Had his vanity been the cause of his death? As the meal came to a close George wondered if the Cairnses would provide the answer to the question.

At Molly's suggestion they drove to the Cairnses' cottage. George was horrified. He thought it immoral to use the car for such a short distance, but she said she was tired. It had been a long day and she was not too proud to admit that she was feeling old. She, too, had been preoccupied throughout dinner. Something Sharland had said took on a new significance and the image of the man described by Cedric flitted in and out of her memory. Despite these distractions she was convinced, like George, that the Cairnses were involved, either singly or together, and she looked forward to the evening's interview with something approaching dread.

Phil and Cathy were waiting for them. Sharland must have phoned to warn them that the relationship between Mardon Wools and Nick Lineham had been discovered. Phil was subdued and washed out. All the energy and bounce had gone. He alternated between defiance and apology, but beneath the occasional blusters he was profoundly miserable.

"You'd better come in," he said. "I thought you'd both be around tonight. To gloat."

"No," George said. "Not to gloat. To get to the bottom of it."

"It's all very well for you to have principles," Phil said with one of his sudden outbursts of anger. "You can afford them, George. If the TCE leak had been made public all those years ago I'd have lost my job. I had a wife and a child to support. I suppose you think I should have gone to the authorities and said what a bad boy I'd been. It wasn't even my mistake!"

"It might have been easier," George said flatly. "In the long run."

"It wasn't even my decision!" Cairns said, pity and self-justification taking over once more. "The directors decreed that the thing had to be kept quiet. If I'd come out into the open with it, they'd have sacked me, made me a scapegoat. I couldn't win."

The three of them had been standing in the kitchen and Phil turned suddenly and led them into the living room, where Cathy was sitting in a rocking chair, staring into the fire.

"Look, love!" he said with mock surprise. "We've got visitors. George and Molly. Isn't that nice?"

She turned slowly, not seeming to recognize the sarcasm, and nodded.

"I suppose you'll feel you have to go to the NRA," Phil continued bitterly. "Do your duty as an environmentally concerned citizen."

George did not say that he had already been to the NRA. Let Phil think, for the moment, that all his information had come from Sharland.

"That's not really my business," he said. "Especially after all this time . . ."

"No," Phil said. "It's not your bloody business."

"If it were an ongoing problem it might be a different matter. . . ."

Still Phil did not respond.

"I was concerned, for example, to discover that there'd been another, more recent leak."

Phil was astounded. "How did you know about that?"

"Jimmy told me. In a way. And then there was that swan on the shore."

"So it was a guess," Phil said. "Is that it? You've no proof. I know you've not got the swan. I disposed of that myself."

"There is proof," George said. "Jimmy had proof. He took a water sample from the Mardon Wools outfall."

Phil was silent.

"It was an accident and it's sorted now," he said at last. "You can do your own test if you're worried. You can forget it."

"But Jimmy couldn't forget it, could he?" George said. "You asked him to think again about publishing the story of the cover-up in his autobiography. And he might have done. You were friends and anyway it was ancient history. But then he took the sample from your outfall and realized that it wasn't ancient history after all. All he needed was a few dying swans and publishers would be falling over themselves to pay him a hefty advance for the book."

"He didn't say that was what it was about," Phil said. "He said it was the corruption that was important, the attempt to bribe NRA officials and the way anyone who was prepared to come out into the open was threatened with the sack. Hypocritical bastard."

"He came to tell you that on the afternoon of his death?"

Phil nodded. "I suppose I'd expected it. But I thought we were friends. I thought I could get him to change his mind."

"Did you go and see him later that night to make him change his mind?"

"Of course not!" Phil shouted. "I knew it would be no use. He had little enough respect for me, anyway. I wasn't going to grovel to the man."

220

There was a short silence.

"What about you, Cathy?" George asked. "Did you go to see Jimmy later that night?"

She shook her head. It was a gesture of resignation, not defiance.

"But you must have gone at some time," George said. "Either late that night or the next morning."

"It was the next morning," she said.

"What are you saying?" Phil demanded. "That Cathy murdered him? You're mad. I had more reason to do that than she did."

"I'm not accusing Cathy of anything," George said. "Not at this stage." He turned back to her and she faced him, strangely compliant.

"So you went into the Mill that morning?"

She nodded. "Meg had gone with the ambulance. They must have realized that he was dead by then, but they'd called an ambulance. The rest of the place was in chaos. Nobody saw me, but if they had I don't think it would have registered. I went to his study and took the autobiography and the Lineham notes, everything that referred to the pollution incident."

"Did you find the anonymous letter that started the investigation?" George asked.

"No," she said. "But I wasn't looking for it. I thought it would still be in London."

"You were burning the notebooks, weren't you?" he said. "When I came to see you on that first day. I thought there was a lot of paper in the bonfire."

She nodded. "I wasn't sure what to do with it," she said. "I didn't want it published, but I couldn't bring myself to destroy it. It represented, I suppose, so much work. Then Meg told me that you were coming to investigate, so I knew I had to get rid of it."

"Why didn't you tell me?" Phil said.

She shrugged. "You were in enough trouble," she said. "I didn't want you implicated."

"Why did you do it?"

"For you," she said simply. "Because I owed you so much. To do something to pay you back."

"How did you know Jimmy was dead," Molly asked, "if you didn't kill him?"

"Because Ruth phoned me. She thought I should know. We were quite close, Ruth and I. She used to stay here when Hannah was alive. It would never have occurred to Meg." She paused. "Really," she said, "I didn't kill him."

Something about the inflection of the last phrase, a slight emphasis on the last word, made George look up sharply.

"Perhaps you had better tell us," he said quietly, "how Aidan Moore came to die."

"He knew about the first TCE leak," she said. "Jimmy sent him up here to snoop around when he first got wind of it. Aidan was only a lad, but he dug up enough dirt to make Jimmy take it seriously."

"Yes," George said. "I'd realized that."

"Did you?" she asked. "Yes, I suppose you would." She looked at him closely. "He thought Phil had killed Jimmy," she said. "When you started stirring things up, making everyone believe Jimmy was murdered, he thought Phil must be responsible. Who else could benefit from Jimmy's death?" She smiled wanly. "He was even frightened of Phil. He was planning to run away."

"And make Jimmy's story public himself," George said.

"Yes," she said. "He wanted to put the record straight. He thought it would be some sort of memorial." She looked at her husband with affectionate irritation. "Jimmy was his hero, too."

"How did you know what he intended?"

"I didn't know," she said. "Not definitely. But Ruth told me he was going away. I explained that Ruth and I were close. She finds it easier to talk to me than she does to Meg. She's rather lonely and had grown very fond of Aidan." Her voice, which had been controlled,

222

suddenly faltered. "I never meant to do it," she said. "I wouldn't have hurt either of them on purpose."

"When did Ruth tell you that Aidan was leaving?"

"That night. The night Aidan drowned. He'd taken her to the pub. She had expected, I think, some declaration of love. Instead he told her he was going home. She came here to cry on my shoulder." Cathy paused. "I thought that was suspicious. I had to know what he intended doing with all the information on Mardon Wools."

"How did you try to find out?" George asked.

"I phoned him," she said. "At the Mill. I said I wanted to talk to him. He thought I was prepared to pass on information about the recent TCE leak. He'd heard about that from Jimmy. He agreed to meet me on the shore." She smiled bitterly. "He thought I was prepared to betray my husband. Phil didn't know anything about it. I told him that all the uncertainty over Jimmy's death had upset me and that I needed a walk to cool down. Then I went out."

"Why was it so important to see Aidan?"

"I've told you. To find out what he knew and what he intended. To persuade him, I suppose, to leave the thing alone, that no good would be done to rake everything up."

"Did he listen?"

"Oh, he listened," she said, "but he didn't take any notice. It was ridiculous—I should have known that it would be no good. Jimmy might be dead, but Aidan Moore was still under his spell." She paused and started to describe the scene: "It was very cold. We were standing on those boulders that stretch out towards the spit. I didn't want anyone at the Mill to see us and I'd switched off my torch. We talked by moonlight. I got there first and I saw him come over the bank and watched him walk across the shore towards me. He was shy, you know, but quite determined. Jimmy had told him there'd been another TCE leak. He'd been very excited about it, apparently. Aidan wanted to know all about the pollution, demanded to know who was responsible. He said he was planning an article to go in *Green Scenes*. He thought Jimmy would have appreciated that. 'And I've even got a drawing to illustrate it,' he said. . . .

"When he realized that I had nothing to tell him, he said I was wasting his time and he turned away to go back to the Mill. I ran after him to try to persuade him. I caught hold of his arm and pulled him back. I thought if he would only hear what I had to say, if he realized the misery he would cause, he would understand."

"And did he?"

"No," she said flatly. "He called Phil a murderer. He wouldn't believe that Jimmy had committed suicide. That was your fault, George. You started all this."

"What happened then?" George asked, implicitly accepting the criticism.

"I was still holding on to his arm. It had made me so angry. That anyone who'd known Phil could think him capable of that! I pushed him away. He was standing awkwardly and the boulders were uneven. He fell back and hit the side of his head on a rock."

She was suddenly very pale.

"Was he dead then?" Molly asked gently.

"I don't know," Cathy said. "It never occurred to me. He'd tripped, that was all. It was a silly accident. And I was still furious. If he'd knocked himself out I didn't care. I thought he deserved a sore head. I just walked home."

"Didn't you turn 'round later to check that he was all right?"

"Yes," she said. "But a cloud had gone over the moon so I couldn't see."

Phil Cairns was looking at her in horror. "Why didn't you tell me what happened when you came in that night?" he said. "I would have gone to see him. I might have saved his life."

"I didn't know his life was in danger," she shouted. "It was a silly accident, he tripped. How could I know it would end like that? I'd made a fool of myself out there on the shore, pleading with him for favours. I wanted to forget all about it."

There was another silence.

"You'll have to tell the police," Phil said. He took her hand. "I'll come with you. We'll see it through together."

She did not answer.

"It would look better," George said tentatively, "if you went in voluntarily and offered to make a statement. You can explain that shock and panic caused the delay in reporting what happened."

"We'll go now," Phil said. Something of the old energy had returned. He turned to her. "Did you do all that," he asked, "for me?"

"Oh, Phil," she said, smiling despite herself, despite her tears. "You are a fool."

Late that night George had a jubilant phone call from Reg Porter, the detective in charge of the Moore case.

"I thought you'd like to know," Porter said. "It was an accident, that drowning earlier this week. Or an accident of a sort. I don't know what conclusion the coroner will come to in the end. Cathy Cairns was involved. There was an argument. The lad wanted to publish an article that reflected badly on her husband. I don't know the details."

Why not? George thought. Why didn't you ask?

Porter was continuing breezily: "That bitch did herself no good by keeping quiet for so long, but they're like that, aren't they, brainy women? They tend to get hysterical. We've bailed her anyway and we'll see what happens. But murder it certainly wasn't."

He laughed unpleasantly, concerned only that he had been proved right.

He paused, hoping perhaps for congratulations or an admission of defeat.

"So you'll be able to go home now with a clear conscience, won't you?" he said when none came. "I told you it was suicide and accidental death. No conspiracy and no murder. So you can go home and forget all about it."

George replaced the receiver without speaking, but he thought it unlikely that they could leave immediately. Aidan Moore's death had been a distraction. It had little to do with the real issue. On the drive back from Salter's Cottage, Molly had suddenly remembered where she had seen the person who fitted Cedric's description of the man who had met Jimmy Morrissey the weekend of the accident. They had discussed the possibilities the identification suggested and had come to the conclusion that the answer to Jimmy's death lay even closer to home. It was all about families, Molly had said, and it could be found at the Mill.

20

After breakfast the next day Meg called George into her flat. She told him that the investigation was over. She had decided that no more good would come of it.

"But you asked us to come for a reason," George said, "and we haven't fulfilled our commitment."

"You're upsetting everyone," she said. She was at her most regal, dressed in a navy twinset and a navy pleated skirt. She was even wearing pearls. "I can see it's not your fault, but I hadn't thought there would be so much disruption. Then there's that business with Aidan. Poor Ruth is heartbroken. And now you tell me that dear Cathy had to go through the trauma of a police investigation."

"Don't you want to know how Jimmy died?" he asked.

"I'm not sure," she said. "Not any more."

She was standing by the window looking out and she would not meet his eye. She seemed to come to a decision and turned back towards him.

"Can I be frank, George?" She sat down. He saw that it was confession time and it would not come easy to her. "Perhaps I was a little impulsive when I decided to call you in. Overemotional. Of course I wanted to find out how James died. I'm still not convinced that he would have committed suicide. It was not like him. But

227

if I'm honest that wasn't my main motivation." She hesitated. Somewhere in the building Caitlin was playing the flute and the sound, piercing and shrill, seemed to be mocking her. "I was frightened," she said at last. "It was the missing autobiography—I was afraid it had got into . . . unsympathetic hands. Now I know that it's been destroyed that concern is no longer relevant."

"What do you mean by 'unsympathetic hands'?"

"People who would have published pieces out of context. The press, I suppose."

"You were afraid that the Cairnses' role in covering up the pollution incident in the Marr would be made public?" He would not have thought her so altruistic.

"What?" She seemed surprised. "Oh no. It wasn't that. I knew about the incident at the time and I thought it was a mistake for James to be so high-handed. I tried to persuade him to drop it—we were friends, after all—but to be truthful I thought it was a fuss about nothing."

"Why were you so worried then that the autobiography would be published?"

"I was never allowed to read it," she said resentfully. There was a silence filled again by the laughing notes of Caitlin's flute. Meg seemed suddenly irritated by the noise. She got up and shut the living-room door. The music faded. "I suspected that James might have made some rather scathing remarks about the family," she said. "Our family. It never had the same priority for him as it did for me. He might have been tempted to ridicule our ideals. Without realizing, of course, quite what he was doing."

"And that would never have done," George said with gentle sarcasm. "Would it? To make fun of England's favourite mother."

"It would have been embarrassing," she said. "James could never see it. He never took my work seriously."

"And when it was stolen you thought someone had sold it to the press?"

"It occurred to me," she said. "Some of the less principled rags would have paid something for it, I suppose. I panicked on the evening of the memorial service. There were all those people involved in the media. It seemed unbearable that they should be given the ammunition to mock me. I decided then that something would have to be done."

"And who did you think had stolen it?"

"I don't know," she said. "One of the students perhaps. Rosie? Jane? I thought you would find out."

"And now that you know Cathy Cairns burned it on her bonfire you've decided you don't need us any more."

"I don't think I do," she said graciously, her natural self-confidence returning. "I'm very grateful for all your efforts, of course. And Molly's, too. But I think now it's time to stop grieving and to look forward. I have to consider the children in all this. I don't think it's healthy for them to live with this uncertainty."

"I think Jimmy was murdered," George said. "You were right about that."

"All the same," she said, dismissing him, "I think we'll accept the inquest verdict after all. I think that would be best. Stay on until the end of the week, George, as our guests. I wouldn't want to be inhospitable. But enjoy yourselves. Pretend that you're on holiday. No more detective work!" And she smiled at him chidingly, as if he were one of her younger children. "You will promise, George? I insist."

"Of course," George said, "if that is what you want."

It was easy for him to make the promise. They had decided already that Molly would play the role of detective that day.

Molly walked to the Dead Dog straight after breakfast and arrived there before opening time. There were still dirty glasses from the night before on the bar and ashes in the grate. There was a smell of stale beer. A woman, presumably Cedric's mother, was making an energetic attempt to clear up. She tut-tutted at the mess and began to polish the tables with a vigorous circular movement of her cloth. She was very small and neat and despite the domestic work she was rather smart. Her hair was permed and her face was made up. She wore a flowery overall on top of a matching brown skirt and jersey. It was still very cold outside, but she had opened the door to let in the fresh air.

Molly stood in the doorway watching her, waiting to catch her attention.

"Excuse me," she said at last. "I wonder if it might be possible to speak to Cedric."

The woman stopped her work and looked up. Cedric might be approaching middle age, but her first instinct was still to protect him.

"Why?" she said suspiciously. "What's he done?" She was clear-sighted enough to know that her son wasn't quite normal. She would always be anxious about him.

"Nothing," Molly said quickly. "Nothing at all." She walked away from the door and up to the bar. "We were talking in here a couple of nights ago and he gave me some interesting information. I was hoping he might help me again."

"Oh." The landlady wasn't quite sure what to make of this scruffy little woman with her round John Lennon specs and her parka tied at the waist with a frayed string. "Who are you then?"

"My name is Molly Palmer-Jones. I'm staying at Markham Mill."

She understood then. "Your husband's that detective."

Molly was tempted to reply that they were partners, that she, too, was a detective, but she simply nodded.

The woman's curiosity was aroused. The pub had been talking about James Morrissey's death and the arrival of the mysterious detective all week. She hoped, through Cedric, to have some news to contribute and she regarded Molly more kindly.

"I'll get him," she said. "He was just having his breakfast. If you don't mind waiting here."

Molly took a seat.

Cedric bustled into the bar soon after. He had dressed hurriedly and he had the tousled look of a small boy. People seldom took him seriously and Molly's request for help had excited him. His mother followed him, but this was *his* moment of glory and he didn't see why she should listen in.

"We'll go into the lounge, shall we?" he said, giving his mother a brief, spiteful look. "It'll be warmer in there."

He took Molly into the other room and with a gentlemanly flourish, lit a calor gas heater. The smell of the fumes filled the place. He settled himself heavily on a leatherette bench. "Now," he said. "How can I help you?"

"You told me that Jimmy Morrissey met a man in the pub on the weekend that Hannah died," Molly said. "It was a long time ago, but I wondered if you'd manage to recognize him again."

"Why?" he demanded. "Why do you want to know?"

She hesitated. She did not want to offend or disappoint him. "I'd rather not say at the moment," she said. "We have a duty of confidentiality. You do understand?"

He nodded proudly. Of course he understood. They were private detectives like on the telly. It would all have to be hush-hush. You couldn't expect anything else. He would have liked to be in on the secret but was glad just to have the attention.

Molly spread a number of photographs over a table. Some were of the Morrissey family at different times in their lives. Caitlin had provided them from the family album the night before without asking why Molly needed them. Others had been obtained in a more underhanded way. There was even one of George as a young man, which for some foolish and sentimental

231

reason Molly kept in her handbag. It was the nearest she could come, she supposed, to an identity parade.

Cedric considered the photos seriously. His stomach prevented him from leaning over the table to get a closer look, so he stood up. He pored over the smiling family groups, the birthday parties, the days out with friends. She thought that he probably recognized the man immediately—throughout the episode he had an air of confidence—but he wanted to prolong the excitement. There was something of the showman about the way he moved the photographs over the table with his fleshy fat fingers, like a magician moving cards.

"That's him," he said when he could spin it out no longer.

"You're sure?"

"Definitely," he said. "I told you I've got a photographic memory." He paused. "I can see now why I thought I'd seen him again recently. Uncanny, isn't it?"

"You won't say anything?" she said quietly. "Not yet. Just for twenty-four hours. It won't matter after that."

"You can trust me," he said, nodding violently and touching the side of his nose with his fingers. "You can rely on old Cedric."

She thought, as she walked back to the Mill through the frozen countryside, that she probably could.

In the schoolroom Meg was supervising the children's lessons. Tim and Emily were moving on from Vikings to the Tudors and Stuarts and Meg was showing them how a family tree worked. She set it out on the blackboard, marking all the Tudor kings and queens in different-coloured chalks.

At first Ruth took no notice. She was writing an essay on *Northanger Abbey* and Meg's voice was only a distraction. Then Meg asked Emily to come and draw their family tree on the board. The child held the chalk in her fist and carefully printed JAMES X MEG. Then a line and four rods leading to each of their names.

"Very good!" Meg said. "That's quite right."

But it's not right, Ruth thought. James wasn't my father. Mother is so keen to make us appear one big happy family that she seems to forget that. Caitlin and I have deserted him.

They considered it a chore now to keep in touch with him. They had to be reminded of his birthday and when he phoned to talk to them they pulled faces at each other as if to say: What a *drag*. What have we got to say to him? He still taught at the same school as when Meg had walked out on him, with his two young daughters, to set up home with James Morrissey. He had never come to the Mill. Whenever he phoned to suggest it Meg put him off and the girls were grateful to be spared the awkwardness. Despite his profession he wasn't very good with teenagers.

But now, looking at the family tree from which he was excluded, Ruth considered that they had treated him unfairly. She thought of Rosie, who seemed so close to her mother despite the hardships of her childhood, who still mourned her father after all these years. If my father were to die, Ruth wondered, would I care at all?

Molly spent the rest of the morning in James's office, making phone calls, building up a pattern of what must have happened. When the bell went for lunch it was almost finished, though there was no proof. If that was needed it would have to come later.

"Family values," she muttered to herself as she went in to the meal. "Bloody family values."

21

$George$ found lunch an awkward meal. There was an air of forced jollity. Meg seemed to feel there was need for a celebration. It had been a dreadful time for them all, she said, but they had to put it behind them. She looked around her fondly.

"You children have been *so* brave," she said. "I want you all to know how much I've valued your support since James died. And I'm sorry if George's questions have made things more difficult. I can see now that there's no purpose in taking it any further." She leaned forward across the table. "If you feel up to it I thought we'd open the Mill for business again next week. I've phoned Laura Sutherland about the Wildlife and Photography course and I'll try to get in touch with all the prospective students this afternoon. What do you say?"

The children nodded dutifully, surprised by her mood. Then she asked Rosie to bring wine, unheard of at lunchtime, and she even allowed Caitlin to take two glasses.

"Molly and George will be leaving tomorrow," she announced. "We're very grateful for their efforts, but I can see now that it was a mistake to ask them to come. We've spent too long agonizing over the past. Perhaps we should drink a toast to the future."

George thought it was all in dreadful taste. Even if Meg had come to terms with her husband's death, she should be mourning Aidan Moore, a brilliant young man with so much to look forward to, who was supposed to be a family friend. Besides, George knew that it was not all over and that by the end of the day there would be a tragedy of a different sort.

When lunch was finished Molly went back to the study. There was one phone call to wait for. George spent the afternoon in the common room looking out at the shore. Tim was beachcombing, walking along the high tide line, pulling out treasures then throwing them back into the sea. Time passed, but George felt none of his usual restlessness or impatience. He was not tempted to seek Molly out, to find out why it was taking so long. He watched the boy walk up the shore until he was a speck against the sky, then turn and make his way slowly back towards the Mill.

Molly came into the room.

"I'm sorry," she said. "There was a case conference. They were late phoning back."

"Well?" he said sadly. "Is it how we thought?"

She nodded.

"Where is she?"

"I don't know," Molly said. "I haven't seen her since lunch-time."

They sat for a moment in silence. George still seemed overtaken by lethargy. He thought there was no hurry. Not now. They watched Tim walk back up the beach towards the Mill. He was dragging a piece of old fishing net behind him. He stopped and seemed to be greeting someone else not yet in their line of vision. He disappeared over the bank and his place was taken by a small figure, shapeless in her padded jacket, bare-headed, her long hair tied back in a plait.

"Do you want me to go?" Molly asked.

"No," he said. "I'll do it." He felt that he owed it to Jimmy to finish the thing properly. He raised himself slowly and stretched.

"There's still no proof," she said. "But I don't think you'll need it. She'll be glad to talk."

"What do you take me for?" he said lightly. "A social worker?"

"Nothing wrong with that," she said automatically. They smiled for a moment before the tension returned.

When he got outside the light was beginning to fade and the Salter's Spit light was already flashing. She was still there, sitting on one of the large, round boulders. It was almost as if she was waiting for him. She must have heard him coming, his boots crunching on the shingle, but she did not turn around. He sat down beside her.

"You know, don't you?" she said without looking at him.

He nodded. "How did you guess that I'd found out?"

"I noticed that the photograph was missing from my room this morning. I always thought your wife was brighter than Meg made out."

"Why did you do it, Rosie?" he asked.

"Because James Morrissey ruined my life," she said simply. She turned then to face him and he saw that her control was very fragile.

"Why don't we go for a walk and you can tell me about it," he said. He wanted to talk to her before Reg Porter was let loose on her, and that had nothing to do with social workers.

She hesitated and he thought she would refuse, might even attempt to run away. But she stood up and they walked, almost like father and daughter, following the high water mark as Tim had done earlier.

"My father thought James Morrissey was wonderful," she said abruptly. "He'd seen him on the television, read his books." she paused. "Famous people should realize," she blurted out. "Take some responsibility."

"Why don't you tell me about your dad?"

"He was a bit before his time," she said. "A conservationist before it became fashionable. He used to take *Green Scenes* every month, read it like the Bible."

"You must have admired him very much."

"Very much." She kicked out suddenly at a stone, which clattered over the shingle.

They walked on for several minutes without speaking, in step with each other.

"He worked for Mardon Wools, didn't he?" George prompted at last.

"Yes," she said. "He'd worked there since he was a lad. He didn't know anything else. All his mates were there."

"And he found out about the TCE leak?"

"You know about that?" She wasn't surprised. "Yes. He knew what had happened. It was a matter of cutting corners, he said. That made him angry. He'd warned the boss that it might happen, and there was no guarantee that it wouldn't happen again. And there was a cover-up." She stopped sharply and turned to face George, wanting him to understand. "He wasn't telling tales," she said. "There was nothing like that. But he wasn't the sort to compromise with his principles. Perhaps it would have been better all 'round if he had been. He knew he'd get no joy from the management, so he wrote to Mr. Morrissey."

"He wrote an anonymous letter making allegations of pollution and corruption," George said. "Jimmy arranged for Aidan Moore to come up and meet him. Eventually he was so excited by the stuff Aidan turned up that he decided to come himself."

She nodded.

"Your father met Jimmy in the Dead Dog," George said gently. "Cedric remembers seeing them together. And you look so like him that when you first went in there he thought your face was familiar. When Molly took your father's photograph to him this morning he picked it out at once."

"Did he?" she said, pleased. "Did he really think I

looked like Dad?" Then in mild surprise: "I never realized they met in the Dead Dog."

They walked on again in silence.

"My father trusted him!" she cried suddenly. He saw she had been brooding, reliving the imagined crimes and insults. "Dad thought he would do what was right. And he promised to be discreet. He said Mardon Wools would never find out where he had got his information. The very next month my father got the sack. That was the first the rest of us knew about what he'd been up to."

"I'm sure Jimmy did try to be discreet," George said, though discretion had never been one of Jimmy's qualities. "But he had to discuss the pollution incident with the management to check his facts. It wouldn't have been difficult then for them to find out who had access to the information he'd received."

"Oh," she said angrily, "Mr. Morrissey discussed it with the management. He discussed it with his old friend Phil Cairns. My father must have been daft to expect any justice from them. They shared a wife, after all. So they got together and decided to hush the whole thing up. My dad would be in the way, so he was made redundant. It was all very convenient!"

"I'm sure it wasn't like that," George said. He felt in a strange position defending Jimmy Morrissey to his murderer. Shouldn't Rosie herself be on the defensive? "Jimmy did intend to publish the story although it would damage his relationship with Phil and Cathy Cairns. Even Meg tried to persuade him to leave the thing alone, but he insisted on following it through. It was only after the car accident that he felt he had to drop it."

"Why would the car accident make any difference?" she asked suspiciously. "James hurt his leg, didn't he? Shook himself up. That was all. It wouldn't stop him working."

"Didn't you know?" He saw then that there was no
238

reason why she should be aware of Hannah's death. She'd known nothing of the Morrissey family at the time of the accident, and though it had been reported in the newspapers it would hold no interest for her. Her father had passed on only his bitterness. Later, working at the Mill, she'd been considered a domestic. There would be no intimate conversations with Meg about the family's past.

"James had a daughter called Hannah," George said. "She was about the same age as Ruth. When he and Cathy separated she lived with her mother, though she spent some of her holidays with the Morrisseys. That weekend, the weekend your father met Jimmy in the Dead Dog, he was going to take Hannah back to London with him. He was impatient to get back to start his story and he'd had an argument with the Cairnses. He was driving recklessly, much too fast, and Hannah died. You can understand why he didn't want to cause Phil and Cathy any more grief. He felt responsible."

She began to bite her fingernails furiously and he saw that she did not want to understand. She did not want to lose her justification for killing Jimmy Morrissey. She preferred to see him as a heartless fiend.

"I don't care!" she cried. "It wasn't my dad's fault that the girl died. Why should he have to suffer?"

George said nothing and they walked on. When he thought she was calmer he said: "What happened when your dad was made redundant?"

"We moved to the bloody Midlands," she said. "We all hated it."

"And soon after that your father died?"

"Don't you see?" she said earnestly. "Jimmy Morrissey killed him. It was just as if he'd shot or strangled him. It was Jimmy Morrissey's fault."

"Then your mother had a nervous breakdown."

"She'd been dependent on Dad all their married life," Rosie said. "She'd never been strong. She became severely depressed." She gave a strange little laugh. "Just

239

like Jimmy Morrissey, you might say. Ironic, isn't it, that they had so much in common? But she wasn't really like Mr. Morrissey. He was pissed off because Meg had made him give up his television appearances and move up to the Mill. I suppose he had a crisis of confidence. But he wasn't really ill. Not like my mother. Not screaming, barking mad."

"The crisis of confidence was about killing his daughter," George said. "And the Mardon Wools incident. He knew he should have followed it through. After Hannah's death he was in a state of shock and he couldn't decide what to do. Meg decided for him. He regretted it afterwards."

"I don't care," she cried again. "He had everything, didn't he? He had money and a family to look after him. He had it all."

"He tried to put it right," George said. "In his auto-biography."

"I know," she said. "Why do you think I waited for it to be finished before I killed him?"

They walked on again without speaking. It was dusk, but George's eyes had become accustomed to the gloom. There was a soft sucking and gurgling sound as the tide came in, and the crunching of their footsteps on the shingle.

"You were ill, too, weren't you?" he said carefully. Molly's phone calls had been to social-work colleagues in the Midlands. She had found out about Rosie being committed to local authority care.

"Not ill," she said at once. "Angry. I was angry."

"You attacked a social worker who was trying to help you," he said gently. With a bread knife, he could have added, but didn't.

"She didn't help! She couldn't understand. I told her that we had to come home, back here to Mardon. Mum would be all right then. But she couldn't see it." She paused. "I lost my temper," she said.

240

"And that's why you got taken into care," he said. "They put you in a secure unit."

"It was dreadful," she said. "Hellish. That's where I planned my revenge. It was the only thing that kept me going."

"You can't have known that Jimmy Morrissey would need a cook," he said.

"No," she said. "Not that. That was luck." She stopped walking. "I did enjoy the cooking," she said. "I really enjoyed that. It was creative, you know? It was the only good thing to come out of that place."

He nodded.

"When I saw the advert in the magazine it was like a sign."

"Didn't Jimmy recognize you at the interview?" George asked. "You look so like your father."

"Do I?" She was distracted again by the thought. Then: "You don't think Mr. Morrissey interviewed the staff? That was below him. Meg saw to all that."

"And later? Did he recognize you later?"

"No," she said. "That shows the arrogance of the man, doesn't it? My father had no impact on him at all. He didn't even recognize the name. If he had, you know, if he'd said sorry, everything would have been different probably." She paused again. "I quite liked him in a funny sort of way. But I couldn't go soft. Not after all that planning. All that waiting."

"What happened then?" George asked. "You said you waited until the autobiography was finished. How did you know?"

"He told me," she said simply. "He came into the kitchen that afternoon pleased as punch. All smiles and laughter. 'That's it,' he said. 'I'll have to read it through, of course. It's just a first draft. But I've got all the facts down. It's all straight now.' It was what I'd been waiting for. I'd been planning it for months. I knew those pills would kill him. My mum had the same sort at one time. The doctor told me to keep an eye on her. 'They're useful because they have a sedative effect that the more modern drugs don't have. But there's always the danger of overdose. Don't leave them lying about where she can get hold of them.' "

"How did you know that Jimmy had been prescribed the same tablets?"

"I looked," she said. "The flat was never locked. I wanted to know all about his bloody loving family. When they were out I went up and poked around. They never knew, never suspected."

"And that night you stole his tablets from the bathroom."

"That's right," she said. "While they were at dinner. They thought I was in the kitchen skivvying. I crushed them up using two wooden spoons. I got a really fine powder."

"Did you put them in his food?"

"No," she said. "I couldn't be sure he'd eat that. I thought about the coffee, but sometimes he even left that to go cold. But he'd always drink the whisky."

"But didn't he keep the bottle in his study? Wouldn't he have helped himself to a drink? He wouldn't have needed you to get that for him."

"I'd cleared all the glasses away," she said. "He always started on the whisky after dinner, so when I went to get his tray I knew he'd ask me to fetch him one. 'Bring one for yourself,' he said. 'You can have a drink to help me celebrate.' He was still reading through his manuscript when I came in. I could have tipped half a bottle of bleach into the glass and he wouldn't have noticed."

"So there *were* two glasses in the study the next morning," he said. "The second one was yours."

She nodded.

"What was Jane doing when all this was going on?" he asked.

"You leave Jane out of this," she said sharply. "It's nothing to do with her."

242

"Didn't she even suspect?"

Rosie shook her head. "She thinks the best of everyone, Jane. I've told her, she'll get hurt in the end. She'd have to toughen up or folks'd walk all over her." She paused. "I wasn't going to let that happen to me," she cried. "I couldn't let that happen to me, could I?"

It was almost dark. George took her arm gently and guided her back to the Mill. Molly would be waiting for them.

22

Later Molly sat on the bed in Rosie's cell-like room and read the letter that the girl had been writing two nights before. It still lay, face down, on the dressing table:

Dear Mum,

This afternoon I went for a walk along the shore to the place where we used to go on Sunday afternoons for a picnic. Do you remember? Dad built a fire with driftwood below the tide line and we'd cook potatoes wrapped in foil. They were still hard as stones when the time came to go home and we always ended up chucking them into the water, seeing whose would go the furthest. Dad's always seemed to go for miles, up into the sky and beyond Salter's Spit. Halfway to Scandinavia we used to say.

I'm sorry you've been feeling a bit low lately. I'll bring you back to Mardon as soon as I can. We'll find a little house, just big enough for the two of us with a view of the river. You say I've deserted you but you know that's not true.

Did you see the pictures of James Morrissey's memorial service on the television? You said you'd get better if James Morrissey paid. I did it, just like you always told me to. I did it for you.

* * *

The letter was unsigned, unfinished. At that point Rosie had been interrupted by Molly and Jane and the bottle of wine. Molly replaced it on the dressing table. The police would find it and use it in evidence at Rosie's trial. Molly hoped that a skilful defence lawyer would make use of it, too.

She was roused by the sound of the distant dinner bell. Meg was obviously determined that the ritual of the Mill would go on.

They sat for dinner at the same single table as on the night when George and Molly had arrived at the Mill. Jane had set the table before she had heard of Rosie's arrest and the neatly arranged cutlery, the empty glass held their attention. The younger children kept glancing surreptitiously towards the place before picking again at their food. They ate in silence. Only Meg seemed insensitive to the general mood of sadness.

"So it was Rosie!" she said brightly, speaking rather loudly because of her position at the head of the table. "I can hardly believe it. She was a good enough worker. And to think we always treated her as one of the family! She must have been unbalanced, deranged. What can one expect with parents like that? It's in the upbringing, of course."

She seemed to bear the girl no malice for killing her husband, only for taking them all in. Now that she had got used to her role as widowed mother she was starting to enjoy it. It would always elicit sympathy and she no longer ran the risk that her marriage would be exposed as less than perfect. Molly saw that life would be more convenient for her in many ways without James around.

Meg had come in to dinner still carrying the typescript of an article she had been correcting. It was entitled "Coming to Terms with Bereavement." Molly thought Meg had lost no time in sharing her experiences with the nation's women and supposed she would be even more in demand as a contributor to women's magazines after the publicity surrounding Rosie's trial.

"I saw that dreadful man Porter arrive to take her away," Meg went on in the same conversational tone. "I could see it wasn't the time to intrude, but I shall insist on an apology from him for not taking my allegations more seriously. Perhaps I should write to the chief constable. What do you think, George? I'm so grateful that you proved me right in all this."

George said nothing. He found Meg's righteous indignation almost unbearable.

"Are you all right?" Molly said quickly to Jane. The housekeeper was red-eyed, drawn. She made no attempt to eat.

"I wasn't much of a friend to her, was I?" Jane said abruptly. "All this time and she couldn't trust me enough to tell me what was bugging her. I knew she wasn't happy, but I could never persuade her to talk. I should have seen how angry she was. I could have stopped her. . . ." She paused. "Now she's ruined her life and there's nothing I can do to help. She wouldn't even let me go to the police station with her. Perhaps she thought I'd make a fuss. She probably thought I'd be useless."

"She wouldn't let anyone go with her," Molly said. "She wanted to see it through on her own. It had nothing to do with you."

"Besides," Meg interrupted, "Jane, my dear, that would have been quite unsuitable. The police station! What would your mother say? It's bad enough as it is. Poor Celia. She sent her daughter to me for safekeeping and you became friends with a murderer!"

"We were friends," Jane said quietly to Molly. "Whatever she's done somehow that's still important."

"I think I'd better phone Celia and explain before she reads about it in the press," Meg continued, as if Jane had not spoken. "I suppose there will be a lot of press coverage." She seemed lost in thought for a moment and Molly guessed uncharitably that she was picturing headlines like 'Brave Widow Fights Police Indifference. Justice at Last.' "I hope Celia doesn't expect me to send you home to her, Jane. I don't know how we'll manage as it is if we're opening for business again next week. Rosie was a competent cook. One must give her that. I must say it will be a relief when we get back to normal."

Ruth looked at her mother with astonishment. How could she talk so glibly about things returning to normal? She was tempted briefly to make a grand gesture. She could walk out, leave home, tell Meg that she could not stand the hypocrisy and pretence any longer. She could live with her father or find a flat of her own. But she knew she would never do it. In the end she did not feel strongly enough. She would stay here, one of the children, pretending to be a dutiful daughter. She would read bedtime stories to Tim and Em, prevent Caitlin's wilder excesses, be polite to the students. She would even answer the visitors' questions about Aidan Moore.

"Yes," she would say. "Of course we knew Aidan. It was a terrible tragedy. He was a brilliant artist. And a good friend."

Eventually she would go away to college, but even then she would return, every holiday, to the Mill. That was how most families worked. And perhaps it was healthy, the detachment, the dependence on show and form. Look at Rosie, after all. Look what a close and loving family had done for her.

It was left to George and Molly to make the grand gesture. When the meal was over they stood up and said that they were leaving.

"Surely not, George," Meg said, ignoring Molly. "Not at this time of night. At least stay until tomorrow."

"We've done what we came for," George said. "We've no more reason to stay."

"I was hoping to entertain you in the flat this evening, to say—you know, thank you for all your help."

"There's no need for that," George said. Then brutally: "We'll send our bill in the post."

He saw his rudeness had got through to her, but she would never have been impolite in return. Not in front of the children. She turned away and composed herself, not allowing her irritation to show.

"Well, if I can't persuade you . . ." she said. "Perhaps we'll see you at the Mill again in happier circumstances."

George said nothing. He knew they would never go back.

Coming to bookstores everywhere in
March 1995.

KILLJOY

A Detective Stephen Ramsay mystery

by Ann Cleeves

Published in paperback by Fawcett Gold
Medal.

If you enjoyed reading how George and
Molly Palmer-Jones solved *their* latest
mystery, you'll also want to try Ann
Cleeves's series featuring Detective
Stephen Ramsay.

Read on for the compelling opening pages
from
KILLJOY . . .

1

At seven o'clock on November 30 the Grace Darling Arts Centre was busy. The fog seeped inland from the Tyne and hung around the horse chestnut trees in Hallowgate Square, but the building had a light in every window and the carpark behind the house was full. Hallowgate had once been a prosperous Victorian suburb. The wealthy middle classes from Newcastle who made their money from ships or coal built houses there. Then the connurbation spread and Hallowgate became part of the North Tyneside sprawl. Its fortunes declined. It had never been as smart as Tyneside or Martin's Dene to the east and was too far from the metro line and the main road to be taken up by serious commuters. From attic windows in the solid red brick houses there were views of the cranes along the river, a rope factory, the remaining skeleton of a boatyard. Hallowgate was close to the Tyne, but this part had an identity of its own: quiet, shabby, forgotten.

The rest of the square was quiet. Most of the residents were elderly. Recent news reports of skirmishes with the police on the Starling Farm, a nearby council estate, kept them inside. The talk in the pubs was of joyriding, ram raiders. The streets seemed dangerous. On the corner of Anchor Street the Bengali grocers' shop was still open, but the languid teenage girls behind the counter had no customers to serve and spent the

251

evening reading magazines and sucking sweets. By then the fog was so thick that even with the streetlights they could not see the visitors to the Arts Centre in any detail. Even if the visibility had been perfect they were unlikely to take any notice.

Evan Powell drove into the Grace Darling carpark, saw that it was full, and drove out again to find a space in the square. It would not have occurred to him to cause inconvenience by double parking. The manoeuvre took longer than he had anticipated, and it was just after seven when he opened the door to the small music room where the other members of the choral society were arranging chairs and music stands. Punctuality was important to him, and he had been faintly anxious that they might have started. It came as a relief to see that three other people came in after him. Before the conductor called them to order he wondered briefly if John had remembered that he would be here tonight to give his son a lift home. It was a bad time for youngsters to be out on the streets alone.

In the main hall the Tyneside Youth Theatre had just begun its rehearsal. The teenagers were limbering up to loud rock music. The windows were covered by black out curtains and the room was dimly lit by coloured spots. They moved barefoot, across the wooden floor, jumping and twisting, dressed in cycle shorts or lycra leggings and loose, sexless T-shirts. Prue Bennett, sitting on the stage and watching them, admired their youth and energy, with a trace of envy. She switched off the large cassette recorder.

"Okay everyone," she said. "Relax."

Then she turned to the theatre's director, who was too grand, it seemed, to take the exercises, but who came in now once the real work of the evening was to begin.

Gus Lynch was a local man. His dad had been a draughtsman at the Swan Hunter Boatyard, and he had been to school in Wallsend. The trustees of the Grace Darling thought it was local pride that had brought him back to run the centre and direct the Tyneside Youth Theatre, but he was too canny for that. Soon after Drama School, he had starred as a token Geordie in an ITV sitcom. The series had run for years to a dwindling audience, and when it came to an end Gus was virtually unemployable. He had no experience of the serious stage and in its final years the series had been something of a joke; advertisers and the producers of the new, slick comedy programmes were not interested in anyone associated with it. Gus was an ambitious man, and although he had played hard to get he had welcomed the approaches from the centre's trustees. He recognised the potential the post had for reviving his image. It made him the North East's most prominent media man. He was invited onto late night television shows to discuss provincial theatre. The money was crap, he had to admit, but in the scheme of things the Grace Darling Centre was performing a useful function. The situation comedy had almost been forgotten and he was already looking forward to something new.

He cultivated the part of the famous actor. Despite middle-age he wore a lot of denim and he swore at them all. The teenagers thought he was wonderful. They gathered together to listen as he joined Prue on the stage.

"Let's do some work on the last scene," he said, "when Sam Smollett rescues Abigail from the crowd around the gallows, don't forget I want real menace, not just a lot of shouting and abuse."

He was very thin and his head was the shape of a skull, Prue saw now, prompted by talk of the gallows.

The group had devised the play—*The Adventures of Abigail Keene*—from stories they had grown up with since childhood, and from a folk song performed still in clubs and pubs all over the region. Abigail Keene had been an eighteenth-century rebel, the daughter of a Hallowgate merchant who had run away from home to travel and see the world. She had taken up with a rob-

253

ber and highwayman, then been caught and sentenced
to hang, rescued only at the last moment by her lover.
There was no real evidence of her existence, but her
story had survived in the area through song and myth.
The group had turned it into a roistering melodrama,
full of black humour and sexual innuendo, interspersed
by music. Prue Bennett described it to her friends as
Richardson's Clarissa crossed with Monty Python.

Gus looked down at the expectant teenagers and felt
the sudden exhilaration of power. This might be a small
pond, he thought, but he was a bloody big fish in it.

"Okay," he said. He moved restlessly over the stage.
"Let's set it up. John and Gabby to their positions, the
crowd over here. We'll try it without the music first.
Don't forget, we've our first dress rehearsal next week."

The young people were using the stage and the front
of the auditorium below it. They had placed blocks to
separate the space and give a variation in height. They
milled around to find their starting positions.

"Right!" Gus said. "Now, can we have more light?"

The hall was suddenly lit by a series of white spotlights. In one, on the stage, stood a dark, muscular boy
in a track suit. He held one hand to his face to shield
the glare from the light.

"Gabby's not here," the boy said flatly. "I haven't
seen her all evening."

"Bloody hell!" Gus Lynch said. "We can't do much
without her. Prue, where the hell is Gabby? She lives
with you, doesn't she? What have you done with her?"

"I haven't done anything with her," Prue said calmly.
"I'm her landlady, not her minder."

"Well, we can't wait any longer for her. Anna, you
can play her part for tonight. Let's get on with it."

Prue Bennett watched her daughter move from the
shadow, sensing her nervousness. In the circle of light
John Powell stood, moving his feet and shaking his
hands as if her were some athlete warming up before a
big race. She wondered if Gus Lynch had hoped to

254

cause her some awkwardness by choosing Anna as Gabby's understudy for Abigail Keene. He knew that the girl worked well as part of a group but became shy and diffident when she was the centre of attention. Was this an attempt to give her confidence, or just an opportunity for him to exert his authority over Prue?

Gus produced in Prue, as always, mixed feelings. She knew he was an arrogant bastard, but she enjoyed her work in the Arts Centre. She had been there for three years and still thought she was fortunate to have the job, that Gus Lynch had in some way been kind to employ her. She had applied for the job at the Grace Darling with enthusiasm but with little hope of success. She had little enough experience—a year in rep between university and getting herself pregnant. She had had no real work since then. First there had been Anna to look after, and just as the child grew more independent, her elderly parents had begun to make different and more cruel demands. Even now, three years later, she felt a remnant of gratitude to Lynch for not choosing one of the eager and attractive young actresses she had met at the interview. She was still uncertain why he had gone for her.

Prue watched John Powell put his arm round her daughter. She knew it was acting. John was Sam Smollett, the highwayman, hero of the piece. But still she felt a twinge of possessiveness. Something about the guarded tension of Anna's face made her anxious, reminded her of the turbulence of her own teenage years. She fancies him, she thought suddenly. She's excited by the physical contact. Then, almost immediately: I hope nothing comes of it. Not with John. He's too reckless. He's more Gabby's type. Then: What has it got to do with me anyway. I always promised myself I'd never interfere.

The thought of Gabby produced her to more irritation. Where was the girl? She could be unreliable at home but usually took the Youth Theatre seriously. She had never been this late before. For the first time she began to worry, influenced, despite herself, by the lurid news reports. *Perhaps Ellen knows something,* she thought without much hope. *I'll speak to her after the rehearsal.* Then she felt resentful. She had responsibility enough without having to take on someone else's child. She forced herself to concentrate on the teenagers in the body of the hall.

Ellen Paston was Gabby's aunt, her dead father's sister. She had worked part-time in the cafeteria in the Grace Darling Centre since it had opened, had worked there in fact before that, cleaning for the old lady who had owned the big house. On November 30 Ellen Paston began her shift at six o'clock. She got a bus from the Starling Farm to the end of Anchor Street and walked the rest of the way, staring in at the shop windows. Most of the shops were shut, but the windows were bright with gaudy Christmas decorations. Outside the pub a thin-faced man sold flimsy sheets of wrapping paper twisted into tubes. He smoked roll-up cigarettes and his eyes were alert, all the time, for the police. Ellen was heavy, big boned, and walked with a slow, lumbering gait. She took in all the details of her surroundings.

By seven o'clock Ellen Paston was panning coffee for the Hallowgate Writers Circle. They met in the cafeteria, then moved on to the small lecture room to share news of rejection slips and to massage bruised egos. The membership was composed mostly of middle-class women who drove in from the more affluent suburbs. Ellen Paston listened to their conversation without apparent interest. Despite her size she managed to be unobtrusive, and though they met her each week, the Writers Circle hardly noticed she was there. The woman's competitive boasting about their grandchildren's achievements left Ellen cold, but she listened just the same. You never knew when you could pick up something worthwhile. She was single, always had been, and realised that being single put you at risk. There was a danger that you would miss out on what was due to you. Ellen knew instinctively that information gave you power, and she was determined always to know what was happening in Hallowgate.

It had been inevitable that John Powell would be chosen to pay Sam Smollett, the hero of *The Adventures of Abigail Keene*. He had been given a leading role in every production since he was fourteen. Even then, sullen and covered with spots, brought by his father who thought it would be good for him, Gus had recognised something special about him. Something moody and reckless. He saw that John would not be afraid of taking risks. The character of Sam Smollett suited him down to the ground.

Tonight John's performance was not up to its usual standard. It lacked the pace and swagger needed for the part. His mind was not on the role. Gus blamed Gabby's absence for the lack of energy, but John knew that his inability to concentrate was at fault. He was ashamed of some of the trivia that distracted him. The lousy mark he'd got for the last history essay, for example. He couldn't hide it from his father any longer. The old man was already asking about it—not angrily but with that hateful, compassionate interest that made John want to hit him.

"How did you get on with that project you were researching?" his father had asked the night before. "Cromwell, wasn't it?" He had come in from a late shift and looked tired, but still he made the effort to take an interest in his only son's work. When he was eleven John's form teacher had said he was Oxbridge material, and Mr. Powell had never forgotten that.

"I don't know," John had muttered. "Haven't had it back yet."

And Powell had shaken his head in disappointment. "I suppose they're overworked," he had said, "but all

257

the same . . ." He wondered if they should have sent John to a private school after all. Jackie had been all for it, had offered to go out to work to pay the fees, but Evan hadn't been keen on that. In his work he saw too many kids allowed to roam the streets without proper supervision. That wasn't going to happen to his son.

John stood, waiting for the crowd to move back to their places so they could rehearse the movement again. It was the climax of the play, a piece of comic melodrama. He appeared, disguised as the hangman, and at the last moment pulled Abigail to safety through the crowd. Usually he enjoyed the scene, but today he was preoccupied, wondering why his father bugged him so much. He wasn't unreasonable, not compared with some other kids' dads, but he left John always with a sense of vague and uneasy aggression.

And there was the same unease wherever he thought about Gabby. . . .

Anna Bennett touched his shoulder to move him back to their starting place, and he jumped with a start. He was getting nervy. That wouldn't do. In this game he needed to keep his nerve. He breathed deeply into the pit of his stomach as he did in the relaxation exercises Prue set them before they started rehearsing.

"Are you all right?" Anna whispered. "Is anything wrong?"

"No," he said, smiling, super cool. "It's just a drag, isn't it, Gabby not being here?"

She turned away, and he saw with irritation that he must have offended her. He should be more careful, keep his feelings under control. It wasn't her fault. He saw himself as a modern Sam Smallett, gallant and daring, a gentleman of the road. He flashed her a smile.

"I'm sorry," he said. "I didn't mean that. You know what it's like when you get used to working with someone. It's bound to make a difference. Let me buy you a Coke later, to show there are no hard feelings."

Gus Lynch looked at his watch and saw gratefully

that it was a quarter to nine. He felt like giving the whole thing up now.

"We'll go through it just one more time," he called unenthusiastically. "Try to be aware of each other. We need a coordinated movement. It's not a rugby scrum. God knows how we'll be ready for performance. And what happened to you, John? Let's have a bit more dash and pace."

"Sorry, Gus!" John shouted. "I'm feeling a bit off to-night."

Gus Lynch shrugged and gave the cue to start them off. He watched the dispirited, disorganised performance with irritating annoyance. This play was important to him. For God's sake, he needed a bit of media attention. Especially now. He wouldn't allow the bloody kids to let him down. If John Powell didn't pull his finger out he'd be replaced with someone more committed.

The rehearsal rambled on to its close. The lights were switched up and the young people stood in groups, blinking and shamefaced, expecting an angry lecture from Gus. The old lecture about how he'd given up a good career to come and work with them and he expected some guts and energy in return. But he let them go in silence, and they wandered through to the cafeteria where Ellen Paston stood, hunched and unresponsive behind the counter.

John Powell, haunted by the old worries, forgot immediately about the easy promise to buy Anna a Coke when the session was over. He left the centre, ignoring the porter's greeting, and stopped at the entrance to the carpark. He'd always liked cars, and it had become a habit to stop there to admire the smart vehicles left by the centre's patrons. But the fog and the smashed security lights meant that visibility was poor, and he hurried back to the square. The pavement was covered with sodden leaves, and his footsteps made no sound.

Through the mist he saw his mother's car parked outside the grocer's shop. He remembered his dad had said he would borrow it because his was in the garage for a service, and was pleased; it would give him an excuse for not waiting for a lift home. He would say that he'd forgotten about the service, and when his father's car wasn't around, he'd presumed that he had missed the choral society because of some emergency at work. His excuses to his father grew more elaborate every day.

In the cafeteria Anna Bennett pretended not to notice that John had left without buying her a drink, without saying good-bye. The place was busy so she could chat with her friends and ignore her mother's glances of anxious sympathy.

"Gabby wasn't here tonight," Prue said to Ellen as she collected her coffee.

Ellen looked up, said nothing.

"She told me she'd be here," Prue said, trying to contain her impatience. "You don't know where she might be?"

Ellen shook her head, then seemed to realise that some contribution was expected.

"Perhaps she's poorly," she said.

"She didn't say anything this morning," Prue said. "But perhaps that's it. Perhaps she didn't feel well at school and went straight home."

"You don't want to worry about that one. She can look after herself," Ellen said unhelpfully. She began to serve the next customer and added as an afterthought, "No need to fuss."

"All the same," Prue said. "I think we'd better go home and check." She imagined Gabby in the house at Otterbridge, alone and seriously ill. She drank her coffee quickly and called to Anna who was standing at the edge of a group of girls, smiling too brightly, pretending too hard to be interested in what they were saying. With a relief that was obvious only to Prue, Anna gathered up her coat and bag and followed her mother into the lobby.

At an impressive wooden desk sat a short, thick-set, bald man, reading the *Sun*. This was Joe Fenwick, retired boxer, the porter and security man; he looked up from the paper and smiled.

"All right, Miss Bennett?" he said. "Finished for the night, then, pet?"

"Yes," said Prue, then, contradicting herself, "No, I'd forgotten. I must see Gus before I go." She turned to her daughter apologetically. "He's worked out a final draft for the programme, and I want to check it before it's printed. I'll take it home with me."

"Go on, then!" said Anna, long suffering, tolerant of her mother's middle-aged absentmindedness. "I'll wait for you here."

Prue ran up the stairs and paused outside Gus's office door to catch her breath, then knocked and went straight in. She saw first that Gus had a visitor, then that she had interrupted some silent confrontation. Gus was sitting behind his desk facing a middle-aged woman who sat squarely in a leather chair inherited with the house. The woman was well-dressed, confident, classy. Prue recognised her as Amelia Wood, deputy chair of the Grace Darling trustees. Prue composed herself. Mrs. Wood was an intruding presence, and she wondered briefly what trouble the old bat was causing now. She smiled.

"Sorry to disturb you, Gus," she said lightly. "I'm here for the programme. I was hoping to work on it at home this evening."

He jumped to his feet, all tension and nervous energy. He was rattled, Prue thought. Mrs. Wood sat with her gloved hands clasped in her lap and smiled.

"Yeah," Gus said. "Right. Of course. Look, the draft's still in my car. In a file in the boot. Why don't you help yourself?" He took the keys from the pocket of a jacket that was hanging on a coat stand by the win-

261

dow and tossed them to her. "Leave them with Joe at reception," he said. "Save you coming all the way up the stairs again."

Mrs. Wood watched his agitation with amusement. She stood up, offered one of her hands to Prue, and said:

"Miss Bennett! How nice to meet you again."

Resisting the urge to curtsy, Prue left the room and returned to Anna.

When they walked into the carpark the Christ Church clock was striking nine-thirty. Usually the place was brightly lit with security floodlights, but they had been smashed by vandals the weekend before and had still not been replaced. After the warmth and light of the house the carpark was chill and uninviting. The only light came from the orange streetlights beyond the trees and from the uncurtained windows of the cafeteria. From the mouth of the river came the distant, muffled sound of a foghorn and the smell of mud. The carpark was almost empty. The teachers and solicitors who came to the Grace Darling Centre to sing and write, enjoyed its facilities but were nervous about its location. One heard such dreadful stories. At the end of each meeting they were relieved to find their cars still there, intact, and drove back with relief to the civilization of Tynemouth and Martin's Dene.

Gus had his own space in the carpark. He had insisted that Joe Fenwick should paint DIRECTOR in big white letters on the concrete. The blue Volvo was parked at an angle between the parallel white lines as if he had arrived in a hurry. Prue fitted a key into the lock of the door. As she lifted it a bulb inside lit automatically, and she had no difficulty in seeing the contents. There, on top of the file containing the programme for *The Adventures of Abigail Keene*, lay Gabby Paston, curled on her side like a child at sleep. But her eyes were open and bulging. Gabriella Paston was dead.